SONS A

'Aunt Fiona,

the run. The p

'You?' She shook her head disbelievingly. 'I don't believe it.'

John forged on. He had come so far. 'They think I killed someone in Melbourne.'

Fiona's mouth fell open. 'Killed?' she breathed. 'Oh no.'

'I didn't do it,' John said fervently, his eyes fixed steadily to hers. 'I promise you. I didn't do it.'

'I see.' She closed her eyes, then opened them again, preparing herself to hear something unpleasant. 'Then you had better tell me about it. Everything. From the beginning.'

SONS AND DAUGHTERS

Carl Ruhen

From an idea by Reg Watson and based on the scripts of Bevan Lee, Maureen Ann Moran, John Alsop and Christine McCort.

A STAR BOOK
published by
the Paperback Division of
W. H. ALLEN & Co. PLC

A Star Book
Published in 1985
by the Paperback Division of
W. H. Allen & Co. PLC
44 Hill Street, London W1X 8LB

First published in Australia as a
QB Book by Horwitz Group Books Pty Ltd

Printed and bound in Great Britain by
Anchor Brendon Ltd, Tiptree, Essex

ISBN 0 352 31739 6

1

He saw her again — the girl on the horse. The sun was going down and there were coppery streaks behind the long, flat lines of cloud that ranged up from the horizon in almost flawless symmetry. Shafts of dying sunlight shimmered across the greying, gently heaving ocean and were caught in the spume and spray of the surf as it pounded up onto the beach then slid back into the next rising wall of dark green water — endless motion, endless rhythm, and splashing through it now, right at the edge, riding away from him, was the girl on the horse.

He watched her. He could feel the breeze on his face, taste its salt on his lips. The girl was urging the horse forward in a breathtaking gallop through the surf, and each drop of water sent up by the animal's hooves was like a tiny piece of crystal as it caught and imprisoned the light for the briefest fraction of time — sheets of crystal that soared and fragmented and fell away in a wide spatter. it was all so clear, so vivid. The girl's hair, burnished now by the fading sunlight, flew freely, her body lifted from the saddle in a tight but supple harmony with the plunging movement of the horse. She was wild, she was free, the girl and the horse . . . He could feel a constriction forming in his chest, a dryness in his throat, as he watched.

The girl, the horse, the sea and the sand — he had seen it all before, many times. He had seen the sun go down behind the strips of cloud, the luminescence of the waves . . . And now, later — the same night, another night, the sand cool and silvery in the moonlight, and she was running towards him. And it seemed that the closer she came to him, the slower her movements were, although she was still running, her dark hair whipped back across her face by the breeze, her lips moving as she called his name.

And then . . . and then he was holding her, gripping her hands tightly as he spun her around and around in circles, faster and faster, her body leaning out at an angle from him, their feet almost touching, her hair flying, her eyes shining and her small, even teeth gleaming white as she laughed happily. And now the sun was shining as they spun and spun on the empty beach and the surf thundered and roared and rolled ceaselessly up onto the sparkling white sand.

And so, smiling in his sleep, John Palmer dreamt on. The same girl — it was always the same girl. Her features were firmly and indelibly printed on his mind. Even when he was awake she was there.

2

The pencil marks on the frame of the kitchen door told their own story. They were landmarks, each of them representing a stage in the life of the three children in the house. How many times had she made them stand against the door frame while she marked off their height with the stubby pencil? They grew up fast, and there were times when she wondered at the speed it had all happened. The years had rushed by, births and heartaches, scratches and cuts, bruised knees and elbows, teeth pushing through inflamed gums, nappies, measles, mumps, birthday parties, toys, messy bathrooms, broken windows, dismembered bicycles, wet shoes and colds, and mud tracked into the hallway by football boots. These were the things — working, washing, cooking, day after day, making beds, polishing floors — that filled in the spaces between those pencil marks on the frame of the kitchen door. And now there was to be a wedding.

Beryl Palmer looked up at her daughter and sighed. Susan did look beautiful — more than that, radiant, a glow that seemed to diffuse her from within. Another landmark. The first wedding. It was funny. At one moment Susan had been just a child, and then, the next, she was grown up, about to be married and leave home for good. It had all happened so fast, and sometimes Beryl felt she had been left a long way behind.

"Your grandmother was right," she said with a smile. "It fits you perfectly."

Susan's grandmother had been married in that same dress, unique, folds and turns of rippling lace, very old. Kneeling in front of the chair on which her daughter was standing, Beryl deftly brought the needle through the delicate filigree hem for the final stitch. She, too, had been married in this dress. Breaking the thread, she brought herself up onto her feet and stared at her daughter. Marks on the door, all the time growing. All grown up now, more or less, no more marks to put on. What had happened to all those years?

"David," she called. "Come and see your beautiful daughter."

"Won't be a minute," a man's voice called back from the kitchen. "I've just boiled the kettle."

"You'd better get down," Beryl said to Susan. "Let him get the full impact."

Young, glowing, on the threshold of a full, mature life — happiness, kids, thorough contentment. It was a time of hope. Beryl could feel young again, no longer careworn, quite unworried about her weight, the toughening of her skin, the gray strands she was finding more often in her hair. Susan was everything she had ever hoped herself to be.

"What about the veil?" the girl asked suddenly.

Hoped to be — and perhaps was, once. "Oh yes." She raised her voice. "David, don't come in."

"Make your mind up," a grumbling voice came back from the kitchen.

The veil was in a box on the sideboard. Beryl took it out of the box and as she lifted it the light seemed to flow through it, transforming it to pure spun gossamer. She adjusted it over Susan's head and face.

"When I married your father," she said, "there was the biggest panic over this veil. It disappeared."

"Disappeared?" Susan's eyebrows lifted a fraction.

Beryl nodded as she continued to fuss with the veil. "It

was all my fault. You know how slapdash I am. I just bundled it up with a stack of washing and dumped it in the wardrobe. Sometimes I wonder why your father ever married me."

"I'm glad he did," Susan said with a fond smile. "You're the best mother in the world."

Impulsively, she reached out, and taking Beryl in her arms, gave her a hug and a kiss on the cheek. Beryl could feel something brimming inside her, a warmth, a gathering. Tears pricked her eyes, a lump formed in her throat. "Best mother?" Her voice trembled. "Luckiest mother, you mean. Three fantastic kids — and him in there." Her chin jerked towards the kitchen. She sniffed and suddenly the room, her daughter's face, everything, was out of focus. She blinked hard a few times."David, are you coming in here or not?"

Gently disengaging herself from Susan's embrace, she moved across to the kitchen door and opened it. "Now close your eyes until I tell you to open them," she told the man who was coming towards her balancing a large, laden tea tray.

"What are you talking about?" David Palmer demanded. "I'm trying to juggle this tray . . ." Then, as his eyes fell on the vision in the middle of the living room, he stopped and gave a long, low whistle. "Well, will you just look at her," he said softly.

Beryl eased the tray from him. "Here, you'd better give me that before you drop it." She placed the tray on a small table. David Palmer continued to stare at his daughter, then moving forward again, took her hands in his own.

"Your mother's right," he said. "You really are beautiful."

It was a long, tender moment which was abruptly shattered by the sound of the front doorbell. Beryl frowned.

"Now who can that be?"

"If that's Bill, don't let him in," Susan said quickly. "It's unlucky."

"I'll go see who it is," Beryl volunteered, heading for the

hallway.

Then, as if a concerted effort were being made to disrupt the self-containment and pleasure that filled that small, rather crowded room, the telephone rang. With a glance at his daughter, David moved across to it.

"Hello."

"Hello, Bill. We're just having a preview of the wedding dress. Your bride-to-be is really beautiful, you know." He caught Susan's eye and nodded to her. The long lace wedding dress rustled slightly as she came across the room and stood expectantly by his side. "Here she is." David held the receiver out to her.

"Hi, darling." Susan's voice was eager. Her heartbeat quickened and she was aware of the warmth in her cheeks. She pictured Bill at the other end of the line, in his flat, smiling and fond.

"Have you got the TV on?" he asked.

"No," she said, a little surprised. His tone was serious, and she experienced a small flutter of apprehension.

"Then you'd better switch on. News spot. You're in for a shock."

"What is it, Bill? Can't you tell me?" She glanced at her father who stood near the door listening to the voices out in the hallway, her mother's voice, a man's voice, indistinct but somehow conveying a ring of authority into the room.

"Just turn on the TV," Bill said grimly. "You'll see."

She put the receiver down on the table, and with a thoughtful frown, crossed the room to the corner where the TV set was standing. She switched it on.

"He told me to turn on the TV," she explained to her father as the picture leapt outwards, lurched a little then settled into focus; as the voices in the hallway became louder, more distinct; as Beryl, fluttering, concerned, came into the room accompanied by a uniformed policeman.

"David," she said, trying hard to keep down the alarm in her voice. "It's the police."

David tensed. The police were always bad news. When they came to the house like this . . .

"Mister Palmer?"

"Yes." David's expression was stony.

Susan was looking from the policeman to the TV screen. A voice swelled into the room. Then she saw a face on the screen. "Dad! Look! It's Johnny!"

It *was* Johnny — Johnny near the top of a TV transmitting tower, clinging to a steel ladder, grinning, his hair blowing in the wind, and the lights of Melbourne spread out beneath him. Johnny, picked out in the lights that were beamed up at him from the foot of the tower, from the confusion of police cars and outside broadcast vans, of cables and cameramen jostling to get a better angle on the young man perched high up on the tower. A crowd had gathered; barricades had been set up.

One reporter, more intrepid than the others, had scrambled up the ladder behind John, holding on with one hand, and with the other extending the microphone up to the youth who was crouching a few feet above him. In the Palmer living room a silent, astonished group regarded the scene that was being enacted on the small screen. The reporter was talking. He had to shout to make himself heard above the fitful whistling of the wind.

". . . but most people would say this is a pretty stupid thing to do."

John grinned disarmingly, and Beryl felt a pang. He was up to one of his silly tricks again — and this one looked extremely dangerous. Beryl was frightened. She held her hand to her mouth, scarcely daring to breathe and sensing the mounting rage of the man who stood beside her.

"No, they wouldn't," John said happily. "A few people might think it's stupid, but I'll bet most people will probably say it's romantic. Why shouldn't people get invited? Everybody. The trouble is that no one ever bothers to invite them to a great day like this."

Lights popped, the wind carried away their voices and flung them back again out of shape. It buffeted the two figures on the ladder near the top of the transmitting tower. His mouth set grimly, tense, his fists bunched by his sides, David Palmer stared at his son on the screen.

"Let's get it right," the reporter shouted, jabbing the microphone up again towards John. "The invitation's just for the church — not the reception."

Now what? What was this about the reception? Beryl looked helplessly at David, at Susan, but clearly they were as confused as she was.

"Is that your son, sir?" The policeman's voice seemed to boom and reverberate around them. Beryl started. Her hand fell away from her mouth as she swung away from the set and stared wide-eyed at the policeman.

"Yes," David growled. "But what's it all about?"

The policeman was brisk, businesslike. He took a step backwards. "I'll explain on the way to the station," he said.

David took a deep breath. He scowled.

He looked at Beryl, gave her a brief nod which was possibly meant to be reassuring, then walked out behind the policeman into the hall. Turning back to the screen, Beryl heard their heavy footsteps on the hall carpet, the door opening and closing, and more than ever, with the sound of the closing door, she felt as if things were spinning away out of her grasp, leaving her alone and uncomprehending.

Until a few minutes earlier all she had had to worry about was the wedding dress, the wedding itself, the plans that had been made, and now here was Johnny, on top of a tower . . . It was too much. She shook her head and bit down on her lower lip to check the rush of emotion that threatened to break loose. Johnny — how could she ever hope to understand that boy? She had tried so hard.

"Mum!" Susan cried suddenly. "Look what he's done."

She saw now as the camera panned away from the tower and the screen was filled with a huge flapping banner that had printed on it in huge uneven letters the words

SUSAN AND BILL GET MARRIED SATURDAY 28th
ST STEPHEN'S CAULFIELD. YOU ARE INVITED.

Despite herself Beryl smiled. It was something so typical of

John, impetuous, madcap, and — the smile faded — bound to cause a great deal of trouble. He meant well, but . . . but this sort of thing didn't do any good at all.

"If I could afford it I'd invite everyone to the reception as well," John was telling the reporter. "But I'll do that when I meet the right girl."

"Susan's your sister — right?" the reporter queried, and Susan gave a small gasp. Her hand fluttered ineffectually as if she were trying to silence him.

"Yeah." John grinned again. His cheeks dimpled when he smiled. Beryl slowly shook her head. He had always been a beautiful boy, curly hair, blue eyes that gazed with candor and a vague sense of wonder out at the world, those dimples. "Susan's a nurse and Bill's my best mate. We work together and I introduced him to her." He spoke quickly, almost breathlessly. He was excited. "Saturday the twenty-eighth is going to be the happiest day in their lives so I want everyone in the State to turn up for the wedding and enjoy themselves."

Susan gasped again. Her face was pale. She looked stricken. "How can he do this to me?" she moaned.

From his perch on the tower, the reporter was looking straight into the camera. "Well, what do you think?" he addressed his audience, who, from the comfort of their living rooms beneath the vast canopy of lights that stretched out to the Dandenongs, to Port Phillip Bay, the peninsula and the open sea, intently watched the unfolding drama; some perhaps disappointed that the boy obviously had no intention of jumping, although anything could still happen — an accident maybe. "Do *you* find it romantic? Would *you* risk arrest and maybe your life to climb a tower like this to invite the world and his wife to the marriage of your sister and your best friend?" He grimaced in a well-practised way. "Frankly, on a night like this it leaves me . . . cold."

With a strangled sob, Susan gathered up the folds of her grandmother's wedding dress and rushed out of the room. Beryl switched off the set. She had seen enough.

3

The siren wailed, the blue light flashed and David Palmer was thoughtful. Neither of the policemen spoke and for that he was grateful. It gave him time to think, to put his thoughts in order. He needed time for the problem he was about to face, and had in fact been facing for the past twenty years.

The police car weaved in and out of the traffic, its siren going full blast. People stopped on the pavement to stare at it. In the back seat, David Palmer gazed out the window at the tall city buildings ablaze with light, the dark areas of parkland, the broad tree-lined streets, shop windows, cars and trams — he saw all these things, or rather registered them in a part of his mind where it didn't really matter. They were incidental, merely an overlay. He was seeing back much further than that — another time, another place, when he was about the same age as his son was now. Twenty years ago. The siren seemed to fade, to lose its strength and shrillness. Other sounds intruded — a distant ferry horn, the hissing of the surf . . . Twenty years ago, a cold night in Sydney. A street in Manly, a boarding house just off the Esplanade, and Patricia very, very pregnant. That was when she had changed, in a strange city, in a boarding house near the sea, and everything they owned crammed into one battered suitcase — that was when she had fallen out of love with him.

The siren dipped and soared. It sounded wispy now, totally without menace or even urgency. David thought of Fiona, tall, leathery Fiona who hadn't asked too many questions when she had taken them into her boarding house, although she must have guessed that they were running away, that they weren't married. "A remarkable woman," one of Fiona's friends had told David. "One in a million."

It had been Fiona Thompson who had stayed with Patricia when the pains started coming and she refused to be taken to hospital; who had fussed and ordered masses of hot water to be boiled; who had finally come into the kitchen where David was sitting.

"Well, David? What did you want? A boy or a girl?"

"I. . . I. . . don't mind."

"Just as well. You've got one of each."

Twins, two more mouths to feed, work to be found, tramping the streets looking for a job, desperate, money running out fast — things needed, clothes, nappies, baby food, Fiona helping, cooing and clucking, Patricia querulous, unhappy, struggling to cope. The twins crying in the middle of the night, disturbed sleep, bones aching after a day's work at the building site, mixing mortar and rushing it in a wheelbarrow across to the bricklayers, and then, one day, coming back to the boarding house and finding the room empty, Fiona solemn.

"Patricia's gone, David. She left you a note — and something else."

The note — he could see it now, Patricia's neat handwriting. "I'm taking the girl. You can have the boy. Whether you have him adopted or not is your problem. I never want to see either of you again — Patricia."

So went the way of young love — a bright future, they had thought, where the love they felt for each other would over-ride everything, just as it had already proved stronger than their parents' opposition, their lack of money and prospects.

"You've got to find her — you know that."

"No, I won't try to find her. She knows what she wants. She always did. And she certainly doesn't want me — or the boy."

"Okay. What about the boy?"

"I guess I'll have to put him up for adoption. I can't look after him. I know that."

He had wanted to marry straight away. Patricia had wanted to get married in the Church, but in her condition, so obviously pregnant, she would be ashamed to approach a priest about it. As soon as the baby was born — then they would get married. She wouldn't change her mind about that, not even after David had pointed out that they owed it to their child to get married before it was born. One child they had thought then; it was inconceivable that Patricia's swollen stomach could harbour more than just the one. And, of course, that religion of hers had a great deal to do with it. It was there all the time, final, forbidding, feeding her doubts. The dream of a blissful future that had fuelled their resolve to run away had begun to fade for her, to be replaced by visions of drudgery and relative poverty.

The police car cut across intersections, disregarding the lights, and in the back seat David Palmer dipped in and out of time and place, Melbourne now, Sydney then, Fiona Thompson's level gaze.

"If you put this baby up for adoption you'll have to live with the memory for the rest of your life. Look, I'll show you what it's like to live with memories."

And, opening a drawer, she had taken out armfuls of baby clothes, soft and fleecy, and spread them out on the bed. They had looked brand new.

"I had a son once. All these things were for him. I've saved them for over ten years now. . . ah, memories. I was going to give them to Patricia today for the two babies."

"What happened to your son?"

"He died. He was mine for three days — that's all. Ah

. . . David, you're young, you're strong and you're capable of giving this child a good future. Do you want to give him away?"

"I don't know. Anyway, how could I keep a kid on my own?"

"I'll look after him until you get on your feet."

"You mean it?"

"When you're ready, come and get him."

"Thanks. I'll pay you back."

"Have you thought of a name for him yet?"

"Aw, I don't know . . . What do you think?"

"You're his father."

"How about. . . John?"

"John? John Palmer. Yes, John's a nice name. Hello, Johnny. Oooh, you'll grow up to be a fine young man. You'll see — a fine young man."

A fine young man who climbed television transmitting towers and made a nuisance of himself, who was always doing stupid things like that, who lived in a dream world and had a twin sister he knew nothing about — nor would he ever know.

David Palmer sighed and slumped further down in his corner of the seat. The car was slowing down. The siren trailed away into silence.

4

The police station was small and clammy, functional and without a trace of personal adornment that might have lessened its aura of severity and claim to be a place where no nonsense or frivolity could be brooked without bringing down the full force of the law it represented. There were *Wanted* posters on the walls, and the single window was barred. The woodwork was scarred and stained. There were filing cabinets, telephones and typewriters. A door led off from one side of the room to the cells. Another door opened into a poky, austerely furnished office behind the charge rooms. A plain clothes man sat at the desk, laboriously writing out a report in longhand.

"Hi, Dad. I'm sorry."

"Are you?" David snapped. His normally good-natured features were taut as his anger maintained a dangerous pressure inside him.

John's eyes dropped. He made a small, helpless gesture with one hand. "It all got a bit out of hand," he murmured uncomfortably. "I wasn't doing any harm."

"Weren't you?" The plain clothes man behind the desk was reaching forward with a sheet of paper in his hand. "Take a look at this. Tell me what it says."

John took the sheet. " 'Trespassers will be prosecuted',"

he read.

The policeman nodded and looked faintly pleased with himself. "Good," he grunted. "I just wanted to make sure you could read. You obviously saw those signs around the transmitter then?"

"Yes, sir." John was looking shamefacedly down at the floor.

There was a knock at the door and the uniformed policeman who had brought John in from the cells a few minutes earlier put his head around it.

"Spare a moment, Sarge?"

The man behind the desk grunted, then, pushing back his chair so that it scraped across the bare wooden floor, rose and left the room. David and John were left alone. David glared at his son.

"They might want you to have psychiatric tests," he remarked.

"Me?" John laughed unconvincingly. "They're mad."

"No." David shook his head emphatically. It was turning out to be a long day. "They think you're mad. And you know something? After tonight I'm damned sure you are."

"Aw, come on, Dad." John shuffled nervously. "It was only a bit of fun."

"Fun!" David raisd his eyebrows. "You call that *fun*?" His voice reverberated around the small room and hurled itself back at him. He threw his hands up into the air. "I give up — I really do. You've been nothing but trouble from the day you were born." He was shaking with anger; his gestures were tight and savage. "Just tell me. What are you trying to prove by doing stupid things like that all the time? What do you want?"

John turned away from him. "I don't want to talk about it," he muttered sullenly.

"You're going to *have* to talk about it!" David exclaimed. He might have said more if the door hadn't opened just then and the sergeant come back into the room.

"How many sons do you have, Mister Palmer?" he

asked coldly.

"Two."

"The other one named Kevin? Age seventeen?"

"Yes." What now? What were they going to heap on him now? Apprehension lodged heavily in the pit of his stomach.

The sergeant turned back to the door. "Come on in, son," he called.

The young man who came tentatively into the room looked scared. David stared at him in dismay. First John, and now Kevin. His first son, and now his second son. "Kevin, what are *you* doing here?" he demanded.

"He was in it, too," the policeman told him. "Playing funny buggers he was. There was his brother up on that tower while he was ringing up all the television stations putting on funny accents and saying why do they want to arrest this guy when all he's doing is showing he's got a bit of romance in his blood and inviting people to his sister's wedding." He grimaced in disgust. "A little bundle of energy, a one-man spontaneous audience response. They cottoned onto him soon enough, though. He was still in the telephone box when they caught him. He was being a public nuisance, Mister Palmer," the detective concluded reproachfully.

Kevin was dark and chunky, three years younger than John, a year younger than Susan who had been the first child born to David and Beryl Palmer. "I didn't want John to get all the blame," he said, staring defiantly back at his father.

The detective sighed and wearily compressed his chin between his thumb and forefinger. "Seems to me you've got a pretty undisciplined family on your hands, Mister Palmer," he observed.

Undisciplined. The word stuck with David even after he had managed to persuade the sergeant not to charge the boys but to turn them over to him — he would take care of them, he said, they wouldn't be let off lightly, no sir, you could be damned sure of that. Undisciplined. The burden of it was on his shoulders as they were driven back to the house. He had tried, he had done his best, but it just hadn't seemed to work. The contempt in the policeman's eyes had been unmistakable when he told David he had a pretty undisciplined family on his hands. It wasn't fair. He had tried hard enough, worked hard enough, trundling rigs all over the damned place, and maybe it was true he hadn't spent as much time with the family as he should, but a man had to work, had to earn money — he was away from the place sometimes for days on end, but he knew it was a happy house; Beryl made sure of that. There was nothing wrong with Susan, or with Kevin, really, for that matter, although he did tend to be rather heavily influenced by John. And John — there was the problem. He wished he could put his finger on it. Undisciplined. The word mocked him all the way home.

It was after two in the morning when they walked through the front door. Beryl was still up, stitching the wedding dress. David went into the kitchen to make himself some coffee. Susan had gone over to Bill's place, Beryl said. Bill's mother had suggested she spend the night at their place. "We had lots of phone calls," she went on in aggrieved tone. "People kept knocking on the door to tell us you were on TV." She shook her head at John. "You're not Susan's favourite brother at the moment."

John shrugged. Now that they were back home he could try to make light of it. "I thought she'd laugh about it," he said. "You know her sense of humour. She has got one, you know."

"Sure," Beryl said dryly. "Time and place. Some girls don't find their wedding day a laughing matter." She looked across at Kevin who was standing behind and a little to one side of John. "And how did *you* get mixed up in all this? I couldn't believe it when your father phoned to say you had been arrested as well."

Kevin looked sullen. "I don't know what all the fuss is about," he said peevishly. "We didn't hurt anyone, did we?" His voice rose as the injustice of it all made itself felt.

"It'd be different if we were throwing petrol bombs and mugging little old ladies. All we tried to do was make people happy for a change. Any other family would have laughed about it."

David came in from the kitchen carrying a mug of coffee. "Any other family would have thrown you out into the street," he growled. "Now get to bed, both of you."

John gestured half-heartedly. "Can't we talk about this sensibly?"

David snorted. "I don't think you can do anything sensibly," he snapped.

John held his ground, glaring at his father. Beryl, sensing an outburst, moved between them, once again in the role of peacemaker. "Come on," she said to John. "You've got to get to work in a few hours. We can talk tomorrow night."

She kissed John lightly on the cheek and much of the tension seemed to ebb away from him. "Night, Mum," he said. He nodded to David. "Night."

There was no response from David. John left the room. Beryl kissed Kevin. "And I'll talk to *you* over breakfast," she said.

Kevin turned to his father whose face was expressionless. "Dad, it wasn't all John's fault. We thought it up together."

"That's right," David said wearily. "Protect him. Now go to bed."

Then Beryl and David were alone in the living room, with the comfortable, solid, not very stylish furniture they had gathered together over the years, a couple of nondescript watercolour landscapes on the wall, the sideboard where Beryl kept her best china, to be brought out only when they had visitors. David slumped down on the couch which groaned a little beneath his weight. Beryl sat down beside him, and slipped her arm around him. David sipped his coffee.

"The police think we're a family of ratbags," he remarked.

The laughter lines around Beryl's eyes deepened as she smiled. She smiled often. "Well, maybe we are."

David wasn't amused. "You wouldn't joke if you had been there," he said harshly, then sighed. "What am I going to do with that boy, Beryl? John, I mean."

"You could try understanding him," she said gently.

"Understanding him!" David retorted. "He's a lost cause — you know that? If he isn't doing stupid things like this caper tonight, he's living in a ridiculous dream world of his own. And you always end up defending him. He isn't even your son."

Beryl slid her arm from around him and touched his hand. "David," she said placatingly. "When you first brought that rebellious little boy back from Sydney my heart went out to him. We've all grown to love him — very much. But you . . . you treat him like a stranger and you're his father. It may be that he does these crazy things to make you notice him. Have you ever thought of that?"

"Oh, I notice him all right," David said bitterly, rising to his feet.

With a sigh, Beryl also stood up. "Come on," she said, taking his hand. "Let's go to bed."

Down the hallway, in the room he shared with his half-brother, John Palmer dreamt again of the girl on the horse.

5

John was late for work. Leaping down from the tram before it stopped, he sprinted the two blocks to the warehouse, hesitated in the open doorway, peered into the gloomy, cavernous interior of the building, saw no one, breathed a sigh of relief, then hurried across to where his overalls hung from a hook on the wall. Hauling them down, he quickly began to climb into them. He had one leg into them when he heard the engine start up behind him.

He swung around and saw the forklift truck bearing down on him along one of the alleys between the piled crates. It was coming fast. He flattened himself against a crate as the huge forks lunged in on either side of him, effectively pinning him there. Bill Todd switched off the engine and coolly regarded his captive.

"Had some fun last night, didn't you?" he said flatly.

John gave him a quick, nervous smile. "Look, I want to apologise for that. Mum says Susan was upset."

"Yeah." Bill Todd nodded grimly. "Susan was upset and I was upset. My mother's upset and I should think your old man's upset as well."

"Sorry, Bill," John said contritely, completing the job of putting on his overalls. "It was just going to be an invitation on the top of the TV mast. Then they caught me climbing up and I got carried away. That's why I invited the whole of Victoria on TV."

Bill grinned. He couldn't help it. His teeth were strong and white. "God help you if *you* ever get married. I'll get even, don't you worry."

Relieved, John grinned back at his brother-in-law to be. "You'd never get even," he laughed. "I'd be too smart for you.'

He ducked out beneath one of the forks and ran along the alleyway to a large cleared area in the middle of the warehouse. Starting the forklift Bill spun it around and headed after John. John waited, legs apart, arms raised, in an exaggerated kung-fu stance. The forklift roared towards him. John stood his ground until it was only a couple of feet away from him, then leapt gracefully to one side. The forklift came round in a circle, and once more Bill was aiming it at John.

"Switch that thing off. You hear me? Switch it off!" Yelling at them, gesticulating wildly, a large red-faced man ran into the clearing. Bill stopped the forklift and switched off the engine. "What the hell do you two lunatics think you're doing?"

"Sorry, Sam," John said.

"Bloody fools!" Sam Selmer raged, glaring from one to the other. "I warned you about all this horseplay. You arrive late for work, you clown around with tens of thousands of bucks worth of stuff in those boxes." His face was mottling dangerously. "Now you two get your fingers out and do some work or you're fired. Understood?'

"Yes, Sam." John looked suitably chastened.

"It won't happen again, Sam," Bill quietly assured him.

"Not if you want this job it won't," Selmer shouted, as he stormed back along the alleyway between the stacked crates that reached almost to the ceiling. John and Bill looked at each other. Bill raised his eyebrows. He was plainly worried.

They were Sam Selmer's only employees. Bill was already working there when John was taken on at the import-export warehouse. Before long they had become fast friends. It was through John that Bill had met Susan, and things had snowballed from there. They had fallen in love, had become engaged. Bill had scraped together enough money to put down a deposit on a house, and now they were about to be married.

John and Bill worked well together. If Bill did have one fault, John had decided quite early on in the piece, it was the quickness of his temper. When he lost his temper — and fortunately, that happened very rarely — he could be frightening. John knew that at one time he had been a keen footballer who had his eye on a professional career. He had been so good, in fact — this was what Bill had told him once — that he was just at the point of being signed up for a league team when a knee injury had put him out of the game for good. He had cause to be bitter. Although it had not been definitely stated, John guessed he had gone off the rails for a while after that. There were dark areas in Bill's life on which he wouldn't be drawn.

About halfway through the morning they were hoisting large crates of china to a rack near the high ceiling. John and Bill were on the floor, straining on the rope which ran through a pulley on the ceiling. Sam Selmer was standing on the rack, ready for the crates as they swung in towards him. They had already lifted three crates in this way. They were now on their fourth. With John and Bill pulling on the rope, it swung in towards Sam.

"Steady," he called down to him. "That's it. . .steady . . ."

Then something happened. It was John. He shouted suddenly, and letting go the rope, leapt back and covered his face with his hands. Even afterwards he couldn't say what had caused him to do this. All he could say was that there had been a very real sensation of panic, a reaction to an emergency which had nothing to do with the warehouse or with anything that was going on inside it — something totally unrelated, yet with which he was inextricably bound up. Was there, in that sudden rushing moment of fear — was there just the faintest overlay, the faintest suggestion of a woman's scream, the squeal of locked tyres? He couldn't say for sure. His heart pounded and thumped. He was trembling all over. It was all over in a fraction of a second — but by then it was too late.

When John let go the rope, Bill was unable to hold the extra weight that was so abruptly thrust on him. The rope slipped through his fingers, and above them the crate swung outwards from the rack where Sam was waiting, teetered, then came hurtling down just as John and Bill sprang clear. The crate hit the concrete floor and broke apart. The sound of smashing timber and crockery was deafening, echoes rebounded on echoes, and all John could do was stare at the wreckage in horror. What had happened? His heart was still beating rapidly. Bill swung on him angrily.

"What the hell's the matter with you?" he demanded.

"I don't know," John whispered, shaking his head helplessly. "I don't know."

Then from above Sam Selmer's furious voice cut roughly across the dying echoes. "Okay, that's it," he shouted. "Get out — both of you. You're fired."

They waited until he had scrambled down from the rack. Bill was angry. His jaw muscles worked, his eyes were narrowed. "You can't fire me for something that wasn't my fault," he said, trying to keep his voice level, free of the hurt and outrage he felt.

A vein throbbed in Sam Selmer's temple. His eyes were wild and staring. "Don't argue," he cried in a strangled voice, his finger jabbing in the direction of the door. "Just get out. Both of you. I don't want to see either of you ever again."

John felt as if he were about to be sick. "But it was an accident, Sam," he said weakly. "I let go of the rope, not Bill.

But Sam was not to be placated. His body was shaking with rage. He looked as though he might have a heart attack at any moment. His face was almost purple.

"Listen," he roared, pointing down at the wreckage that was strewn around their feet, "The stuff in that crate was worth thousands. Fine china — what do you think?" He brought the edge of his hand up level with his throat. "Now I've had you two clowns up to here, so just get out. Now! Do you hear me?"

Abruptly he wheeled away and stomped away from them towards his office at the far end of the warehouse. In a quick, convulsive movement, Bill turned on John. All the colour drained from his face, his eyes were furious and his mouth set in a straight, grim line. "You know how much I need this bloody job." He spat the words out viciously. "I could kill you, you stupid bastard!"

6

It was a sparkling day in Sydney. The harbour gleamed, as did the white sails of the Opera House. Light was reflected in the windows of the buildings that piled down to the water's edge. Sailing boats darted and skimmed across the placid surface of the light-filled water, ferry boats chugged sedately. Puffs of cloud floated lazily across the clear sky. It was a day to be alive, doing things.

As they headed north across the Bridge, Angela Hamilton rested her head against the back of the seat and closed her eyes. She felt the breeze on her face, a gentle touch on her cheeks. The sun was warm on her face. She felt tired, but quite deliciously so — more lazy than tired, really, like the day itself. Lazy and floating perhaps — yes, floating was a much better word for the way she felt.

She opened her eyes and glanced at the young man beside her deftly guiding the open Mercedes sports in and out of the traffic, smooth, assured, totally relaxed. Yes . . . tanned, blonde, attractive, rich, spoilt, a part of the set, indistinguishable, a stud — a lazy afternoon, full and drowsy, lunch at Double Bay, chic, a discreet murmur like the sound of bees on a lazy summer's afternoon, conversation, a soft chinking of cutlery, the touching of glasses, a ripple of laughter, gliding waiters, the scratch of a signature scrawled across an expense account, subdued lighting that gave everyone's face a faintly roseate glow, people eating, people drinking, toasting each other, making promises, closing deals in an atmosphere of flawless elegance, spotless white napkins of the purest linen, flowers, unobtrusive music, chardonnay, tournedos, more wine, plenty of wine — yes, perhaps she had drunk a little too much.

When they had left the restaurant the bright sunlight reflected from the water had hurt her eyes and she had hurriedly fumbled in her bag for her sunglasses. A wave of dizziness had passed over her, and as she moved a little unsteadily, Simon had grabbed her arm, and laughed. "Hey, hey, watch it, people might think you've had too much to drink." Good old Simon.

"Whoops," she had said and the dizziness had passed as quickly as it had come.

Now they were driving home. After Simon had dropped her off, she thought she would go up to her room and rest for an hour or two. Rest a while. The contented purr of the engine, the sensation of speed, the sun, a distant humming in her head, a sense of unreality, of floating. . . She was aware of the beginnings of a headache, a tightness around her eyes and temples.

Another lunch out of so many — a succession of lunches and parties, familiar faces, telephone calls, things to arrange, fitting in with her mother's plans — oh yes, she *did* approve of Simon, very much, "eligible" was the word she liked to use — hints here, hints there, all the time hints. So, lunches and dinners, first nights at the theatre, unflattering pictures in the social pages, riding and pool parties, all with the right young people — people of whom her mother certainly approved. Day after day — it was seldom when there was nothing to do, when time hung heavily on her hands.

And yet, while she had everything she wanted, and a certain amount of freedom which even her mother couldn't suppress — though, God knew, she tried hard enough — there was still something lacking. Angela realised this, and there were even times when she felt she could put her finger on what it was — moments, perhaps, when she had had a little too much to drink and felt herself to be on the point of revelation. On those occasions all the pieces fitted neatly into place and there were no longer those moments of uncertainty when she felt lost, somehow out of place in that spotless house where everyone in it seemed to be drawing farther away from each other, turning into strangers, becoming lost in the luxury with which they had surrounded themselves. They were careful people, daunted by symmetry and a cleanliness that bordered on the antiseptic; people in control of their emotions, who acted out their lives with precision as though in the centre of a spotlit stage.

But was that entirely right? Angela thought she was possibly exaggerating a little. Perhaps she was letting herself be subject to impressions that weren't there — or at least in the form in which she imagined them to be. She smiled to herself. She was letting herself be carried away again. Everyone was just preoccupied — that was all. Her father was a busy man, with so many responsibilities that took up so much of his time, and her mother — well, she could see right through her mother. And Wayne — she quickly banished the thought of her brother. She didn't want anything at the moment to spoil her mood of contentment and well being.

Heading north, away from the city, her hair stirring in the breeze and the sun warm on her face, drowsy, drifting . . . she could not help remembering the surprise party her mother was organising for her birthday. Only it *wasn't* a surprise because she was all the time on the 'phone about it — "The guests enjoy it more that way, dear."

"Are you sure you don't want to go for a swim?" Simon's voice sounded as if it were coming from a vast humming distance. "It'd clear your head."

"No, no." She shook her head. "Just take me home — that'd be fine."

"Yeah, okay." He was obviously disappointed, but she

knew he wasn't going to argue about it.

There was a time, not so very long ago, when she had broken out. She had seen it then as an adventure, a focal point for her rebellion. She sighed. Now she wasn't so sure. It had been illicit, and at the time she had enjoyed it, the secrecy, the elaborate precautions, the motels where there were no questions asked, moments grabbed whenever they could be. It was all over now, of course, and that had been no surprise to either of them; neither of them had expected it to last — or had even wanted it to. A fling, and all the time Angela had believed that she was the one who was pulling the strings, turning it off and on, perfectly in control of the situation. And then she had gone too far, and felt the compelling need to flaunt her triumph. And now all that was left was a bitter, lingering taste.

She hadn't really loved Bernard. She had wanted him — and everything she wanted, she got. But had she really got what she wanted? Again, she wasn't so sure. Bernard had been mature, caring, and there had been some good times — times when Angela had felt herself in danger of losing that wonderful control she thought she had. He had been different from the boys she had known — those quick, eager, fumbling, disappointing boys who were always panting over her. But the affair had ended as a closed chapter.

She didn't think it was fair, though, that she would have to feel so guilty about it. Bernard had gone into it with his eyes wide open. He had known what was at stake, and if his marriage had fallen apart because of the fling, then it didn't say much for the strength of that marriage in the first place. It must have already been falling apart when the affair began.

They were coming up through the leafy North Shore, heading towards Dural, and home, sweet jasmine and black tiles. Bernard was out of her mind now, finished, a dead issue. Her head felt empty. She would feel better if she had another drink. She shouldn't drink so much at lunchtime — a perfect sunny day, and she should have been out riding, or swimming, or playing tennis. Thoughts jumbled, tossing and tumbling, and a faint, very faint buzzing sound inside her head, coming from deep dark recesses . . .

She opened her eyes suddenly — some warning, some instinct, a rush of panic, the sun very bright, shimmering through the leaves, massive trees forming an arc over a side street, and a truck coming out of it. Simon yelled and slammed his foot hard down on the brake. The anguished blast from the horn jolted right through Angela as the locked wheels screeched their own agonised protest. The car swerved in towards the bank and the truck loomed closer. Angela screamed . . .

. . . many hundreds of kilometres away, in Melbourne, a crate of china crashed down onto a warehouse floor.

7

David Palmer was angry. He was frustrated and disappointed. He paced up and down the small comfortable living room, his jaw muscles clenched, and every now and again his fist slammed into the palm of his other hand. John Palmer sat in one of the armchairs, staring up at his father — with a sullen expression.

"I give up," David yelled. "I really do. Ever since you were a kid you've been in trouble. You dropped out of school when you could have gone in for a successful career . . ."

"I dropped out because this family needed money," John broke in. There was defiance in his eyes and angry red spots on his cheeks. "That's why. You should remember that. We were broke — or near enough. Or don't you *want* to remember?"

David Palmer made a curt, dismissive gesture. "And what happened?" he demanded with a trace of sarcasm in his tone. "One job after the other — that's what happened. In and out. You either walked out or they fired you." He stood over his son, his arms hanging by his sides, his face thrust forward, his eyes hard and unrelenting. "So what is it you want, mate?" he said with cold deliberation. "What the hell do you want out of life?"

John avoided looking at his father. His eyes flicked around the room, resting briefly on familiar objects and finding no reassurance from them. "I don't think you'd understand," he murmured at last. How could he explain? What *was* there to explain? Something had happened in the warehouse that had made him let go of the rope holding the crate of china — a split-second of inexplicable panic.

"You're damn right I don't understand," David Palmer said bitterly. He stared down at John for a long moment. "Now let me tell you what to do," he went on more quietly but just as deliberately. "I got you that job with Sam Selmer, and now what you're going to do is get right back down there, apologise and ask for your job back — right?"

"Dad, it's a *lousy* job," John cried out in dismay.

David shrugged. His mouth turned down slightly at the corners. "So is driving a truck all over the country," he observed drily. "But you don't hear *me* complain, do you. It's a job and I have to do it."

"Oh no." John gave a short humourless laugh. "No, I never hear *you* complain. All I ever hear *you* say is hello and goodbye. You know something? This is the longest talk we've had in years."

"Don't get smart with me, son," David said tersely. "If you don't like it here you can always move out."

"Okay." Slowly, John rose to his feet. "Okay, I'll ask for the rotten job back." He turned to the older man. "Just tell me one thing, though." He gulped and with an effort held his father's baleful stare. "Why don't you like me?"

David's chin jerked towards the living room door. "Just get that job," he snapped, "or find somewhere else to live."

Beryl Palmer was just coming in through the front door with a bag of groceries when John stormed past her.

"What's wrong?" she called after him.

"I am." He was almost in tears. "Everything I do is wrong."

It was true. He couldn't do anything right, it seemed, even when he tried — and he tried very hard. But, somehow, his father seemed to have some sort of grudge against him, as if he, John, had once done something really bad to him. It was as if his father resented him for being . . . well, just for being what he was, his son. There had been times when John was tempted to grab his father by the front of his shirt, to yell at him, scream at him, and demand an answer. But he knew there would be no answer; nothing would change.

The worst of it was that it was different with Susan and Kevin. With them, he really *acted* like a father — and right from the beginning, from the time he had been brought down to Melbourne from Sydney to live with them, he had always felt that his father regarded him as a stranger, that he didn't truly belong there. Everyone else — Beryl, Susan and Kevin — had accepted him for one of their own. It was only his father who didn't — and John didn't know why.

He thought about it on the tram that was taking him back into town. He looked out at the rows of buildings, houses and shops as they slid silently by without really seeing them. He was nervous. He was going back to the warehouse to *plead* with Sam Selmer to let him have his job back — he knew only too well he was going to be humiliated. He shook his head. No use, no use. He could get off the tram now, walk around for a while, have a drink or two, waste some time, then go back home and tell them that Sam had refused to give him his job back. But what if his father checked it out with Sam, decided to plead with him on his behalf . . .? No, better see the thing through.

The bell rang, the tram started and stopped. People climbed on, people climbed off. They passed factories and sales yards. John thought about his father — his father's obvious dislike of him. It went right back, this attitude of his father's. It went further back than the time John had taken his father's car for a joy-ride and pranged it. He had been furious then, had called John a useless bludger and all the rest of it. That was when John had decided to leave school, take a job, and pay his father back the first $250 David had had to fork out for repairs in order to keep his no-claim bonus.

Factories and grimy streets. They were almost there. Next stop. Reluctantly he stepped down from the tram and walked slowly down the street towards the warehouse, hands in his pockets, shoulders hunched, putting off the moment of confrontation for as long as he could. He kicked an empty soft drink can and it rolled away into the gutter with a resounding clatter. He turned a corner.

The warehouse was silent. John stood in the main doorway and blinked into the gloomy interior, taking in the rows of shelves, the piled crates and the narrow alleyways between them. He listened, but heard nothing. It still wasn't too late. He could always turn back now, say there was no one there. Summoning what was left of his resolve, he stepped in through the doorway and made his way between the towering rows of crates towards the rear of the building. A dim light from the office reached towards him as he drew closer to it, but he still heard nothing. He hesitated. There was something almost eerie about that silence, and as he stood at the end of the row looking across at the lighted office where there was no sign of life, John experienced a very real sense of foreboding.

"Sam?" he called weakly, and yet his voice seemed to fill the cavernous interior of the warehouse, to whip away down the rows behind him then fling itself back at him with a renewed force. "Sam, are you there?"

There was no response. Cautiously, John moved across to the office. He stopped in the doorway.

The scene in the office semed to insinuate itself on him, to build up slowly, component by component, until at last, it was all there, laid out for him in unmistakable perspective — and even then it was unreal.

The first thing he saw was the overturned chair, then the telephone receiver dangling over the side of the desk. He saw ragged red splotches on the wall, and papers strewn across the floor. And then the last vital piece of the grisly tableau — the humped body on the floor, lying face down. He saw the crowbar, stained a gleaming red, lying across the man's back.

"Sam?" he whispered. Suddenly he couldn't breathe; all his breath seemed to be caught up in his throat, blocked there, wedged, an immovable obstacle. His heart was pounding, and it seemed to him that the sound of it reverberated throughout the silent warehouse. He crept across the room on the balls of his feet, and knelt down beside the lifeless body on the floor. His hand reached out, hesitated, hovered for a moment, then with an effort closed around the end of the stained crowbar. He lifted the bar from the body. With his other hand, he pulled at the body, gently at first then with more vigour when it failed to budge. He put the crowbar down on the floor and tugged at the body with both hands. His breath was still stuck in his throat and he didn't feel he should dare try to force it loose. He pulled at the body.

Suddenly it moved. It rolled over onto its back, and John found himself staring down into Sam Selmer's bulging, lifeless eyes, stamped indelibly with the terror that had marked the closing moments of his life. John recoiled in horror from the smashed, bloody face. He struggled to his feet, stumbling, falling heavily against the frame of the office door. Mindless panic was taking over, directing him as he ran back through the warehouse, running fast, his only thought to put as much distance as he could between himself and the gory horror he had left behind him in the office. Gritty sunlight filled the warehouse entrance in front of him, grey streets, safety. Huge sobs racked his body.

And then he was out in the street, running. There was a squeal of tyres behind him. Without faltering, he glanced over his shoulder to see the car swinging into the street, black and white, a flashing blue light, a shout, running feet behind him. His heart was pounding, deafening. Possessed, his feet hardly touched the ground, ducking and weaving, an alleyway, more warehouses, factory doors, and even though he could no longer hear the sound of running feet behind him, no longer hear the shouting, he still kept running.

8

The ringing was harsh and strident — each ring went right through him, jarred him. The first ring had made him jump, and now as he stared at the telephone, squat, black and malevolent on the table beside the door, Bill Todd felt leaden and sick. Cold sweat pricked his forehead. The telephone was ringing out his own doom. It accused him. He was trembling. Hunched on the edge of the armchair, he pressed his hands tightly together to try and force himself to stop trembling.

The phone kept ringing. Its sound was insistent and shrill. It echoed inside his head, went around and around inside his head, a wire-thin band that drew painfully tighter. It would have to stop some time, he told himself. Whoever was there would give up in the end.

He shook his head. It could be anyone. It didn't have to be . . . It didn't necessarily mean . . .

They would have found Sam by now. Oh, Jesus, why did it have to happen? Why didn't the phone stop ringing? It *had* to stop ringing. He couldn't stand it any more — the suspense, the not knowing . . . Abruptly, he leapt up onto his feet, and crossing the room, scooped up the receiver. His nerves — he would have to watch his nerves. They could give him away. When he was being questioned —

and it was bound to happen sooner or later — he would have to have them under firm control.

"Hello."

"Bill? It's Susan."

At the sound of her voice the relief surged through him. He took a deep breath. He should have guessed it might have been her. Or someone for his mother. Not about Sam — not yet. "Oh, hi," he said. feebly. His smile was shaky.

"I've just walked in." Susan's voice was concerned. "Mum told me that you and John have been fired."

"Yeah," Bill grunted. "We were fired."

"I need that job, Sam. The accident wasn't my fault."

"Get lost."

"I'm saving up to get married, Sam. I've just taken out a mortgage on a new house."

"You should have thought about that when you and that other fool were horsing around."

"Bill? Are you still there?"

"Yeah."

"Well, what happened? Why were you fired?"

"Ask John. He'll tell you."

"He's gone back to talk to Sam Selmer. He hasn't come home yet."

John! He wiped the sweat away from his forehead with the sleeve of his shirt. But it still sprouted just below his hairline. The office, the single light bulb, and Sam with his back to him, coldly adamant. John had gone back *there?* The little fool! What did he hope to prove by going back down there? Did he expect Sam to give him his job back, to succeed where Bill himself had failed?

"Look, Sam, just give me a chance."

"No way. I've just taken on two new men. They start tomorrow."

Now John had gone down there. Bill could taste the bile that suddenly rose to his mouth. He felt dizzy, weak, and his palms were slippery with sweat. John going to that office, and finding. . . But maybe the police were already there by the time John arrived.

"Bill? Bill? Are you all right?"

There was a leaden weight in the pit of his stomach. "Yeah," he muttered. "I came home straight away — after we were fired. Mum's not well, so I stayed with her." His lips were dry and cracked. He moistened them with his tongue. Nerves, nerves — steady on, try and act natural, as though nothing has happened.

"You owe me a week's money, Sam. I want it."

"Is that some kinda joke? After what it cost me today, you're asking for money? Do I believe what I'm hearing?"

"I've got to have it, Sam. I told you . . ."

"Well, you won't get it here. Now clear out or I'll have you thrown out. You don't think I mean it? You want me to call the police?"

The silent warehouse and Sam with his back to him, picking up the phone, dialling a number.

"Give me the police . . ."

The anxiety was still in Susan's voice. "Would you like me to come over?"

"No," Bill said quickly — maybe a little too quickly. Watch it, act naturally. You don't know anything — remember. You don't know about Sam. "She's got a migraine or something. She's lying down." He took another deep breath, and for an instant, saw once again the expression on Sam's face as he had dragged him away from the telephone, as the receiver had fallen from his hand. "Look, Susie, can we skip going out tonight?"

"Sure. If that's what you want." She sounded a little hurt.

"It's just that . . .well, I've got to find another job, haven't I? So it's probably best if I start going through the papers — that sort of thing."

"All right." Susan didn't sound too convinced. "I'll ring you later on."

"Yeah." Bill sighed. "John's got a lot to answer for, Susie," he said grimly.

"Don't worry," Susan said. "I'll have it out with him when he gets home. Bye, darling."

"Susie."
"Yes, Bill?"
"I love you, Susie."
"I love you, too."

Slowly, Bill replaced the receiver, then resting his head against the wall, closed his eyes. He was exhausted, totally drained. He had come through one ordeal and he was sure that this was only the first of many more to come which would be much, much worse. He doubted at that moment if he would ever find the strength to face them.

9

John Palmer stood in the kitchen doorway, watching them. They were having their dinner and he noticed the place that had been set for him at the table. The room was so warm and familiar, the smell of roasted food caused a pang in his stomach and reminded him that he hadn't had anything to eat since breakfast. As usual, there was lashings of food on the table, plenty for everyone. On a plate, the roast beef had been cut into thin slices. There were roast potatoes and baby carrots, peas, thick gravy. Everyone was talking at once, except his father who sat there with a sour look on his face.

It was Kevin, his younger brother, who noticed him first. He looked up, the laden fork halfway to his mouth, and saw John standing there. His mother, following his gaze, rose to her feet. She smiled at John. "You're home at last," she said cheerfully. "I'll get your dinner."

They were all looking at him now, a little uncertainly, put off perhaps by the grim expression on his face as he stared at his father.

"Dad, can you come in here?" he said quietly.

David Palmer was steadily chewing his food. "What for?"

"I want to talk to you — alone." He moved back into

the sitting room before his father could raise any objections which might serve to lessen the force of his resolve. What he had to say was very important. It couldn't be put off — and even now it might be too late.

He waited in the sitting room, restless and fidgeting, for his father to join him. He had run and run, not thinking, away from the warehouse, not knowing where he was going, obsessed only by the need to escape, his mind full of the battered, bloody object that had once been a living human being. The word had kept beating inside his head as he ran. Why? Who would have done something like that?

The police had seen him leaving the warehouse. They had chased him, but he had managed to avoid them — and even after he had realised this he had kept on running, losing himself in a maze of back streets and alleyways. Gradually, keeping away from the main streets, he had worked his way back home.

"Couldn't this wait until we've finished dinner?" David Palmer came into the room and stopped in front of John.

"No, it can't."

David studied his son for a long moment. "Well?" he demanded at last. "Did you get your job back?"

"I've been walking around for hours," John said earnestly. "Dad, I know how upset you get with the things I do — but I always tell you the truth, don't I?"

David frowned in annoyance. Muted conversation drifted into the room from the kitchen. "Did you get the job back?"

This was it. This was it now. "He's dead," John said simply.

"Who's dead?"

"Sam Selmer." John held his father's gaze. It was important that he believed him — everything depended on it. "I didn't kill him, Dad. I went back there to ask for my job because you insisted. But he was dead when I got there."

David was staring hard at John. "Hold on a minute," he said sharply. "Are you trying to tell me that someone *killed* him?"

John nodded. The blood spattered on the office walls, the staring eyes. "With an iron bar."

David drew a sharp breath. "Jesus!" he whispered. "Did you call the police?"

"No," John told him. "I ran away. They saw me."

The sound of the doorbell startled them both. His heart racing, John leapt across to the window, and parting the curtains a fraction, peered out into the darkness. He saw the patrol car at the kerb outside the front gate, the two men standing on the front porch, one of them in uniform, his cap badge gleaming dully in the wash of moonlight. John flung himself away from the window.

"It's the police," he cried frantically. "Dad, I didn't do it. They won't believe me, but you . . . you've *got* to believe me. I didn't do it."

David looked from his son to the hallway, obviously confused, undecided. "Wait in your bedroom," he ordered.

Beryl came in from the kitchen. "Who's at the door?" she asked, looking uncertainly from her husband to John who hadn't moved.

"Do as I tell you, John," David said firmly. "Get to your room. I'll handle this."

John looked helplessly at his father, at Beryl, and glanced out into the darkened hallway. He felt trapped, but there was nothing else he could do — he simply had to trust his father. There was silence from the kitchen behind him. The doorbell rang again. Quickly, silently, he moved out of the sitting room into the hallway, and down to the room he shared with Kevin. Closing the door gently behind him, he sat down on his bed and held his head in his hands. A light breeze stirred the curtains in front of the partly opened window.

A trapped animal, nowhere to run, and they were closing in on him — and who would believe him, believe it hadn't been him who had picked up the iron bar and smashed Sam Selmer's face almost to a pulp? The door opened. He let his hands fall away from his face and looked up as Kevin and Susan, looking concerned, came into the room.

"What did you do?" Kevin asked in some awe.

"Nothing," John said in a trembling voice.

"Doesn't look like it." There was a curious glittering intensity in Kevin's dark eyes as he stared at his brother. "It's the police. What do they want?"

"Shut up, Kevin," Susan snapped, and sat down on the bed beside John. "Are you all right?"

"I don't . . ." John began miserably. He turned on the bed and looked imploringly into his sister's eyes. "Look, there's been some trouble and you'll hear about it soon enough, I guess. But . . ." His hand reached out and touched Susan's arm, then just as quickly withdrew. "But, look, Susie . . ." He glanced up at Kevin. "I didn't do it, whatever they say. I didn't. I just walked into it, and now . . ." He shook his head, trying to get his racing thoughts into some sort of order. "Susie, please, tell Dad I want to speak to him . . . before anything else . . . before he says anything to the police. I've *got* to speak to him. Please, Susie," he begged. "Go and tell him I want to see him."

Susan looked at him doubtfully for a moment, then with a sigh, rose to her feet. "All right," she said. She opened the door and left the room.

After she had gone, John sat motionless on the bed, his hands clasped together, staring at the floor. Kevin's expression was lively. Clearly he had a lot of questions to ask, and was on the point of asking them, but something about his brother's attitude put him off. So they waited in a silence that just dragged and dragged, before it was finally broken when the bedroom door opened again and David Palmer came into the room.

"Leave us alone, will you, Kev." His chin jerked towards the landing behind him. Then when Kevin had gone, he swung angrily on John. "Why did you do it?" he demanded.

"But, Dad, I didn't." John's voice rose so sharply that it almost cracked. It was hopeless, hopeless — he knew his father didn't believe him, that he really didn't have a chance.

David Palmer's face was pinched. His eyes bore gimlet-like into John. "Oh, come on, don't give me that. Sam Selmer gave them your name."

It was as if somebody had just landed a piledriver into John's stomach, knocking all the breath out of his body. Even the fear that hadn't left him since that awful moment in the warehouse seemed to be momentarily displaced. He gaped at his father open-mouthed. "But . . . but . . ." he stammered. "But he couldn't. He was dead."

"I'm only telling you what they told me . . . down there." David's chin jerked again towards the closed door. "He wasn't dead when you arrived at the warehouse. He died on the way to hospital." He sighed heavily. "What you need now is a good lawyer." He gestured towards the door behind him. "Now you'd better come with me. Get this mess sorted out."

But John didn't move. He was conscious of the hot tears stinging his eyes, a deep rending sense of betrayal. "I'm asking you to say you believe me," he said in a small, shaky voice.

David's face was a pale expressionless mask. His features appeared sharper, his lips drawn in a thin, bloodless line. "Why should I?" His voice was like steel.

"Because I've never lied to you," John cried. The tears welled in his eyes. "I need you to say you trust me."

"*Trust* you?" David exclaimed bitterly. "Just look what you're doing to this family."

There was only emptiness now. "I wonder if you know what *you're* doing to *me,*" John said quietly, hopelessly.

They stared at each other. John bit down into his lower lip to stop it quivering. "Would you ask Mum to come in," he murmured, looking away. "I want to say goodbye to her."

David stared at him for a moment longer, then shrugged. "Okay. I'll get her."

There was nothing else for it. John had already made up his mind. He listened to his father's footsteps along the hallway. He couldn't stay here. He had to move — and fast. They would be back in a minute or two. He moved swiftly across to the window, and careful not to make a noise, opened it wider. He put one leg over the sill, easing himself out and down.

He knew now where he was going. He had some money, not much, but enough to keep him going for a day or two. And when that ran out? Well, he would have to wait until that happened. No time. No time even to take a change of clothing. He was going a long way from here, and he had no idea what his chances were of making it. He didn't think they were very good, but at least he had to try. If he didn't. . . His hands came away from the window ledge and he let himself fall into the darkness of the yard below.

10

The house was silent and full of shadows. It was a long night, and as she waited for David to return from the police station, Beryl Palmer had plenty of time to reflect. It was useless to even think of going to bed. She knew she wouldn't be able to sleep, would start at every sound from the street outside. So she sat in the sitting room, and waited — and wondered what had gone wrong.

It was a happy house — she had seen to that. A house of warmth and laughter. It had been that way right from the beginning, and even when David had brought John down from Sydney, had been quite secretive about him, and John himself had taken a long time to settle down, she had managed not to be too upset. Perhaps she had been a little hurt, because David hadn't fully taken her into his confidence, but the placid routine had been shaped quite satisfactorily around the new addition to the family. Susan had been three at the time, and Kevin almost two, and they had eagerly taken to their new brother — as Beryl herself had eagerly taken to him. It was only David who had shown any reserve towards him, and she wondered why. There were times, she noticed, when David seemed positively to dislike the boy, and on those few occasions when she tried to draw him out about it, David seemed to withdraw more deeply into the shell he had created about himself. It worried her — in fact, it was the only cloud in the comfortable, settled, happy world she had made for them all, an extension as it were of the happiness she herself had known as a child.

It wasn't as if David was an insensitive type of man. Very much the opposite. That trait was what she had first noticed about him all those years ago when he walked into the roadside diner where she worked. He wasn't at all like the other drivers, rough and ready but with hearts of gold, and she had been able to hold her own with the best of them. David was quiet, withdrawn — he had depth, she recognised that, and every time he stopped off at Ararat on his way to and from Adelaide, she had become increasingly more fascinated by him. A long time ago. A secretive man.

John and David — they just hadn't seemed to hit it off together. Now John was gone, with a murder charge hanging over his head. He hadn't eaten, he must be tired and hungry . . .

She started at the sound of a key turning in the front door lock, and for an instant the wild hope that it was John surged within her. Then David came into the room and she tried not to let her disappointment show. She smiled up at her husband who looked drawn and pale.

"I don't suppose he phoned, or anything?" he said, lowering himself in the armchair opposite her.

"No." She shook her head. She was relieved now that he was back, but some of the tension remained.

"The other two gone to bed?" David asked.

"Yes, Susan's on the early shift tomorrow." She leaned forward in her chair. "What did the police say to you?"

"They questioned me for hours," David said in disgust. "Or it seemed that way. Of course, spending so much time there last night didn't help either, but I think I managed to convince them that I had nothing to do with him running away like that."

What would her own parents have done, what would

they have said? Always laughter in the house — no money, but plenty of laughter. And if something like this had happened . . . ? There were five Keegan kids, including herself, and not one of them had gotten into real trouble — certainly nothing as bad as this.

"David, do you think John did kill that man?" she asked quietly.

David thought about this for a few moments. "I don't know," he said finally, shaking his head. "He kept telling me he didn't . . . but I don't know what to believe."

"He's never lied to us — you know that," Beryl reminded him firmly. "I know he's a bit wild at times . . ."

"Wild!" David snorted, slamming one hand down on the arm of the chair. "Wild! What an understatement." His voice rose angrily. "He spent most of last night in a cell for trespassing, disturbing the peace and God knows what — and now this! He just can't stay out of trouble, Beryl." He spread his hands in a gesture of hopelessness. "I should have been tougher on him when I brought him here from Sydney, but you were always protecting him." He glared at her accusingly. There were dark smudges under his eyes. He looked exhausted.

Now it was Beryl's turn to be indignant. She felt the warmth spreading in her cheeks. "He *needed* someone to protect him," she retorted. "You were harder on John than you've ever been on young Kevin."

David's eyes were fixed on the sideboard. "Kevin's different to John," he said, and Beryl could sense his unease. "So is Susan."

In the silence that followed, Beryl steeled herself for the response to the question she was about to ask. It was one she had asked before, but she couldn't help asking it again. "What *was* John's mother like?"

But instead of shouting at her this time, David merely sighed and shook his head. "Beryl, don't start that again," he said reproachfully.

"I need to know, David," Beryl persisted, leaning forward in her chair. He was so stubborn, so caught up within himself, and if only she could draw him out, break down the wall he put up between them at times like this . . . Of course, she knew she was only dashing herself futilely against that wall, hurting herself. He would never change. She went on, less fervently. "I think you must have hated her very much . . . for some reason that you're just too stubborn to talk about." The other woman, the one who had borne David's first child, and Beryl didn't know what she looked like, couldn't even imagine. "Maybe it's because John reminds you of her all the time." She paused. David was looking even more uncomfortable. "You know, that woman . . . the one I've never seen, the woman you won't talk about . . . she's beginning to haunt this family."

Abruptly, like a suddenly released spring, David jerked to his feet. His face was flushed and he spoke with barely suppressed anger. "Look, I told you before — I told you when we first met that I'd never talk about it." He moved towards the kitchen door. "And I never will."

That was it, conversation closed, the wall well and truly up again. Beryl slumped back in her chair and watched her husband as he walked stiffly out of the sitting room into the kitchen.

11

"Now, in case you get lost — what's your name?"

"John Palmer."

"And where do you live?"

"I live at number twenty-two Manly Terrace, Manly."

"Good boy. . . oh, you're a good boy. Now off we go. Off to school."

Fiona straightening his tie, making sure his cap wasn't crooked, handing him his lunch, fruit, brown bread, nutritious, always knew what was best for him. Years and years ago. He remembered it all so clearly.

Even more so now, vividly, as the prow of the ferry sliced through the cool dark water. Leaning against the deck railing the strong breeze whipped through his hair as he looked across at the Heads, and Middle Harbour. Slowly they drew closer to Manly.

It was inevitable, of course, that he should have thought of coming back to Manly. He had never really left it. Even during all those years in Melbourne, part of him had remained right here, on this isthmus that separated the Harbour from the ocean beyond, the crowded hills that bounded it, the small harbour beaches, and the cliffs and bushland of North Head. Even the air here was different, something special.

He was coming home, to the place of his childhood, to the long sweep of ocean beach, to the wharf and fun fair, Marineland and the Norfolk pines, the beach bums and the lorikeets that made an enormous racket in the trees at sunset. It was all looming up now as the ferry approached the wharf — a world apart, Melbourne a long way behind him, and even Sydney. What did they say about Manly? "Seven Miles From Sydney And A Thousand Miles From Care." At this crucial turning point in his life the slogan was very meaningful. He had come a long way, and now he was almost there.

There had been times when he had thought he wouldn't make it, cold nights, moving under the cover of darkness, at any moment expecting to feel a hand on his shoulder, hear a shout. He had finally smuggled himself on the back of a truck heading north, shaking, rattling, on and on, it seemed forever, the miles slipping out from beneath the massive wheels. He had known where he was going.

"Where do you live?"

". . . twenty-two Manly Terrace, Manly."

Home — and safety. He hoped. If Fiona still lived there . . . it was thirteen years . . . she might have moved, anything was possible. But he was coming back — crowded beaches, hordes of holiday makers streaming off the ferries and drifting in swarms and eddies along the Corso to the ocean beaches. Here he could lose himself, be anonymous, be someone else.

Johnny, do you know who this is?"

Staring, gaping at the stranger, shaking his head.

"This is your father. Remember how I always told you he would come back one day? Well, here he is. He's come to take you back to Melbourne with him."

Hot stinging tears. "No! No!" he had screamed. "Aunt Fiona! No! Don't let him take me!"

He had struggled and tried to throw himself at Fiona for protection from the strange man who had come to take him away — and he had seen the tears glistening in her eyes. But she had made no move to help him.

Water churned and foamed up from the ferry's propellers as the engines were thrown into reverse. The wharf shivered and groaned as the side of the ferry nudged it. Gangways scraped across the concrete. There was the smell of fish and salt water, a heady mixture John had almost forgotten but which now returned to him with bitter-sweet poignancy.

He walked the familiar streets, noting the changes, heading towards the street and the boarding house where he had spent those earliest, happiest years. The sun was warm on his face and neck. A variety of smells from the takeaway food places drifted and mingled. He walked quickly. He wasn't yet out of danger.

Then he was standing in front of Fiona's house. The street was quieter. The house looked exactly as he remembered. He glanced quickly up and down the street, then with a sense of homecoming threaded through with apprehension, he walked through the open front door into the dark hallway and pressed the bell beside the door of Fiona's flat. He waited, his heart beating faster, wondering, hoping. Then there was a click, and the door opened.

"Door's open," a voice called from inside — and John almost shuddered with relief. Fiona's voice was unmistakeable.

Pushing the door open, John stepped into the bright, well-furnished lounge room. He looked around, registering both the objects that were familiar to him and those that were not; at the framed photographs of himself as a baby and onward that stood ranged on the mantelpiece and sideboard; the rugs and cushions, the record player, the colour television, the lamps, bookcases and cabinets — absorbing it all, drawing in the atmosphere which again was so sharp as to be almost painful. There was no one in the room.

"Hello?" he called.

"Hello yourself," Fiona's voice called back from another room.

John smiled to himself. Very little had changed. "Where

are you?"

"In the bedroom, of course. Where else would I be?"

Yeah. He moved across to one of the doors that opened off the main room. It was ajar. He pushed it open, and hesitated in the doorway.

The bed was enormous. In the middle of it, regally, in complete command, and in a long dressing tgown, Fiona sat on the rich satin bedspread, surrounded by bills, an open chequebook on her lap, engrossed, scribbling. Looking at her, John experienced a rush of warmth and gratitude — just for her being there, being herself, unchanged.

"Just get yourself ready," she said without looking up, "and I'll be all yours. If I don't get these damned cheques off today, they'll . . .

Then she did look up and her voice trailed away as she stared in obvious surprise at the young man in the doorway. Then, slowly, she took off her glasses. Her eyes were cold and unblinking.

"Who are you?" she demanded in a deep, controlled voice.

John grinned at her. "You haven't changed a bit," he said. It was true. *He* was the one who had changed, but Fiona — never. How could she? She was impermutable, like a rock, magnificent, a tower of strength. John gazed fondly at that seamed face with the high cheekbones, and the deepset eyes that were now glacially regarding him.

"What the hell are you doing in my apartment?" she snapped.

John was still grinning — he couldn't help himself. Nothing — not the way she was looking at him, the severity of her tone — could take away his sheer elation.

"You said to come in," he said. His smile wavered a little. "You don't remember me, do you?"

She stared at him for a few moments, then gradually, the angular planes of that weathered face seemed to soften. Her eyes lost their coldness.

"Johnny?" she whispered.

John nodded.

"Oh, Johnny," she cried. "Johnny, I didn't know . . ." Her eyes widened and glistened, and there was a tremor in her voice. "I can't believe it. Johnny." The tears welled, overflowed and ran down her cheeks. "I don't believe it." She held her arms out to him. The tears rolled more freely. Crossing to the bed, John bent over her, and as her arms went around him in a tight, fleeting embrace, he kissed her on the lips. "I'd never have recognised you in a million years," she said excitedly through her tears. "What are you doing here?" She suddenly thought of something. "Oh my God. Don't tell me. Your father's dead."

John sat down on the bed beside her. "No, he isn't," he told her. "You made me memorise the address when I was a kid — twenty-two Manly Terrace. You made me say it over and over. How could I forget?"

She clasped his hands in her own thin, dry ones. "It's been thirteen years since I last saw you — do you know that?"

"Yeah." John nodded. "I wrote to you a couple of times."

"I know," Fiona murmured. "But your father wanted a complete break. I had to go along with that." She smiled shakily. "Are you still living in Melbourne?"

"I was." This was the moment. He had to take the plunge. "Aunt Fiona, look, I'm in trouble."

She stiffened and her eyes narrowed. "Oh?"

"And . . . if you want me to go," John said earnestly, "just tell me. I don't want to cause any trouble."

"Hey, whoa there," Fiona said with a laugh and squeezed his hand. "What are you talking about?"

He regarded her levelly, watching for her reaction. "I'm on the run," he said. "The police are after me."

"You?" She shook her head disbelievingly. "I don't believe it."

John forged on. He had come so far. "They think I killed someone in Melbourne."

Fiona's mouth fell open. "Killed?" she breathed.

"Oh no."

"I didn't do it," John said fervently, his eyes fixed steadily to hers. "I promise you. I didn't do it."

Fiona seemed to rally. "Who was it?" she asked, her tone crisp and to the point.

"A man I worked for."

"I see." She closed her eyes, then opened them again, preparing herself to hear something unpleasant. "Then you had better tell me about it. Everything. From the beginning."

And in that bedroom, with the papers spread out all over the covers, holding the woman's dry hand in his own, John told her what had happened. She listened to him intently, her eyes never leaving his face, as if she could read there all those things he might leave out. As if, through him, she could transform herself back to the scene of those happenings he was quietly telling her about so that she would be in a position to make her own solid judgements.

"I begged Dad to believe me," John said. "I know I've been in trouble a few times — you know, silly things — but I always told him the truth. I don't think I could kill anyone — certainly not poor old Sam Selmer. He was right to fire me, I suppose. Like I told you, I was responsible for all that valuable stuff being smashed. Anyway, when Dad left the room to go down to the police, I jumped out the window and just ran."

Fiona was watching him shrewdly. The house was silent. They were insulated from the outside world, from the thronging holiday makers, the beaches and the circling gulls. "Let me get this straight," she said. "You really ran because your father said he didn't believe you — is that right?"

John shrugged his shoulders. "It meant a lot to me. We've never been close and I thought, just this once, it would prove I meant something to him. Besides, if your own father won't believe you, then who will?"

"I might," Fiona said quietly.

She would. Looking at her, John was certain she would. She had always had a strong sense of fair play; always had the ability to listen, to evaluate, and when she came up with an answer she stuck by it implacably.

"It's the truth, Aunt Fiona."

"John," she said deliberately, "if I asked you to give yourself up, would you do it?"

The disappointment was crushing. He was hurt, bewildered. He had come all this way, taken all those risks, because he was sure there was one person at least who would believe him — and now it looked as if he had been wasting his time. If giving himself up was what Fiona wanted him to do. . . He sighed deeply.

"If you think that's what I should do," he said in a strained voice, "then I guess I will. I guess if I yell loud enough that I'm innocent, *someone* might believe me." The words seemed to be damming up in his throat. He stood up and tried to mask the tumult of his feelings with a smile — but it was a very weak one. "Well, it was nice to see you again. A little talk . . ."

"Come here," Fiona commanded, patting the bed beside her. John couldn't be sure, but there appeared to be a lightly mocking glint in her eyes which at times could be steely. Tentatively, he moved back to the side of the bed. Again she reached up, and placing her hands around his neck, pulled him down towards her and kissed him lightly on the forehead. Then holding him away from her, she gazed at him with a soft, misty look in her eyes. "I didn't say you should give yourself up," she said softly. "I only wanted to know if you *would.*" She smiled. "I'm a good judge of character, Johnny," she went on after a brief pause. "You're wild — you've admitted it — and I guess I was too, in my time. But I won't see you arrested for something you didn't do. You're staying here with me until this mess is sorted out," she told him, her tone indicating that she would brook no argument.

John was touched, he was grateful. He was tired. Long sleepless nights, the police looking for him, Sam Selmer's face bashed in, blood everywhere, dead — not dead. "Sam Selmer gave them your name," his father had said. The weariness was creeping down over him in stages. A lump had formed in his throat.

"Thanks," he murmured.

Then the doorbell rang and all the weariness was gone. He was tense again, every nerve-end alive, burning. "Nick?" Fiona called.

"Yeah," a voice called back.

"You can relax," Fiona said to John, and pressed a button at the side of the bed. There was a faint whirring sound as the outside door opened. John looked about him with rising desperation. This was no place for him to stay. "Where can I go?"

"What do you mean — go?" There was a chuckle in Fiona's voice. "You'll stay right here and hold my hand while he does it."

"Does what?" Now he was truly alarmed.

She laughed outright. "I haven't had time to tell you, have I? Look, I'll show you." She pulled back one side of the dressing gown. John saw that the leg she revealed was encased in a plaster cast covered in signatures, scribbled messages and sketches. Fiona's smile was broad. "If I told you how I broke it, you wouldn't believe me." She looked past John. "Ah, Nick, there you are."

The guy who came into the room was tall, dark, well built and somewhere in his late twenties. He was carrying a small bag. "Morning, Fiona," he said, placing the bag down on the bed, and opening it. "I hope you realise I wouldn't do this for anyone else."

"Of course you wouldn't," Fiona said heartily. "You'll get your reward in heaven — you'll see."

The newcomer took a pair of cutting tongs out of his bag. "What's he going to do?" John asked quietly.

Fiona looked at him in surprise. "Remove the plaster, of course. There's no way they'll get me up that hill to the hospital . . ." Her eyes moved from John to Nick. "Oh Nick," she said. "I haven't introduced my little nephew.

This is Scott — Scott Edwards — from Brisbane."

The two young men shook hands. "Hi Scott," Nick said. "This is some aunt you've got here."

"Oh yes." John glanced at Fiona who was innocently smiling back at him. Scott Edwards — silently he savoured his new name. It didn't sound at all bad — quite distinguished, in fact. "She sure is," he said.

12

Patricia Hamilton smiled in quiet satisfaction. Everything was going along just fine. The near miss car accident had been a lucky escape for Angela — thank heavens that nice young man Simon was such a skilful driver. Yes, life was looking pretty good — which was really a way of saying it was going exactly how she wanted it to go. It had been luck at the beginning, when she hadn't really had much in the way of options. But from that basis, shaky at first, very doubtful, it was generally acknowledged that she had managed things very well.

She smiled at Angela, who stood between her and Gordon with her eyes closed. From the stables behind them, a horse snorted and whinnied. "Now keep them shut until we tell you to open them," she told her daughter.

"Okay." Angela giggled a little in anticipation. Her eyes were squeezed shut, a kid just about to receive a very special birthday treat.

It was a perfect day. The sky was almost completely cloudless and the distant hills were blue, sharply outlined The sun was warm, and after the recent rains the grass at the stud was rich and plentiful. The horses looked sleek and well fed. The business was doing well. Patricia looked from Angela to Gordon, who was staring fondly down at his stepdaughter, and thought that here, too, things were not nearly so bad as they might have been.

They had come to some sort of arrangement which

suited her just fine. They lived quite separate lives; they didn't interfere with each other. She had pushed him, chivvied him, and now they were rich. Gordon still had Woombai, the grazing property at the far north-west of the State, and the transport division of which Patricia didn't really approve but had to admit was virtually the lynchpin of the organisation that had been built up from it. But he most prestigious part of the highly diversified business was the horse stud. Patricia had seen to it that Gordon's son, Wayne, had been given responsibility for it. Gordon had hedged at first, had been reluctant, making it plain that he didn't share Patricia's high estimation of his only son — but in the end, weary of Patricia's persistence, had given in against his better judgement.

"Ready? You can open your eyes now."

The horse was pure Arab. It was magnificent. When she opened her eyes and saw it, Angela gasped in delight.

"Happy birthday, darling," Patricia said softly.

How different it was for Angela now than it had been for Patricia. Angela wanted for nothing; Patricia had wanted for everything. She had been cold, hungry, young and vulnerable. And now that part of her life was sealed away, and if not exactly forgotten — how could it be, with Angela there all the time to remind both her and Gordon that she was the daughter of another man? — certainly something that had no part in their lives. It was something dead — a distant memory that had no substance or even truth any more. Now . . .

Angela was laughing, shaking her head, patting the horse's smooth flank. "I can't believe it," she cried. "Do you mean . . . he's *mine?*"

"All yours," Gordon said with an indulgent smile, placing his arm around his stepdaughter's shoulder and giving her a hug. "Happy birthday, Angela."

Patricia hadn't looked at Gordon as he hugged her daughter. He could easily have been Angela's real father. There was no reserve with him, no holding back, as might have been the attitude of other men towards children not their own. And yet, in the eyes of those children those men were their real fathers — just as Angela believed Gordon to be her real father. And why shouldn't she? Gordon had done more for her than her real father could have ever done. He had brought her up as his own child, and neither Angela nor Wayne had any reason to believe that they were anything other than half-brother and half-sister.

And now Angela was just at the right age — and Patricia had plans for her. Careful steps all the way, the plans laid, the contacts nurtured.

"Isn't he wonderful," Angela cried, skipping up to her and kissing her eagerly on the cheek. "Just look at him. Beautiful." Spinning away from her mother, she took hold of the horse's reins, and patted the animal. The stable hand who had led the horse out of the stable stood near the open doors, watching her.

"Now where's the camera?" Patricia said brightly. "I must get a photo of this."

"I'll get it." Gordon turned away towards the car, then stopped abruptly when he saw the dark, saturnine young man watching them from the corner of the stables.

"Wayne!" he exclaimed.

The young man waved casually. He looked very sure of himself, very confident. "Hi, Dad," he said.

The laughter lines deepened around Gordon Hamilton's eyes when he smiled. "Wayne. When did you get back?"

"This morning," Wayne replied easily, looking at Angela who had stopped at the sound of his voice and was now regarding him with an expression of distaste. "I flew in a day early so I wouldn't miss my little sister's birthday." Moving across to Patricia, he kissed her on the cheek. "Hello, Mother."

"Hello, Wayne." Over his shoulder, she saw the stricken expression on Angela's face and sighed inwardly. It would be so much nicer, she thought, if those two could get along better.

13

It looked increasingly obvious that John wouldn't be home for his birthday, but Beryl bought his present anyway, a pair of jeans which she wrapped in gift paper and put to one side. But no one had any idea when John would be around again to receive the gift. Nobody could even guess where he might have gone. There had been a birthday card Beryl wanted everyone to sign, but when it had come to David, he had torn it up. How could anyone wish John a *happy* birthday, he had demanded, with a murder charge hanging over his head?

It was shortly after this that Bill Todd paid them a visit. If anybody really noticed — and perhaps it was only Beryl Palmer who did — the slight changes in Bill, the nervousness, the hesitation in his manner, they would naturally have put it down to a bad case of pre-wedding jitters. The day was getting closer, and of course he had a right to be jittery. It wouldn't be natural if he wasn't.

No, there had been no word from John, David Palmer told him, and Bill nodded thoughtfully.

"The police keep coming around home to ask questions about him," he said with the air of a man sorely inconvenienced. "I told them I couldn't believe he'd do a thing like that to Sam. He was a tough boss and he was mad at

John, but as I told John. . . I said we could always find another job."

Beryl was watching him closely. Bill looked away. The tip of his tongue flicked at the corner of his mouth. "Susan said you had an interview today," Beryl said. "How did it go? Any luck?"

Bill shrugged. "Nope," he grunted. "Mention you worked for Sam Selmer and they don't want to know." He turned to David. "It's hard to work out why John went back to the warehouse," he said in a puzzled tone.

"I told him to," David said crisply. "I told him to apologise and ask for his job back."

Bill's smile was sad. "Susan probably told you," he said. "I almost did the same thing myself, but my mother was ill. That's why I haven't been around for a while." He shook his head woefully. "Poor old John. He was always so happy-go-lucky."

"He's not dead, Bill," Beryl reminded him firmly.

"Yeah, I know," Bill said quickly. "But if they catch him, he might as well be. I know I couldn't hack being locked up like that — for years and years."

Beryl's eyes were cold. "They'd have to prove he was guilty before they could do that." Her eyebrows lifted inquiringly. She glanced at her husband. "Wouldn't they?"

Bill was momentarily put out. "Yeah, sure," he murmured. "Of course. But. . . well. . . for his sake I just hope they *don't* catch him." Both Beryl and David, Bill's future in-laws, were watching him. His face was flushed and he looked ill-at-ease. "Yet on the other hand," he said, floundering a little, "I keep thinking of him hiding out in the bush, or in some crummy room somewhere — and that'd be pretty miserable, too, I guess."

14

From the large lounge chair in which she was ensconced, Fiona smiled fondly at the young man who was busily trying to open the bottle of champagne that had been chilling in the fridge for some hours. How people grew, she thought, and how fast. It made her feel old, and yet . . . thirteen years and it all came rushing back, those years compressed, the memories so vivid, and the only thing that had changed, it seemed, was the boy himself. That same little boy who had cried and cried because his father had come to take him back to Melbourne, and she had cried too because she hadn't wanted to lose him, although she had known there was nothing at all she could have done about it. She had tried to put him out of mind, that little boy with the engaging grin, to forget him, and gradually, over a long period of time, she had managed to do this.

But perhaps not entirely. Sometimes she still thought back to that cold, blowy winter's night, when she had stood in her doorway looking out at the young couple, a girl blonde and extremely pregnant; the young man — God, no more than a kid — nervous and carrying a battered suitcase. The girl had gazed back at her with very cool, very large serious eyes that were the colour of sapphires. Over twenty years ago now.

Oh yes, they had told her, they were Mr and Mrs Palmer, and she had known with the instinct of her years and experience which had never let her down in the past, that they were not — the girl was too defiant, the boy too nervous. Anyway, she hadn't said anything about it. It wasn't her business.

There was a loud, popping sound. Fiona started. The champagne cork hit the wall. John clapped his hand over the top of the bottle to stem the foamy flow. Fiona laughed. She was feeling very happy, almost lightheaded.

"Always put your hand *under* the bottle, darling," she told John, who by now had the situation under control and was pouring the bubbling amber liquid into two glasses. With a deep, exaggerated bow, he handed one of the glasses to Fiona. "Ah, I adore champagne." She raised the glass in a toast. "Here's to my freedom and the nicest surprise I've had in years."

John raised his own glass. "I'll go along with that."

"We'll finish this bottle, and then do you know what we're going to do?"

"What?"

"We're going shopping."

"What for?"

"Some clothes for a start," Fiona said. "And anything else you might want."

John smiled ruefully and shook his head. "No go," he said. "I've only got about twenty bucks."

"Hah!" Fiona snorted. "It's only money. I've got plenty."

John stood in front of the chair smiling down at Fiona. She sipped her drink, and some of the bubbles went up her nose.

"I couldn't do that," John told her, and she thought what wonderful clear skin he had. A little bit of tan . . .

"You're just like your father," she growled good-humouredly. "So damned independent."

His face tightened. "I don't *want* to be like my father," he said stiffly.

Aha, my boy, Fiona thought, there are some things you

just cannot help — and anyway, methinks you protest far too much. It was hard to say, looking at him now, catching him at different angles, in light and shadow, whom he resembled — his mother or the father with whom he had no wish to be compared. There were flashes, but little more — the bold stare of his mother's; his father's set to the mouth. She drank some more champagne and the bubbles tickled her nose. She willed herself not to sneeze.

"Then take the money," she offered.

"No."

"Why not? You can pay it back — as soon as you're rich and famous."

"I'll never be rich and famous," John said glumly.

"Oh no?" Fiona held out her hand. "Show me your palm. Come on. I'll tell you your future."

John grinned at her. Good teeth, Fiona observed, white and strong. His father had had strong teeth as well. He hadn't smiled much — God knew, he didn't have much to smile about, particularly after Patricia had walked out on him, taking the girl and leaving John behind — but when he did his whole face had become transformed, had lit up endearingly.

You mean you read palms?" John asked in some surprise.

"I'm the best there is," Fiona told him with a smile. "So come on. Let me have a look."

Looking doubtful, John nevertheless crossed the room to where she was sitting. Fiona motioned to the footstool in front of the chair. John sat on it, then at Fiona's curt gesture, held his right hand out to her.

"People pay me twenty dollars a pop to do this," she chuckled, "so you'd better be grateful." Taking his hand, she peered down at it. "Now let's see what I can tell you," she murmured.

"Tell me about my mother," John said quietly, seriously. Fiona looked sharply up at him. "I've never met your mother."

"I mean my real mother." John smiled wistfully up at

her and shook his head. "You must have known her."

Fiona bit thoughtfully down on her lower lip. "Yes, I did," she said softly. "I knew her, but not well. She was very young — very beautiful." And very determined, Fiona remembered how Patricia would virtually throw herself in front of young Hamilton when he came to discuss the property with Fiona, and David was slaving his guts out trying to scrape some money together to carry them through. It had been possible then to read what was going through the girl's mind. Help me, she was saying with those large, expressive eyes of hers — please help me and take me away from here. And it had worked — oh boy, had it worked.

Fiona peered down at the boy's hand. She didn't want to talk about his mother. "Now, what's your star sign?" she asked.

"Virgo," he replied.

"Of course you were," Fiona recalled. "What date was it?"

"The fourteenth."

"The fourteenth . . . ah . . ." She studied his palm for a moment, and then something struck her. She looked back up at him. "The fourteenth? Did you say the fourteenth? God, that means . . . it's your *birthday!*" she cried gleefully, releasing his hand and holding her arms out to him, ready to receive him in one more of her fulsome embraces. "Oh, Johnnie, happy birthday." John reached up and kissed her. "Now what we're going to do is celebrate — your palm reading can wait," Fiona said eagerly. "We'll go out, have some fun. Come on, I'll take you to dinner."

"I'm on the run — remember?" John solemnly reminded her. "What if somebody recognises me?"

"Darling," Fiona said with all the confidence in the world, "by the time I'm finished with you today your own mother wouldn't recognise you."

The main change that she brought about in him during the rest of that day was his new short haircut — and it was surprising how that alone could alter his appearance so much.

"How's that?" she asked as he studied the result of her handiwork in the mirror.

"Fantastic."

"I told you I was a good hairdresser."

"Yes, you're the best."

Fiona clapped her hands together. "So goodbye John Palmer, and hello Scott Edwards."

Afterwards Fiona went out, leaving John alone in the apartment. She returned about an hour later and handed John one of the parcels she was carrying. "Here are some clothes for you," she said. "Now you go and change into them."

In the bedroom, John changed into the pair of jeans and T-shirt Fiona had bought for him. Then, bundling up his old clothes he carried them out into the other room where Fiona was putting the finishing touches to a gift-wrapped parcel. She smiled across at him.

"Ah, there you are." She lifted the parcel from the table and held it out to him. "Here's a little birthday present for you."

As he took the parcel from her, she kissed him. "Oh, Aunt Fiona, you shouldn't have . . ."

"Now don't argue," she broke in with a mock-stern expression on her face. "Here, give me those old clothes. I'll get rid of them."

He handed her the bundle. Fiona nodded to the package he was holding. "Well, aren't you going to open it?"

"Yeah." Placing the parcel down on the table, John opened it. Inside the box was a fawn pullover. John whistled softly. It looked quite expensive. "It's . . . great. Thanks."

At Fiona's urging, he slipped it on. It fitted him nicely.

"There's just one word for you," Fiona said admiringly, "and that's sensational. Now let's plan a birthday dinner. We could go somewhere really fancy . . ."

"I can't." He shook his head. "Look, I know what you're trying to do, and that's just terrific — but I can't go running around in public. The police are probably looking everywhere for me."

The smile faded from Fiona's face. "Come and sit down," she said quietly, then when they had done so, "Listen, Johnny, there are two things you have to remember. You're innocent, you didn't murder anyone, so you've got to stop acting as though you did. If you behave as if you're guilty, people will think you *are* guilty. The other thing is that that guy was killed in another State, in Victoria, and the chances are that it won't even rate a mention here. Now, fella, I've given you a new identity, so you better start getting out and using it."

"Okay," John said after a brief pause. "But could we eat here tonight instead of going out?"

"Here?" Fiona's eyes widened. "In the apartment?"

"I'd like to get to know you again," John told her. "I know what you've been telling me is probably true — but if we go out to a restaurant I'll still be looking over my shoulder all the time." He laughed, not very convincingly, and took her arm. "We've got thirteen years to make up," he said. "That's a long time."

Fiona wasn't too happy about John's suggestion. She looked around for excuses — and one did present itself readily enough. "Well . . . yes, I'd like to eat here, if that's what you really want. But I'm not really a very good cook."

"I can cook," John informed her.

"You can?" She was surprised.

John laughed. "Hamburgers — how's that?"

"Hamburgers?" Fiona was outraged by the thought. "For your *birthday?*"

"Just the thing," John said easily. "We'll need mince and stuff like that. Oh . . ." his face fell . . . "that'll mean going to the shops," he added weakly.

"Good," Fiona said triumphantly. "Just the thing. You've talked yourself into it. Now you're going out to do some shopping and you're going to behave as though you're just a young guy on holidays from Brisbane. Understood?"

John nodded. He didn't look too happy about it, though. "Do you need some money?" Fiona asked him.

"No," John answered definitely. "I owe you enough already — and I'll pay you back, Aunt Fiona, I promise."

She knew he would — some time. The sternness of her expression masked the rush of emotion she felt for him. "Will you go and do that shopping?" John nodded again and moved toward the door. "And Johnny," she called. He stopped and turned back to face her. "There's a public phone just down the street. If you do decide to call your parents that would be a safe way of doing it."

John hesitated in the doorway. A smile flickered briefly across his face. Then he opened the door and left the room. Fiona sighed. She really was worried about him. Just a kid and he had got himself into so much trouble.

15

Angela Hamilton's birthday had been celebrated with considerably more style than that simple meal of hamburgers shared by Fiona and John in the Manly boarding house. There had been food and drink, and lots and lots of people who flitted about and chatted gaily. Her mother had been in her element, playing the role of gracious hostess to the full, and perhaps even at times overdoing it a little. There had been a group to provide the music, and lights had been set up around the swimming pool. It had been a good party — and now, in the morning, with the sunlight flooding in through the windows, Angela regretted having drunk so much. There was a dull, throbbing ache in her head and she felt particularly fragile as she made her way down the stairs with extreme care.

In the dining room, Wayne Hamilton was reading the newspaper. He looked up as Angela came into the room. "Ah, there you are at last," he said with a smile that held its own special brand of malice. Angela groaned inwardly. He was just what she needed to see first thing in the morning, a terrific boost for anyone's hangover. "Walking gingerly, I see," Wayne went on. "Very delicate. Our little beauty with a hangover."

He picked up the paper and held it up to her. It was open

at the social pages, and there, where Wayne was pointing, was a picture of Angela being kissed on each cheek by her mother and father.

Angela grimaced. It was too much — cosy, schmaltzy, and trust her mother never, never to overlook any single opportunity to get her picture in the social pages.

Wayne began to read the caption beneath the picture. " 'The beautiful Angela Hamilton receives birthday kisses from her mother and father at a party given in her honour yesterday'." He looked up at Angela, the quirky little smile still playing on his lips. "That's only half of it. They should get a shot of you now, the morning after — before and after. Oh boy."

Angela grabbed the paper from her brother, glanced at the picture, then tossed it down on the table. She glared at Wayne.

"When are you going away again?" she demanded.

"I'm not sure." His smile annoyed her. Everything about him annoyed her. "Why?"

"I thought we made a deal," she said coldly. "That you'd get out and stay out."

"So?" He raised his eyebrows. "Are you going to tell on me?"

"I might." Her head was still throbbing. She had already taken a couple of aspirins, but they didn't seem to be doing much good. "Daddy's always given you everything you wanted. How could you cheat him like that?"

"I told you," Wayne said offhandedly. "I needed the money. And it's not going to hurt him — not if you don't tell him about it."

Angela's voice quivered with emotion. She wasn't feeling at all well. "I'll never trust you again as long as I live," she said angrily.

"Tough." Wayne chuckled, and it was just too infuriating. "Why don't you have some black coffee? You'll feel better."

Enraged, Angela was about to round on him, lash out at him, when her mother came into the room. She smiled sweetly at them both. “Good morning,” she said, then to Angela, “Oh dear, don’t tell me the birthday girl has got a hangover.”

Angela made a face. “Your picture’s in the paper,” she said drily.

“Oh, really.” Patricia made it sound such a great surprise. “Let me see.” She picked up the paper, and with her head a little to one side, critically examined the photograph. “That dreadful profile shot of me,” she groaned. “Not my best side at all. Oh well, I don’t suppose it can be helped.”

Angela looked at her mother — cool, collected, not one strand of her hair out of place, her clothes just right — an integral part of this gleaming house, spick and span, rich, polished, chic, everything perfect, and the only thing lacking was the human touch. Her mother did mean well, Angela supposed. She did try — and perhaps it wasn’t so wrong for a woman to have ambitions for her children, only Angela wished she wouldn’t be so heavy-handed about it.

“What are you going to do with yourself today?” Patricia asked Angela.

“Not much,” Angela replied. “I’ll probably go riding later, but that’s about all.”

“Be careful,” Wayne said in a syrupy voice. “We wouldn’t want anything to happen to you, would we?”

Angela glared icily at her brother.

16

It was the same girl — the one whose features he knew so well, and she was smiling at him, lazily, as she ran her fingers through her hair. Her lips — full lips, sensual lips — were parted, and she was whispering something to him. Her eyes were bright and full of promise. What was she saying? He strained, trying to make it out, but he heard nothing. He tried to follow her lips, but that was no use, either. He knew that what she was saying was very important, but she might as well have been on the other side of a thick glass partition. Her eyes, her hands, her moving lips, reaching out for him, smiling, and now another sound, a tinkling sound, sharp, insistent, and seeming to come from somewhere else, from another dimension than that occupied by the girl who was trying to communicate with him. He opened his eyes.

He saw the girl, but it wasn't the same girl. She was standing beside his bed, lightly tapping the side of a cup with a teaspoon. He had never seen this girl before, and for a brief, startled moment he thought he was still dreaming. Somehow or other she had come and supplanted the other girl, the one he knew so well, who had been trying to reach out to him.

"Hi, Scott," the girl said, and he knew now, at the sound

of her voice, that he wasn't dreaming. "I'm Jill. Breakfast in five minutes."

Jill? Breakfast? He blinked up at her. She was dark, pretty, but not as pretty as the other girl. She smiled at him and placed the cup down on the bedside table. "There's some coffee to wake you up."

"Thanks."

Turning away from the bed, the girl moved across to the door. Nice, John thought — nice body. Then she was gone, and he was alone again in the room, awake, the room slowly coming into focus, his clothes on the floor where he had carelessly tossed them. Throwing back the blankets, he swung his legs out of the bed and sat up. He was beginning to wonder if the girl — Jill, she had said her name was — had actually been in his room. Then he saw the cup of coffee on the table. He drank it. It was still hot. It tasted good.

Five minutes later he was in the kitchen. He could smell toast and bacon. Jill was whisking eggs in a saucepan. She glanced up at him as he came into the room, barefooted and tucking his T-shirt into his jeans.

"That was quick," she observed.

John grunted. "Who are you?" He needed a shower and a shave — but breakfast first. The familiar smells stirred his gastric juices.

"I told you," she said levelly, placing the saucepan on the stove. "Jill. Jill Taylor."

John was puzzled. Aunt Fiona had told him nothing about a girl. She seemed to be perfectly at home here, in the kitchen, making breakfast. "But. . .what are you doing here?"

Her back was to him. "Making breakfast. I always make breakfast. I rent the apartment across the hall."

It made sense. "Is my aunt awake?" John asked.

"She's gone."

"Gone? Where?" He was surprised. It was still early.

Jill shrugged. "Who knows? She told me to let you sleep until eight-thirty — and so. . . " She turned away from the stove to face him ". . . it's eight-thirty. I hope you like scrambled eggs. I'm very good at scrambled eggs."

John looked at her appraisingly. She wasn't tall, but was neatly built, nice proportions, jeans fitting snugly over her slender hips and thighs, smallish well-defined breasts beneath the thin shirt, a pleasant smile that showed small, even white teeth. "Sure," he said, "scrambled eggs will be fine. Hey, why do you always make breakfast?"

Her smile broadened. "We've got an arrangement, Fiona and I." She gestured towards the table which was already set. "There's muesli and fruit. Help yourself."

"Thanks." John sat down at the table and poured milk from a jug over the muesli that was piled up in the bowl in front of him. Jill watched him.

"What would you like to do today?" she asked.

"Do?" John looked up at her.

"Yes. Fiona said she'd be away for most of the day. She suggested I show you around a bit."

John put down the jug. "Don't you have to go to work?"

"I work nights," she replied. "I've got a car — a beat-up old VW. We can see the sights."

It sounded a good idea. John had nothing planned for the day. "Sure," he said. "That'd be great."

Jill stirred the eggs in the pan. John stared at her, still confused, still wondering just where she fitted in. "Whoops," she said suddenly, putting down the wooden spoon and quickly crossing to the door. "I almost forgot. Excuse me." A moment later she returned with a folded newspaper. "The morning paper, sir," she said, putting it down in front of him.

John looked at the paper, then up at her. He was suddenly suspicious and apprehensive. So what was so special about the paper? Why was she so keen to give it to him? Was there something about him in it? Hurriedly, he unfolded the paper, and opening it, flicked through the pages, his eyes skimming the columns of local news, overseas news, sports news, pictures, comics and weather reports — but there was nothing about him, nothing about a murder in Melbourne and a young man the police were anxious to question about it. He breathed a sigh of relief and put the paper down, open at the social page, pictures of smiling well-dressed people. Jill glanced at him over her shoulder.

"Don't tell me you've finished already."

"I'm on holidays," he muttered. "Don't need the papers. Bad news all the way." He picked up a spoon and began to eat the muesli.

"How long will you be in Sydney?" Jill asked him.

"Don't know yet. Maybe a week or two." His eyes drifted over the open page of the newspaper in front of him; all those confident well-groomed people who looked as though they didn't have a worry in the world, rich people with swimming pools and houses in the country, people who kissed and congratulated each other, who . . . Suddenly, he saw something that made him freeze, the laden spoon halfway between the bowl and his mouth — a face, a girl smiling, being kissed on each cheek by two older people, obviously her father and mother, *her* face. There was no mistake about it, the same girl, not someone who just looked like her, the same eyes, the same mouth . . . John was shaken. The girl on the horse, on the beach, galloping into the sunset, her hair flying. He stared at the picture. Jill was still talking.

"Fiona said you were from Brisbane. I've never been there. Where do you live?"

Inwardly, John shook himself back to the present. "Mmmm?"

"Where do you live in Brisbane?"

"Oh . . . just outside," he said distractedly, then pointed to the picture of the girl whose face he already knew so well. "Do you know this girl?" he asked sharply.

Jill came to his side and looked down at the picture he was indicating. "Her?" She shook her head. "You're joking. Do *you* know her?"

"No, no." Leaning forward, he read the caption beneath the picture. "It says Dural — that's where she lives."

"That's a fair way from here," Jill told him. "Up the coast and inland."

The girl's name was Angela Hamilton. Her birthday, the caption read. The same day as his own. Coincidence. His nerve-ends were tingling, adrenalin flowed. "Could we go there?" he said eagerly. "To Dural? I'd like to see it."

"Sure," Jill said, obviously puzzled. "If that's what you want. We'll go the long way, up the coast, and show you a few of the beaches Sydney's famous for."

The girl's face stayed with him all the way as they drove up past the northern beaches — and now the face had a name. Angela. Angela Hamilton. Angela . . . Silently he repeated the name over and over again. It had class. Angela. Jill's old car rattled and vibrated, the engine made a terrible noise. The sun was shining and there were crowds on the beaches. Angela . . . calling to him . . . only a few hours ago, her face as clear as anything, he could even recapture her expression, her lips moving. Not a cloud in the sky. A perfect day.

They drove in silence. The sea was smooth, like dark green glass. At the Narrabeen Lakes fishermen stood waist deep in the water. Seagulls circled overhead. Heading north in an old bomb of a car that needed a new muffler. They left the coast at Mona Vale and headed inland through the Forest, cut across the leafy North Shore and finally reached the country-like greenness of Dural itself.

They had no real trouble finding the house. Jill pulled up at the side of the road, and they climbed out. The house was in the distance, on a rise, almost hidden among the trees, and must have cost a fortune. A house for rich people, tennis court, swimming pools, long sloping lawns that would be looked after by a gardener, a garage large enough for four cars. Angela was very lucky. She would have everything she wanted. Now he not only had a name for the girl on the horse, but he had a setting for her as well.

"I don't get you." Beside him, leaning on the car, Jill was watching him with a strange expression. "You say you don't know the girl and yet you've gone to all this trouble to check out her address. Now that's what I call mighty strange."

"Sorry." John smiled at her, and pushed himself away from the car. "She just reminded me of someone, that's all." He knew he didn't sound very convincing. "Shall we go?"

"Sure. Okay." Jill slid in behind the wheel. "Where to?"

John moved around to the other side of the car. Someone was using a motor mower in the distance. "You're the driver," he said, getting into the car.

Jill looked across at him. "Sure you don't want to drive?"

He shook his head. It would be too dangerous. Anything could happen, an accident, a faulty brake light, anything, and he could be pulled over and asked for his licence. "No," he said. "I haven't got a licence yet." That was all right. It was a perfectly natural excuse which would stop her from asking any more questions.

They drove some more. The road was narrow and winding. The houses were thinning out. There was more open country.

"You know," Jill said, breaking a long silence, "you're not a bit like what I expected when Fiona told me her nephew was in the spare bedroom."

"Oh?" John smiled. "What *did* you expect?"

"Oh, I don't know." She pushed out her lower lip as she negotiated a tight bend in the road. "Someone more like her, I guess. Although I can't imagine anyone else quite like Fiona."

The road ahead of them was straight. On one side were open fields. In one of them a girl was riding a horse, and there was something about the way she was sitting, her bearing, the economy of her movements as she urged the horse forward . . .

"Look!" He pointed. "Over there."

"Yeah," Jill said unenthusiastically, glancing in the direction John was pointing. "It's a girl on a horse."

"Not just a girl on a horse. The excitement was back.

"No, you don't understand," he cried. "It's *that* girl, the same girl. Can you stop the car?"

Jill sighed. "Sure, sure, I'll stop the car," she said in a tone of infinite patience.

As soon as the car drew up to a halt on the grass verge at the side of the road, John leapt out and moved quickly across to the fence. Yes, there she was, bringing the horse around, galloping toward a stand of trees, her hair flying, the same girl, just as she had appeared to him in his dreams, in a white shirt and a pair of tight-fitting cream jodhpurs, her body lifting tightly from the saddle.

"Scott, is there any insanity in your family?" Jill had come up behind him.

He didn't take his eyes from the girl on the horse. "It *is* her," he said almost to himself. "The same girl."

Jill's voice and expression showed her exasperation. "Look, you know her name," she said. "If it means so much to you, why don't you just go back to her house and say, 'Hi, you're Angela Hamilton. I saw your photo in the paper and spent the best part of a day looking for you'."

The horse had disappeared into a dip. John waited for it and its rider to emerge on the other side. "Hey, Jill, I'm sorry," he said. "I'm sorry. It's just that I had this dream, you see. Always the same dream."

The girl and the horse were still out of sight. They should have come out of the dip by now. Something had gone wrong — he was sure of it.

"Well, go on," Jill pressed him. "You had this dream."

Panic thudded. "Something's wrong!" he cried.

Jill gestured impatiently. "What do you mean — something's wrong?"

"I don't know." But he was sure — sure something had happened to her, she was hurt. He could almost feel the pain, sharp and stabbing. He groaned. Then he saw the horse cantering up the rise, riderless, the reins hanging loosely. "Come on!" he yelled desperately, clambering over the fence and sprinting towards the spot where he had last seen the girl.

He ran, silently praying, pleading that she would be all right, but aware of the pain that had somehow transmitted itself to him, warned him. He came to the top of the bank and stopped. Below him the girl was lying beside a small creek, very still. With a barely stifled cry, John launched himself down the bank, stumbling, sliding in a cloud of dust, only just managing to keep his balance. At the bottom, he flung himself down beside the girl, and the first thing he noticed was a rush of relief that she was still breathing. That was something, but he didn't know how badly hurt she was, what damage had been done. Gently, hardly daring to breathe, he eased her over from her side onto her back. There was blood on her face. He touched her forehead with the tips of his fingers. Her eyelids fluttered, and the grief welled strongly in him. Stinging tears filled his eyes and he fought them back as he raised her from the stony ground and took her in his arms.

17

The hospital corridor was dark green and gloomy. The walls were stained and permeated with the smell of antiseptic. Nurses and doctors in white coats moved soundlessly along the corridor. Doors opened and closed. Telephones rang. Angela Hamilton had already been wheeled away on a trolley, guided by a doctor and a nurse.

"Relax," Jill said as John sat down on the scarred wooden bench beside her. "The doctor said it's probably only concussion."

"Yeah," John said glumly, looking down at his joined hands. He didn't want to talk. There was nothing to say. All he could do was wait.

"You said you didn't know her," Jill challenged.

"I don't."

"That's not the way it looked to me."

John hesitated. He had to tell her something. He owed her that much at least. "I told you before. I dreamt about her," he said quietly, earnestly. "Sounds crazy, huh?"

Jill raised her eyebrows. "Yes, it does."

She didn't believe him. "I'm not kidding," he went on fervently. "I kept dreaming about a girl on a horse. It was a family joke. But all the time it was her — Angela Hamilton. That's why I freaked when I saw her picture in the paper."

"Yeah." She was still looking at him with a cynical expression, and he decided there wasn't much point busting a gut trying to convince her. "We might as well go. It'll be ages before she can see anyone."

"I'll wait," John said stolidly.

But it wasn't a long wait. About half an hour later, a nurse came up to John and told him he could see the girl. She led him along a series of corridors to a room in which there were two beds, both of them occupied. Angela was in one of the beds; a plump middle-aged woman was sitting up comfortably in the other, reading a book. There were flowers in the room, a television set, and a telephone on the table betwen the two beds. John sat down on the chair beside Angela's bed. She lay back against the pillows, her eyes closed. Her face was pale. Then, slowly, she opened her eyes and looked at John. He smiled at her.

"Hi."

Her own smile was wan. "Hi. The doctor said you found me."

John nodded, and tried to think of something comforting to say to her. "Your mother's on the way. The hospital called her."

"Oh." She closed her eyes, briefly, then opened them again. "And the horse?"

"It's okay," he reassured her.

She looked relieved. "I don't know your name," she said. She sounded tired. There were dark smudges beneath her eyes.

"Ah . . . it's Scott. Scott Edwards."

There was another flickering smile. "I'm lucky you came along." Her dark eyes were studying him with such intensity that he felt embarrassed and looked away. He shrugged. "Yeah."

The sunlight was streaming in through the window. There were brisk footsteps in the corridor outside. They stopped in the doorway. John turned to see a tall, well-dressed woman standing there, and recognised her from the picture he had seen in the paper of Angela being kissed by her father and mother. She was very attractive in a cool sort of way. She didn't look old at all. Thirty something, he thought. He stood up, but she didn't appear to see him. She moved across to the bed and looked down at Angela with a slightly peeved expression.

"Are you all right, darling?"

"You know me," Angela said with a wry smile. "It takes more than a bump on the head . . ."

"I told your father not to give you such a high-spirited animal," her mother said reproachfully.

"It wasn't the horse," Angela said quickly. "I think the saddle slipped or something."

"We'll see." The woman turned to John and regarded him coldly. "I don't think we've met," she said.

"This is Scott Edwards, Mother," Angela told her. "Scott found me."

"How do you do." Her expression didn't change. Her voice was distant.

John felt rather intimidated by this woman who was looking at him as if from a great height. "Hi," he murmured.

The pale eyes were fixed on him. There was no warmth in them. "If you leave your address I'm sure my husband will want to thank you."

"Don't worry." He looked away from the woman to Angela. "Can I see you again?"

Angela smiled. "I'd like that. Give me a call."

"Sure." He raised his hand in a sort of goodbye wave. "See you soon then." Feeling rather awkward under Mrs Hamilton's haughty gaze, he backed across the room to the door. He nodded to her. "Bye, Mrs Hamilton."

She didn't reply. In the corridor outside the room, John hesitated. From the room behind him he heard Mrs Hamilton begin to lecture her daughter.

"I understand you're grateful to that boy, Angela," she was saying deliberately, "but you were wrong to encourage him like that. I mean you know nothing about his family. Or where he's from."

John didn't wait to hear any more. It didn't matter. He was feeling elated. He had made contact with this girl at last, the girl of his dreams, Angela Hamilton — who now had a name, a home, and, it looked like, a mother who was a bit of a dragon. He hurried along the corridor towards the hospital entrance.

18

Susan decided the best thing to do was call the wedding off. She hadn't spoken about it yet to Bill, but she resolved to do that as soon as she saw him. It was all too much. Bill was out of a job, and was spending most of his time looking for another one, without much success. Somehow, whenever Sam Selmer's name was mentioned, those people who might otherwise have hired him, suddenly didn't want to know.

And apart from that, the neighbours had stopped talking to them, and that made things rather difficult because the girl next door, Lynn Hardy, had promised to be Susan's bridesmaid. Then Kevin was getting himself into trouble at school, getting into fights with the other kids who jeered at him about his fugitive brother.

The whole thing was being played up on TV and in the papers. The incident of the banner John placed on top of the TV tower to invite everybody to Susan's wedding was revived more than once — and every time she saw it on the screen, in those few seconds before she hurriedly switched it off, Susan winced. Of course now, half of Melbourne would probably turn up at the church just to stand there and gawk at the sister of the guy who was wanted for questioning over a particularly brutal murder.

When she mentioned her fears to Beryl, her mother agreed it wasn't easy now, but it was bound to be different on the day itself. Because then she would have eyes only for Bill, and the rest wouldn't matter, certainly not all those crackpots who were hanging around the church making a nuisance of themselves.

"The day I married your father it was as hot as all get-out," she reminisced. "Hundred and two in the shade, and half of Ararat was there. Plus all the truckies I used to know from working in the cafe. They turned up to form a guard of honour we could've well done without." She smiled at the memory. She added more water to the gravy she was stirring. The pan sizzled and steamed. "They didn't half have a go at me," she went on, "because they knew how I'd been chasing your dad from the first time I saw him."

"And you weren't going to let him get away," Susan remarked, for the moment not wholly absorbed in her own problems.

"No fear," Beryl chuckled, handing Susan the spoon. She nodded to the gravy that still needed to be stirred, and started to set the table. "But the hard part was getting him to notice me in the first place. Your Dad wasn't at all like all the other truckies. They were all bold as brass, and they'd cheek you as soon as look at you. But not your father — not David." She shook her head. "He was so serious and quiet. I couldn't get two words out of him — and the things I got up to to try and make him notice me. I short-changed him, then gave him too much change — extra helpings of food — you name it. Anything to get a conversation going. What finally did the trick was an accident. I was pretty upset, you see, about another boy Mum and Dad were keen on me getting engaged to. I knew it wouldn't work, but I'd made up my mind to say yes."

She straightened up from the table. "I suppose my mind was miles away," she continued, "but I was at work and carrying the biggest pavlova you ever saw up to the main counter." She laughed. "Then what does Awkward Annie do but drop the whole thing down the front of her dress. I felt such a fool. I just stood there crying. That's when your father came over. He made me go and clean myself up, then sit down and have a cup of coffee with him. I poured out all my woes to him, and he listened — and that's how it all started."

Susan was touched. It was a nice story, but she didn't see how it could affect the decision she had reached to put off the wedding.

Beryl was beaming at her. "So you see, on the day, there was nothing a few yahoos could do to spoil our wedding. And *you* won't notice anything, either, the day you marry Bill."

"It isn't just that," Susan murmured uncomfortably.

"Talk about it with Bill," Beryl suggested. "You should sort out your problems together."

Her mother didn't understand — Susan could see that. She belonged to another world — more open, less complicated, where the issues were so positively clear-cut. She saw there was no point in arguing with her. "Okay," she said, "I'll think about it."

"Oh dear." Beryl was looking down at the table she had just set. She seemed annoyed. "I'm always doing it. It's habit." She took up the cutlery and the plate from one of the places. "I just set a place for John," she explained.

Bill's reaction, when Susan told him she wanted to call off the wedding for the time being at least, was unexpecedly fierce. He stamped, stormed and ranted. They were in Bill's flat where he lived with his widowed mother.

"You know what your problem is?" he shouted, jabbing a finger at her, his face contorted with anger. "You haven't got the guts to ignore what people are saying."

"I'm just postponing the wedding," Susan said, trying to keep her own temper in check. "I'm not calling it off altogether. Just for a little while."

"That doesn't matter!" Bill yelled. "You're still giving in."

"Keep your voice down." Susan glanced at the door that opened out of the living room into the rest of the flat.

"We'll upset your mother."

Bill gave a wry laugh. "You think she's not going to be upset anyway?" he asked bitterly.

"She'll see my point." There was a rising edge to Susan's voice. "She's not as unreasonable as you."

Bill was very tense. His mouth was set in a crooked line and there was a wild look in his eyes. "All that stuff about me not having a job," he growled, "that's all so much bull."

"Oh sure," Susan remarked drily. "We could live very comfortably on a trainee nurse's wage."

"If you loved me we could," Bill said sourly.

That stopped her for a moment. Of course he was right. If they loved each other strongly enough then nothing else should really matter — should it? No, no, surely not. They had to live, they had to survive. All the same, she wished he hadn't said it. It wasn't making things any easier.

"Okay," she began slowly, trying to get her thoughts into some sort of order. "Maybe it did start with worrying about John and what people were saying, and . . ." Her voice trailed away. What was it she was trying to say? She rallied. "Well, there are other things on top of that. I want everything to be just right — can't you see that, Bill?" She touched his hand and gazed at him earnestly. "I don't see why waiting a few months makes so much difference," she said gently.

Bill's anger had subsided, but he was still sullen. "It's giving in," he muttered.

Susan's exasperation returned; it had never been far away. What was wrong with him? Why wouldn't he listen to her? "You won't even *try* to understand, will you?" She moved towards the front door. She'd had enough. She had done enough talking. "I'll talk to you tomorrow. I'm not in the mood for any more tonight."

"I'm not going to feel any different," Bill said stubbornly.

"Neither am I." She could be quite as stubborn as he was. She pulled open the door, and stepped out into the hallway.

"Susan," he called behind her, but she ignored him and walked quickly away, expecting him to chase her, to catch up with her — but all she heard was the sound of the telephone ringing in the flat she had just left. Idly, she wondered who it might be.

19

It *couldn't* have happened. It was impossible. Fiona just stared. She couldn't have heard John right — or it could be any girl with that name. Surely it couldn't be *too* uncommon. There must be a few girls around with the name of Angela Hamilton. Angela — yes, common enough; Hamilton — oh, that was a reasonably common name, too. So . . . Angela Hamilton? A coincidence?

So who was she kidding? Even when John had mentioned the name, she had known, had *felt* the inevitability of it all. If she hadn't felt so sure about it, she could have placed on it as much importance as she had the rest of the story up to that moment when John had suddenly thrown in the name Angela Hamilton — and it had been as if someone had poured a bucket of ice-cold water over her.

"Look, here she is." John was holding out a newspaper which had been folded back to show half the social page. His finger stabbed at one of the pictures. "That's the one." Picking up her glasses, Fiona slipped them on and peered at the photograph.

"Oh," she said in a small voice. Her hands were shaking. She clasped them together. Of all the girls in Sydney he had to go and . . . Oh no, there it was, the girl being kissed by her parents, at her birthday party — and how could

Fiona forget *that* date? — no mistaking the girl's mother, Patricia Hamilton, and Gordon . . . and here, right in this house, was where it had all started. She lowered the paper and took off her glasses. She felt weak. She needed a drink. After all those years it was all coming back with a vengeance. What was it John had told her just now? He and Jill had gone for a drive in Jill's old bomb of a car. A girl had fallen off her horse and knocked herself out. They had taken her to hospital — and the big coincidence of it was, John had told her, that her picture had been in that morning's paper — and her name was Angela Hamilton.

"She asked me to call her," John said now.

"I don't *want* you calling her!" Fiona said with more vehemence than she had intended. "I don't want you to have anything to do with her."

He was looking at her in a puzzled way. He didn't understand — but what could she say? No, John, you stay away from that girl because she's your twin sister . . . Oh, marvellous, terrific, it would go down like a dose of salts. He wouldn't believe it because it was too far-fetched. But one thing was for certain — it couldn't go any further. She would have to stop this right now, if there was no damage to be done.

"You don't even know her," John protested.

Hah! If *you* only knew what I know. "I know *of* her," Fiona said tersely. "Her family is very wealthy and influential."

"What's that got to do with anything?" Now there was a plaintive note in John's voice.

"I shouldn't have to remind you," she bore in relentlessly. "You're on the run from the police — and obviously, you've got to keep a low profile as they say. If you get tangled up with a girl like that whose family has money and some influence, then I'd say you'd be taking a bit of a risk — wouldn't you?" Fiona was rather pleased with this. It sounded convincing enough, and from the expression on John's face, he must have thought so, too. But he still had something to say about it.

"*You're* the one who encouraged me to get out," he said. "You don't seem too worried about me knowing Jill."

"Jill's different," Fiona said firmly. "Don't think the Hamiltons won't check out anyone who's going round with their daughter. Absolutely top drawer. They won't accept just anybody — no matter what *she* says."

"We're *not* going around," John said petulantly. "We've only just met."

Fiona's lips stretched in a thin line. "Good. So then let's keep it that way."

20

Angela was back home. Her mother had been insistent and had gradually worn down all the remaining protests, although these hadn't been too violent because Angela had been coming along very nicely. Even if it might have been advisable to keep her under observation for a day or two longer, the harmony and routine of the hospital might be much better served if that woman was allowed to have her imperious way and take her precious daughter home with her.

So . . . Patricia was satisfied now that she had Angela at home and could keep an eye on her. She had made up a bed for her on one of the living room sofas downstairs. Here, she would be a part of what was going on in the house, and not feel cooped up and alone which would no doubt happen if she remained confined to her own room.

However, all was not running as smoothly as Patricia would have liked it. There was that boy, for instance — the one who had found Angela. Not at all the type she hoped would attract Angela. And Angela had been interested in seeing him again — oh, that had been so apparent. So there was something to be discouraged — and perhaps with time, hopefully, Angela would lose interest.

The other thing was that Patricia had told Gordon she

didn't want Angela to ride that horse again. One accident was quite enough, and that one could have been considerably worse. But Gordon had smiled that infuriating, secret little smile of his and said, we'll see, and that annoyed Patricia no end because she knew Angela had him wrapped around her little finger.

About halfway through the morning, Angela received a telephone call.

"Angela? It's Scott Edwards."

She had somehow expected it would be him. There had been something in the way he had asked her if he might call her that had made it almost a certainty. "You know nothing about his family, or where he's from," her mother had warned her. Well . . .

"I knew it would be you," she said, smiling. The room was full of sunlight. Freshly picked flowers stood in vases around the room.

"Yeah?" The voice at the other end of the line sounded surprised, and now Angela felt a little self-conscious.

"Well . . . hoped, anyway," she said a little awkwardly.

"Great." She saw his eyes again, grey and earnest. She could see him smiling. What was it about him . . . ? "How about we get together?"

Angela was alone in the room. She glanced out into the hallway to make sure no one was in earshot. "I'd love to," she said, lowering her voice all the same. "But everyone's treating me like an invalid. I have to rest. I can't go out. So why don't you come out here?"

"Sure," he said, then hesitated, apparently struck by a thought. "Only . . . well, I got a feeling your mother wouldn't be too wild about seeing me again."

Angela laughed. She was feeling really quite happy now, fully recovered, no more aches and pains. "Don't worry about her. I'll have the place to myself. Can you make it up here, to Dural?"

"I think so," he replied. "I know someone who's got a car . . . I'm sure I can get a lift. I know where to come."

"Right," Angela said happily. "If you hurry we can have

some time together."

"See you soon," he said and rang off.

Angela waited for him in a welter of impatience. Time moved painfully slowly; every time she glanced at the clock the minute hand seemed to have hardly moved at all. She paced up and down, fiddled with things, picked up magazines, flicked quickly through them, and put them back. She looked out the window, staring down at the road. She tensed every time she heard a car, but none of them stopped at the gate. At one stage she wondered if perhaps he had changed his mind, had got cold feet at the thought of running into her mother again, had decided not to come after all. She quickly dismissed the thought. No, he had sounded too confident, he had virtually promised . . . He had a fairly long way to come. He would be here. Of course he would.

She heard a sound on the staircase, and looked up, startled, as Wayne appeared in the doorway that opened out into the hall. She thought he had gone out. She had heard their father telling him, before he had left the house with their mother, to get the horse back from the man who had caught it, handing him a small cheque to give to the man for his trouble. Wayne hadn't been too pleased about that, muttering something about lunch at the club. But his father had been adamant.

"I thought you had to go out," Angela said coldly.

Wayne smiled. "You mean you don't want company?"

As if she would. As if she liked him. The doorbell rang, the sound shattering the peace that had begun to be ruffled by Wayne's sudden, unexpected arrival from upstairs.

Casually, Wayne moved back into the hallway. "It's probably Doctor Roberts," he remarked.

"I doubt it," Angela said.

"Ah . . ." Wayne stopped and turned in the doorway. His eyes were wide and bright. "Someone else you're expecting? One of your . . . friends, shall I say, for want of a better word?"

Jeering at her, mocking her. He was in the hallway and opening the front door before she had a chance to retort.

Then she heard Scott's voice, and everything was all right. Wayne, her sweet, loving brother, could just go and jump.

"Hi, I'm Scott Edwards. Angela's expecting me."

"I see," Wayne said drily, ushering the visitor into the living room ahead of him.

And there he was, smiling at her. All the tension flowed out of Angela. He was here, and that was the only thing that mattered. Scott Edwards, in jeans that looked quite new, and a cotton shirt that was open enough to reveal the smoothness of his deep chest. Wayne stood back near the door as Scott advanced into the room, and looked from one to the other with a quizzical smile.

"Bringing them into the house now?" he asked smoothly.

If Angela was meant to be rattled, it didn't work. "Ignore him," she told the newcomer. "He's just my brother."

Wayne moved across to the well-stocked bar in one corner of the room. He reached for a glass from the shelf behind it, and held it up. "I'm Wayne. Would you like a drink?"

"No, thanks."

With a shrug, Wayne took down the Scotch bottle and splashed a liberal helping into the glass. He added a dash of soda. "What line of business are you in, Scott?"

"I'm on holidays." He sat down opposite Angela. Wayne took a long, thoughtful sip of his drink.

"I mean what do you do when you're *not* on holidays?"

"Ah . . ." He gave Angela a quick, apologetic smile. "Actually, I'm looking for a job at the moment," he said. "The last one fell through."

Angela frowned at her brother. If she wasn't careful, he would take over the conversation, and that was the very last thing she wanted. "Scott found me when I fell off the horse," she explained brusquely.

Wayne looked at John with an expression of dawning wonder that didn't quite work. "So *you're* the guy?" He tried to sound impressed. Angela winced. "The Hamilton family will be forever in your debt. So what brings you over here today?"

"I invited him," Angela snapped, then turned to John. "We might be more comfortable by the pool," she added pointedly.

Wayne was still watching John. "Sorry," he said, ignoring his sister. "Where did you say you were from?"

"I didn't." John's eyebrows were contracted in a small frown of annoyance.

Angela stood up. "I think we will go out to the pool," she remarked. John stood up as well. Angela glared at Wayne who looked as though he might join them. "Don't you have an errand to run?" she asked crisply. "The horse — remember?"

"I guess I should be trotting along." Wayne finished his drink. "We must have a good long chat some other time," he said matter-of-factly to John.

John grunted non-committally, and followed Angela to the glass doors that opened out onto the patio. "Behave yourselves while I'm away," Wayne called after them.

The pool was spotless and inviting. All around it was colour — greens, reds and yellows, hibiscus bushes, bougan-villea, vivid flamboyants. John squatted down on the tiled coping, trailing his hand through the cool water while Angela returned to the kitchen, filled a pitcher with chilled orange juice and carried it back out onto the patio on a tray with two glasses. John straightened, and walked across to her. His gesture encompassed the pool and its landscaped setting, the shrubs and trees. "Very nice," he observed.

Angela nodded distantly. She was thinking of other things. "I'm sorry about Wayne," she said. "He tends to give everyone the third degree."

"No matter." John's smile widened.

Angela brightened. "Anyway, we should have the place to ourselves," she told him. Hopefully, hopefully . . . No more interruptions. Wayne had gone. He wouldn't be back till much later.

"Good." He was watching her intently now, a long, searching, smouldering look that made her tingle a little. "So . . . how are you?"

"Not too bad." Did he notice the slight tremor in her voice? God, he was attractive. "The odd bruise." She tried to laugh it off.

"You really gave me a scare yesterday."

Oh, those eyes burning into her, caressing her. She occupied herself by filling the two glasses from the pitcher. She handed him one. "I've been riding since I was six," she said defensively. "And the one thing I do know about is how to take a fall." She sipped her own drink. Those eyes . . . so earnest. "Maybe we could go out riding one day."

"Yeah?" He didn't sound too keen.

"That's as soon as I can convince my mother it's safe," she said with a laugh. "She's got a thing about horses."

John was looking around him again, at the pool and its surroundings, with a sort of awe. "This is really different to what I'm used to," he muttered.

"So what *are* you used to?" Angela asked lightly, then immediately noticed the way his expression tightened. Now she was on the defensive again. "I'm not trying to pump you," she said quickly. "We can talk about . . . well, whatever you want to talk about. Just talk."

The moment of tension had passed. She had the impression she had just skirted dangerously close to something he didn't want her to know about, a secretive side to him, and she wondered if she would ever get to know him well enough to try and break it down.

He was grinning at her. "Okay, so why don't we start with you?"

So they talked, and talked. The sun was warm, and Angela told him about herself, about her mother and father, and how happy she had been on her father's property before they had moved to the city when something seemed to have gone out of their lives. She was happy enough now, of course, but when they were living at Woombai, well, there seemed to be more . . . *involvement* with each other. Her father, in particular. He had spent much more time with her then. Now he was too busy, and her mother devoted so much time to her efforts to put the family on the map socially — and as a consequence, Angela saw little of either parent. She had everything she wanted, in a material sense — but was that enough? Her tone grew wistful.

She told him about Wayne — her half-brother, really; her father had been married before, and his wife had died. They just didn't get on. But she didn't go into too much detail about that. Wayne knew too much about her, had something over her, was sly and always making allusions.

As the sun grew stronger, John took off his shirt. A life of ease, with plenty of friends, carefully cultivated by her mother, but superficial. And admirers. Play it cool, her mother kept telling her, keep them at arm's length, plenty of time.

There were other things she didn't tell him about herself. He wouldn't be too impressed. And she *did* want to impress him, to make him want to see her again — and again. She didn't want him to think she led an altogether empty, unfulfilled life.

Then John brought up the subject of their birthdays. A coincidence, he said, that they should have their birthdays on the same day. Small world, Angela agreed.

"What time were you born?" she asked.

John shrugged. His muscles rippled. "Don't know," he replied. "I could ask my aunt, I suppose. She might know."

"What's she like?"

John smiled. "Well, I guess she isn't like any other aunt," he said, and she could tell by his tone that he was very fond of her. She had a fleeting image of a white-haired old lady smiling benignly over the top of her spectacles. "She's fantastic. You have to see her to believe her."

"Can I?"

"Meet her? Don't see why not."

"That'd be nice." She took the plunge. "Besides, I'd like to see you again."

He looked at her closely, perhaps to gauge whether she was pulling his leg or not. She smiled back at him encouragingly. Of course she meant it. He had to see that. He had to be convinced.

"You never get any peace around here," she said a little huskily, with the feeling she was setting in motion a train of events that would steadily gather momentum and end up either in disaster or perfect bliss — who could tell at this early stage? "Maybe we could find somewhere quieter."

John nodded gravely, and then before either of them could say anything more, a bell rang inside the house. "See what I mean?" Angela asked casually, masking her disappointment. "That'll be the doctor."

John picked up his shirt and began to put it on. "When can I see you again?"

He did want to see her again — that was marvellous. "The sooner the better."

"Tomorrow?"

"Yes."

There was a hiatus as they stared at each other, and for that briefest of moments they were caught in a vacuum, from which time and everything else around them, the world itself, had been drawn. Then the moment was shattered by the repeated sound of the doorbell. John pointed to the path that ran along the side of the house away from the pool.

"Can I get out that way?"

Angela nodded. She didn't want him to go — and the time before she could see him again yawned ahead of her like a deep black abyss.

"Thanks for today," John said quietly.

"Thank *you.*"

Then gently, tenderly, John kissed her — a light kiss, a chaste kiss, but from it radiated a great and wonderful certainty. They smiled warmly at each other.

"I'll call you in the morning," he said.

She watched him walk across the patio to the corner of the house. He had a lithe, athletic walk, almost cat-like. When he reached the path, he turned and waved. Angela waved back. She couldn't remember how long it was since she had last felt so happy.

21

It was Wayne, in his usual deadly way, who let the cat out of the bag, and Patricia Hamilton's mood abruptly changed.

She had been shopping, and now with parcels strewn all over the living room floor, she had fixed herself a drink, kicked off her shoes and was relaxing in an armchair near the sofa on which Angela was propped up. She had questioned Angela about her day, and Angela had told her, no, she hadn't done much, watched some TV, read a bit, and really had quite a boring day. And yes, the doctor had come.

Then Wayne had arrived and overhead some of this exchange. He had made himself a drink. He had smiled sweetly at Angela.

"Did your friend stay long?" he had asked, and Patricia thought he was referring to the doctor.

"He gave her a clean bill of health," she had said.

"Oh, is he a doctor as well?" Wayne's voice had been syrupy, and then Patricia had seen the look of pure hatred that had passed between them.

"What are you talking about?" she demanded.

"The guy who helped yesterday," Wayne replied, then gave Angela another of his sweet smiles. "Scott, wasn't it?"

Patricia's face fell. This was too much. That boy . . . and Angela had deliberately lied to her — or lied by omission, it was the same thing. She had firmly believed that the boy — Scott Edwards — was now well and truly out of the picture, and now . . . in a most roundabout way, she realised how wrong she had been.

When Gordon came home she tackled him about it. He had gone straight into his den, a place it was obvious he was regarding more and more as a refuge, and she had followed him there. Angrily, she told him how Angela had *deceived* her, and as he listened he allowed himself a patient smile, which made her even more angry, and she accused him of not taking the matter seriously. After all, Angela knew what she thought of the boy, and that by seeing him behind her mother's back, when she knew full well how her mother disapproved . . .

"I do think you're over-reacting," Gordon said calmly. "Because he's not on your list of eligibles doesn't necessarily mean he's not a perfectly pleasant young man."

"That's beside the point," she snapped. "It's the fact that she lied to me."

Gordon sighed. "All right," he said wearily. "Leave it to me. I'll talk to her."

It was Gordon who had fallen in love with her, she remembered, the same man who sat in front of her now, painfully polite, just wanting to be left alone. A few more wrinkles, flecks of grey in his hair, a more resigned look about him, the same man who had fallen head over heels in love with her all those years ago in Manly when he had come to visit Fiona MacDonald to discuss business. He had proposed to her, but she had been reluctant at first, had hedged, not because she wanted to play hard to get, but because, after David Palmer, she was genuinely concerned about her ability to relate to any man.

"Thank you," she said, then felt the need to explain herself a little more. "I'm not being bloody-minded, Gordon," she continued. "There are plenty of nice boys interested in Angela. I mean, very nice, but they're lucky if they get the time of day with her. Then she turns around and invites a complete stranger into the house." She fixed her husband with a cold stare. He had to do something, had to bear some of the responsibility. "It's about time she got her priorities straight."

But she knew he had already switched off. He was flicking through some papers on the desk. He looked up and nodded to the papers.

"Give me ten minutes," he said, "then send her in."

22

"Is that you, Johnny?"

"It's me."

He had brought her flowers, a peace offering. Standing in the doorway, he saw by the grim expression on her face that she knew. She jerked her chin towards the flowers. "Are they to butter me up?"

"Jill told you?"

"She told me."

Moving into the room, John handed her the flowers. It was a big bunch — the biggest he could find. "I know all the arguments against me going," he said evenly. "But I did go. I wanted to go."

Fiona's attitude seemed to soften as she took the flowers. "That won't be much consolation in gaol, my darling," she said. She sniffed the flowers. "They're lovely. Thanks." She looked steadily at him. "Have you been with her all day?"

He shook his head. "No. I've done a lot of walking . . . a lot of thinking."

"And?"

"And I want to keep seeing her."

He had walked for miles, hardly aware of where he was going. He could only think of Angela. He thought he was in love. Yes, he did want to keep seeing her.

"I'll take the chance," he said, seeing the impatient gesture she made, the cold glint in her eyes, the tightness of her mouth. He paused, then went on more tentatively. "Aunt Fiona, would it sound crazy if I told you I dreamt about her before I even met her?" He shrugged and gave her an abashed smile. "Crazy, huh? I don't know what it means."

"Maybe it's a warning," Fiona said. Very funny, John thought. "All right," she went on in a more brusque, businesslike tone. "Seriously. I've stuck my neck out to help you — and look . . ." Her smile was one of faint derision, ". . . I don't want to see us *both* getting into trouble because you've stumbled across your dream girl."

"What do you mean?" John's eyes narrowed suspiciously. "Are you saying if I keep seeing her you'll chuck me out — is that it?"

"Of course not." Fiona shook her head in annoyance. "I'm just asking you to show a bit of commonsense, that's all."

Yeah. John took a deep breath. "I'll take things slowly," he said with an exploratory smile. "Promise. If I keep it pretty low key . . . you know, don't get too heavy . . . I can't see why her parents should freak." His smile broadened and he was confident again. "Who knows — once I get to know her real well, maybe I'll run for my life." And maybe not. He saw again the face of the girl by the pool, the look of concentration as she poured the orange juice.

"It's happened before." Fiona was smiling now. All was forgiven. All smiles in Manly. But did he see something beyond that smile? Apprehension? A flickering evasion? Careful now, it's been a long day, momentous, wonderful things happening, mustn't imagine things.

"That's a promise, is it?" Fiona asked.

"That I'll take things slowly?"

Her stare was unflinching. She nodded. With one hand John made a cross sign over his heart. "I really appreciate what you're doing for me, Aunt Fiona," he said sincerely. "It's the least I can do for you." Yes, he really did mean it. Moving across to her, he took her hand and squeezed it gently. She returned the pressure and smiled — and again he saw the uncertainty that flickered momentarily in her eyes and died away.

23

It was an eerie feeling — eerie and unnerving, to be back here, in this place with its stacks of packing crates reaching almost to the ceiling, the narrow passages between them, the gloom, with only a little sunlight filtering down through the skylight. It was like a dream, and at any moment he felt he would awake from a particularly vivid dream and lie there in a cold sweat. His guilt was in no way diminished. It would be with him for all time. He would continue to see Sam Selmer's face turned up to him, a hated face blurred by the power of his unreasoning rage, as he raised the crowbar . . . And he had come back here, to the warehouse, to the small office where it had happened.

"So you can see, I'm in a rather difficult position."

The woman was sitting behind the desk, toying with a pencil, watching him. What did she know? Had she guessed the truth of what had happened, bringing him down here to the warehouse, perhaps with the intention of catching him out in some way, of somehow forcing him into a confession? He must be careful what he said, how he behaved. The slightest thing could give him away. Why — why had he come?

"I don't quite see what you expect me to do about it," Bill Todd said uncomfortably.

But he had come, despite every screaming instinct for

survival. He had been weak, he had given in. The phone had rung just as Susan had walked out of the flat, and he was on the point of chasing her. He had listened in disbelief, with rising fear, to the woman telling him it was Margaret Selmer and wondering if he could come to the warehouse in the morning because there was something she wanted to discuss with him. Something important, she had said.

And he had come, his insides knotted into a tight little ball. Sam's wife was playing it cool, she wasn't letting on. Maybe it was a case of giving him enough rope. Careful, the trap could be already set. He shouldn't have come, made an excuse, put her off. There was no reason to come. Just because she had asked him, said it was important . . . He looked across the desk at the woman. She was younger than Sam, in her mid-thirties probably, blonde, regular features. She seemed to be nervous, having trouble finding the right words, but that, too, could be put on.

"Because Sam fired you," she began hesitantly, "and John Palmer . . . on the day he died, I'm left . . . you see . . . I've got to run this place with in inexperienced staff." The pencil tapped on the desk. Margaret Selmer's eyes were solemn as they regarded Bill. "I was hoping you might come back."

Oh Jesus, no. Not here, not this place, not after . . . He had walked right into it. He cleared his throat a couple of times, and when he spoke he was conscious of how strained his voice sounded.

"I don't think I could. Sorry."

She studied him levelly. Again despite himself, Bill looked away. A giveaway. He was acting furtively. He forced his eyes back to her. "I can understand why you might be hesitant," she went on.

Something leapt inside him. He was startled. What did she mean by that? "What do you mean?" he asked weakly.

"Well, you're marrying the Palmer girl, aren't you?"

Oh . . . yes. "It's got nothing to do with that," he said defiantly.

"Do you mind me asking what it is then?" She looked

surprised.

Bill thought fast. It wasn't easy, but he had to come up with something — something plausible. He took the plunge. The warehouse was full of shadows. Traps everywhere. Mad to come. "Ah . . . actually, when Sam fired me I was already thinking of leaving anyway. To look for something different."

Margaret Selmer nodded as if quite satisfied with this explanation. She leaned forward in her chair. "How does this sound?" she said. "If you come back you'll have much more responsibility. I'll want you virtually to fill Sam's shoes. And of course that'll mean more money."

More money. Sam's shoes. Cold sweat, the urge to run, to get the hell out of here, away . . . More money.

"Is that some kind of joke? After what you cost me today, you're asking for money?"

"I've got to have it."

"Well, you won't get it here. Now clear out or I'll throw you out."

"You mean bastard."

"I'll show you how mean I can be . . ."

Voices rising and falling, clear then blurring, Sam picking up the telephone, dialling. Bill's temper — it had got him into trouble so many times before in the past.

"Bill?" Margaret Selmer's voice pushed forward over the echoes of the other voices, the image of Sam picking up the phone and dialling. "What do you say? Does that sound all right to you?"

"Give me the police."

"Hey, wait a minute. This is between you and me."

"Don't make things worse for yourself."

"Bill? Does it sound all right to you?"

Bill shook away the phantoms and insistent, whispering voices. Dying echoes. "Sorry?" He sat up straighter in his chair. "Oh yeah," he grunted. "Fine. I'll . . . ah . . . think it over. Okay?"

"Yes, of course," she said in a pleased voice. "You think it over."

24

Angela was having it out with her mother, who was really going on a bit much about Scott. Their voices were raised.

"Your problem, mother, is that you're a snob."

Patricia Hamilton was moving restlessly around the living room. "What's snobbish about wanting what's best for you?" she demanded.

"Best for *you,* you mean?" retorted.

Patricia was hurt. "I don't think that's fair."

"Isn't it?" Angela moved towards the closed study door.

"Don't disturb your father." Patricia's tone was peremptory. "He's talking business with Wayne."

Angela smiled to herself. Business with Wayne. The stud was going bad — everyone knew that. Well, it was about time Wayne had his comeuppance. She turned back into the living room where her mother stood watching her with a wary expression.

"I'll wait then. At least he's on my side."

Patricia lit a cigarette. Even that small action had her own special brand of elegance. "That's only because you can twist him around your little finger," she said wryly. "If he'd stop and think for a moment he'd see I'm right."

Angela smiled. How pig-headed her mother could be at times. She would never listen. "You know, it'd do you good to speak to someone like Scott," she said. "Maybe then you'd see there aren't two sets of people — us and them."

Patricia smiled archly. "Don't be ridiculous."

Angela was annoyed by her tone and expression that seemed to embody everything that was superior. "I don't think it's ridiculous," she said tartly.

Patricia shook her head and drew on her cigarette. Twin streams of smoke were pushed out through her flared nostrils. "What's the point of giving you a good education," she said, looking very much put upon, "and introducing you to the right people if you go ga-ga about some boy you know absolutely nothing about?" She shook her head again, as if this attitude of her daughter's was something she could never possibly hope to understand. And ingratitude obviously came into it.

Angela stared defiantly back at her mother. It was another bright sunny morning, and Scott had told her — the promise had been inherent — that he would call her. "I like him a lot," she said flatly. "That's all I need to know at the moment."

Then, just as she had been thinking about it, and this alone had been sufficient for a cue, the telephone rang. Angela started, and hurried across the room to answer it, aware of her mother's cold scrutiny as she did so.

"Hi."

"Hi. I had a feeling it would be you." His voice, already so familiar.

"I would have rung earlier," John told her, "but I slept in."

What had he been doing in the time since he had left her? Had he been thinking about her? Much? Dreamt about her? Crass, she chided herself — pure bloody Barbara Cartland. All the same she was suddenly feeling light-headed. "You sound as bad as me," she said with a laugh.

Patricia was sitting on the sofa, impatiently flicking through a fashion magazine. "I really enjoyed yesterday," John said. "I hope you didn't cop too much flak from your parents."

Nothing he needed to know about. No point in scaring him off. "Of course not. They did find out, though."

Patricia looked up from her magazine. Angela caught her eyes. Well, well, we'll see now, she thought.

"They were okay about it?"

"Yes. Fine." She smiled at her mother. Wait for it, wait for it — this will be good. "In fact, more than fine. Mummy was just saying — she'd like you to come to dinner tonight. Can you make it?"

And what a huge pleasure she derived from the stricken look on her mother's face as the sense of what she had just said to the boy she knew as Scott Edwards sank in. Now she had really set the cat among the pigeons — and it was worth it just to see her dear, dear mother lose her composure for once.

25

It was to be a dinner party well within Patricia's parameters of what she considered a properly organised dinner party to be, even if it was such short notice and the only guest a young man who was becoming altogether too persistent and needed to be discouraged in a manner that brooked no misunderstanding. She was determined the dinner would be a success — in more ways than one. It would serve a definite purpose. So, for that reason, she didn't stint on the arrangements. The caterers had been put on full alert, and a maid hired from the agency. The cutlery gleamed, the glassware sparkled, and the best crockery was beyond reproach. There was even a floral centrepiece on the table to provide a particularly striking touch.

In fact, Angela was making the final adjustments to this floral offering when her mother came into the room. They had both changed for dinner. The guest was expected at any moment now.

"What do you think?" Angela straightened and nodded to the floral arrangement.

"I doubt whether he'll notice the difference," Patricia remarked drily, and Angela thought, yes, that was just the bitchy sort of comment she would have expected her to come out with. She glared at her mother. Then Patricia smiled, totally gracious again, and kissed her lightly on the cheek. "Don't be paranoid, dear. All I meant was that men don't notice these things. The same goes for your father."

She was probably right. Maybe Angela was being a bit too jumpy. She knew what her mother thought of Scott, and maybe she had been fearing the worst. "Sorry," she murmured.

They moved away from the table as the maid came in to finish setting it. Patricia took Angela's arm. "I told you — if you want to play your little game, I'll go along with it. At least I'll prove I'm not a snob."

She was charm itself. After the first flush of success that had come with the sudden, impulsive invitation to Scott, Angela was apprehensive. Her mother didn't like to be crossed, and she could use that famous charm of hers to devastating effect when she wished.

"I hope so," Angela said doubtfully.

Patricia let go her arm. "Anyway, your father wants to see you. He's in the study."

In the doorway, Angela turned back to her mother who was watching her with a small, expectant smile. "You will try, won't you?" she pleaded.

Patricia laughed and waved her away. "Of course. I'll be on my best behaviour."

Angela had to accept that. She wondered if it was enough. In the living room, Wayne was standing at the bar with a drink in his hand.

"Want a drink?" he asked as Angela headed towards the study door.

"No, thank you," she replied coldly.

She stopped in front of the door and raised her hand to knock. "What's so special about Scott Edwards?" Wayne asked suddenly.

Lowering her hand, Angela swung back to face him. "What do you mean?" she demanded.

Wayne gave her a crooked smile. "It's not your usual pattern with his type, is it?" he said in a silky voice. "I mean, it's generally one night in the back seat of a car and thank you very much."

Alarmed, Angela glanced at the closed study door, then moved back across the room to stand in front of Wayne. "Keep your voice down," she whispered savagely. She was angry.

Wayne was still smiling. "Sorry," he said easily. "Can't go disillusioning Daddy, can we?"

"No, we can't," she said meaningfully. Yes, she could give him just as good as he gave her. If he had something on her, then she had something on him. Tit for tat, and he got the message.

"All right," he said with a shrug. "It was just a civil question."

"Yeah, sure," Angela said sourly, and turned back towards the study door.

"Well?"

She stopped again. "Well what?"

"So why is he different? Why the dinner invitation?"

"You'll be the last to know," she snapped, then dismissed him by turning her back on him once more and knocking on the study door. At her father's summons, she opened the door and stepped into the room.

Her father was signing some papers, for the moment absorbed. Angela moved around behind his chair, placed her arms around his neck and looked over his shoulders at the very official looking papers that were spread out on the desk in front of him.

"That looks very, very boring," she remarked.

"Of course it's boring," Gordon Hamilton said, signing the final letter with a flourish. Angela kissed him and moved back around to the front of the desk.

"Are you cross with me?" she asked.

He looked up at her. "What makes you think that?"

"Mother made it sound so serious," she explained. " 'Your father wants to see you'." She paused briefly. "I only invited Scott to teach her a lesson," she said, sitting down on the chair in front of the desk.

Gordon Hamilton joined his hands together and settled

back in his own high-backed chair. "It's not really fair on the young man, is it?" he said gravely.

Angela smiled at him. "I think you'll like him."

Her father's expression didn't change. "You didn't answer my question."

Angela's smile faded. "Oh, you *are* angry."

"Angela," he said in a warning tone.

"All right," she said, chastened a little. "I suppose it was unfair." Then she smiled again. Her good spirits weren't easily suppressed. "But I'm glad I did it."

Gordon was watching her closely. He didn't return her smile. "You didn't get the rise out of your mother you wanted."

"The night's not over yet," Angela observed flippantly.

Gordon remained serious. "Listen to me, young lady," he said slowly, punctuating his words with a forefinger. "I'm telling you the same thing I told her. Scott Edwards is going to be a guest in our house. I don't want him ending up as the ball in a ping-pong match between the two of you."

"I'm only joking, Daddy," Angela said, trying to keep her tone light. "I like him too much to do that."

Gordon raised his eyebrows. "Really?"

"Really." Angela laughed, a little self-consciously beneath the intensity of her father's gaze. "It's funny. I've only met him a few times, but I feel as if I've known him for ages." It was the first time she had been able to articulate a feeling that had been growing stronger in her all the time, explaining it not only to her father, but to herself. She laughed again. "Maybe that's what they call love at first sight."

Gordon returned her smile. "Don't let your mother hear that," he warned her. "She'll have a coronary." His smile died away, and he was serious again. "I'm looking forward to meeting him," he said.

"I'm glad," Angela said, and she really was.

The doorbell rang.

26

John Palmer tried to look relaxed, but wasn't making much of a success of it. From the moment Angela's mother had opened the door to him, had greeted him effusively and taken the bottle of wine he held out to her, he had felt rather intimidated. For one thing, she was beautifully dressed, and he was dressed very casually in slacks, an open-necked shirt and a sports jacket. Perhaps he should have put on a tie at least; it looked to be that sort of occasion. Then there was the way she had looked at the bottle of wine, nonplussed, as if not knowing what to do with it, before handing it to the maid who had just come out of the dining room with a tray of savouries. And he had been left with the impression that bringing the wine had been the wrong thing to do. And then there was the warmth of Patricia's welcome; it made him just a little suspicious.

Now he sat in the living room, nursing a can of beer. Angela and her mother were sipping complicated looking cocktails. Angela's brother and father were drinking Scotch. The beer made John feel a little gauche.

"I'm glad you could make it, Scott," Gordon Hamilton was saying. He seemed friendly enough, John thought. A genuine sort of a guy. "I've been wanting to thank you for looking after my girl."

Angela laughed. "Daddy's having a medal struck," she said happily. John smiled appreciatively across at her. She looked fantastic. Her long blue dress clung provocatively to the contours of her full, ripe body, and was cut deep enough at the front to reveal just enough cleavage to make it very tantalising.

"Don't embarrass the poor boy, you two," Patricia remarked, holding the tray of savouries out to Scott. "Scott?"

"Thanks."

Carefully, aware of the woman's eyes on him, John reached for a square of melba toast spread with caviar. He bit into it. The toast crumbled, and caviar spilt onto his chin. He felt the warmth rising to his face as he quickly wiped the caviar away with his finger. Mrs Hamilton was watching him. John felt very small.

"You're not related to the Edwards in Illona Avenue, by any chance?" Patricia Hamilton asked him, still friendly, smiling sweetly at him.

John shook his head. Was she getting at him in some way? His defences were up. "No."

"Just a thought," Patricia said. "I thought you might be visiting them. Dural's a bit out of the way if you don't have friends here."

Like what had he been doing in Dural in the first place? How had he come to see Angela fall off the horse? "I was sightseeing."

Patricia's eyes widened. "Oh? You're a visitor to Sydney then?"

Watch it, John told himself. "Just moved here," he replied. That was safe enough.

"From?" He wished she would get onto another subject, wouldn't try to drag his whole history out of him. It was getting a bit close, a bit awkward.

"Brisbane," he said, wishing he didn't have to lie, because this was the way a person could easily get trapped.

"Nice city," Gordon Hamilton opined, sipping some more of his Scotch.

"If you like overgrown country towns," Wayne said with a sneer, and John knew that Angela's brother didn't like him. He would have to be watched.

Angela frowned at Wayne. "I never noticed you complaining at Woombai." She looked at John. "We've got a property up north," she explained. "We go back for holidays."

This was better. A respite. John was relieved that it was Angela now who was talking to him. "Yeah?" he said interestedly, and recalled a boyhood memory. "My grandparents live in the country. We go there a fair bit."

"Where's that?" Angela wanted to know.

"Ararat." Shit! It had slipped out. His guard had been down, and out it had come.

"That's a long way from Brisbane," Patricia remarked.

Some repair work to be done here. "Yeah . . . well," John muttered. "We don't go there that much. Special occasions — you know . . ."

And that sounded awfully weak. Reaching forward, he picked up another savoury from the tray Patricia had placed on the low table in front of him. It was a momentary distraction which didn't stop Mrs Hamilton moving in on him again.

"What does your father do?" There seemed to be a gleam of amusement in her large, pale eyes, but that might just have been a trick of the light.

"My father?" John took a swig of his beer. "His job?"

"Yes."

Keep it vague, he exhorted himself. Hold back on the details, be evasive. "Ah . . .—manual work," he said awkwardly, and once again the warmth rushed up into his cheeks.

"Oh." And from the way she uttered that single syllable, she made it perfectly obvious what she thought of *that* piece of intelligence. She seemed to stiffen, and it was as if a film came down over her eyes, so that although they were just as clear and sparkling as before, something had happened to the quality of her vision and subtly altered the substance of things. She stood up, smoothing her dress over her slender thighs. "I think we can go into dinner now," she said rather distantly.

Dinner hadn't even started before John made his first mistake. He sat there at that table with its floral centrepiece, shining cutlery and plates, the exquisitely fluted wine glasses at each setting, and while the maid was serving the soup, he reached across and plucked a bread roll from the basket in front of him. He picked up a knife and cut the roll in half, as he had always done. Then, sensing he was being watched, he looked up and saw Patricia Hamilton staring at him with an expression of faint distaste as she broke her own roll fastidiously apart with her long tapered fingers. Then he saw that Wayne was doing the same with *his* roll, and immediately realised his mistake. So, in the better class of place, people just didn't cut their rolls with a knife. Lesson learnt, but too late now, of course.

"I hope you like vichysoisse," Patricia said to John, nodding to the soup in front of him.

"I'll try anything once."

Gordon Hamilton gave John a conspiratorial wink. "Actually, it's just plain old leek and potato soup," he said.

So he had cut open his roll. Now he needed to butter it. Taking up bread and butter knife again, he reached across with it to the butter. Patricia smiled across at Wayne.

"Pass Scott the butter please, darling," she said.

Wayne passed not only the butter dish, but the butter-knife that was alongside it — and John groaned inwardly again. He had done something else wrong, obviously. He looked in dismay down at the butter-knife. This dinner was turning out to be an obstacle course, with hidden traps all along the way, and he would be lucky if he survived it. It was nothing like back home in Melbourne. There it was all in to the tucker, and to hell with the airs and graces. He wondered what they would be having down there tonight. Steak and kidney pudding possibly, or sausages, something tasty and plenty of it.

"I'll have the butter after you, Scott," Angela said, and when he looked across at her, he saw — hey, beauty, what a fabulous girl — that she was deliberately cutting open her bread roll with a knife.

The food was excellent. John hadn't heard the names of the various dishes before, let alone tasted them. The wine glasses were kept full, the chink of cutlery against crockery was muted and discreet. In fact, there was an air of restraint and rather awful politeness about the whole meal. The movements were economical, and the conversation, when questions weren't directly aimed at him, quite over John's head. He felt like an intruder, and a reasonably clumsy one at that. It was only on those occasions when he caught Angela's eye and she gave him a smile of encouragement that he reassured himself it would soon be over. He didn't like the zabaglione at all.

"We'll have coffee in the living room," Patricia announced. John pushed his half-eaten dessert away. "Don't let me hurry you," she said.

"It's okay," John told her. "It was a terrific meal, Mrs Hamilton."

"I'm glad you enjoyed it," she said distantly, then turned to Wayne. "It was an excellent choice of wines, darling," she said. "The Montalcino was just perfect with the fettucini."

Wayne looked smug. "You can't go wrong if you serve an Italian wine with pasta." He smiled at John. "Right, Scott?"

They were getting at him again, another pit opening up in front of him, but it didn't matter. Why should he care? John shrugged. "I always drink local wine," he murmured.

"True blue Aussie, eh?" There was a friendly twinkle in Gordon Hamilton's eyes.

"Scott was kind enough to bring a bottle . . ." Patricia Hamilton turned to John. No warmth in *those* eyes, no sign of friendliness there. "I'm sorry it wasn't right for the dishes I had chosen. But of course you weren't to know . . ."

John saw the opening. Beauty. "That's all right," he said

with a tight smile. "I'll know better next time, won't I?"

Gotcha. He saw with satisfaction how the shot hit home, the barely perceptible tightening of Patricia Hamilton's jaw, the invisible shutter that clanked down over her eyes.

"Let's have our coffee, shall we?" she said in a strained voice.

27

Things seemed to be developing too quickly, and Fiona didn't like it. Dinner at the Hamiltons' was bad enough. John had told her when he came home, and she was still sitting up playing solitaire, that everything was fine except for Mrs Hamilton who had struck him as being a bit of a snob and didn't approve of him. That had given Fiona some encouragement and made her think that, with opposition like that, John would soon give up. But when she learned from Jill Taylor the following morning that John had already left to visit the Hamilton stud, she was dismayed. Apparently Gordon Hamilton had invited him — and even though there was some grim satisfaction in knowing dear Patricia wouldn't be at all pleased about that, the fact remained that she wasn't pleased about it, either.

And Scott had gone without telling her. If he *had* told her, she would have done her best to dissuade him, of course. But how much would she have to tell him? Everything? No, no, not too much too soon — the thing to do was gradually wean him away from the idea of the Hamiltons, from that girl who . . . she shuddered. It didn't bear thinking about. If matters took their natural course . . . she had to do *something*. She had to think, and think hard — and as always, she found she could do this best by going down to the beach for a swim. It was a brilliant day, and a swim would make her feel much better.

It did. When she returned to the house, John was in the kitchen, fixing himself a sandwich.

"You must have worked up quite an appetite out at the stud," she said, fixing him with a fierce glare, and quietly relishing the look of guilt on his face.

"Yeah," he muttered, slicing a cucumber.

"You promised to take things slowly," she reproahced him.

The sandwich he was making was a bulky one. Piled haphazardly onto the slice of brown bread were cheese, tomato, devon, onion and cucumber. John pressed the other slice of bread down on top of them. "I'm trying."

"Trying?" She raised her eyebrows. This was choice — it really was. "Dinner last night, a visit to the stud today — you call that trying?"

He was uncomfortable. He was concentrating on his sandwich. "I didn't plan it," he said, not very distinctly. "It just happened." Fiona snorted, and a note of defiance crept into John's voice. "I got to talking to Mr Hamilton about the place last night . . . after dinner . . . just before I left, and he invited me." He looked up at Fiona. "I couldn't say no without being rude, could I?" He held her eyes for a long moment, and then suddenly he grinned, the dimples appearing in his smooth cheeks, and he looked so boyish and cheeky that her heart couldn't fail to soften towards him. She tried hard, though. There were still things she had to say to him. "Okay," he said. "I wanted to be with Angela."

Fiona's heart sank. How hard was this going to be? "Why didn't you tell me last night when you came home?" she demanded. "I was still up, and you could have told me then."

John was still grinning. The sandwich had been forgotten for the time being. "You wouldn't have slept if I'd told you," he said shrewdly, and she had to acknowledge the truth of it.

"It's for your own good," she said flatly.

Now John was serious again. "I know."

There was a short silence. John hadn't touched his sandwich. "Okay," Fiona said at last. "A deal. No more calls to Angela till the end of the week." John looked unhappy and remained silent. "You promised." Fiona drove the point home, hard.

John sighed. "Okay," he muttered.

Fiona was pleased. It was something at least, a start. "Good," she said briskly. "Slowly does it. You'll see that I'm right. You just can't rush into things — you being here, what happened in Melbourne." She placed her hand on his shoulder and looked deeply into his eyes. "My friend, we've got some talking to do, things to sort out. You've got a new name — right. Now we've got to give you a bit of history to go with that name — and I don't want to see you risking everything just for the sake of being with a girl like Angela Hamilton."

28

Beryl Palmer did her best to remain cheerful at all times, to keep smiling and put up a jolly front, but it wasn't easy. There were so many things nagging at her, foremost among them John and where he might be. When she was alone as she was now, with David out on the road again and not due back for a couple more days, she allowed the mask to slip and let herself be taken over by the worries that crowded in on her and refused to go away despite all her efforts to banish them.

At such times she thought back to what her life had been back in Ararat, working in the diner, before she had met David and broken off her engagement to Frank. What would have happened if she had married Frank? Probably they would have stayed on in Ararat, raised a family, and she would have been quite happy. She dismissed the thought abruptly, and some wistfulness had been creeping in, because it wasn't fair to David. She loved David, there was no doubt about that, and there was the family. Mostly she couldn't have wished for any better, and the things that were worrying her now, well, they would soon go away as things sorted themselves out. But Johnny . . .

The marriage between Susan and Bill Todd was on again. They had talked it over and agreed to go through with it. But it wasn't to be a full church wedding — Susan had decided against that. She didn't want a fuss, for fear it turned into some sort of freak show, what with all the publicity about Johnny. What she wanted now was a quiet wedding at home, with only family and a few friends along. Susan had explained to her mother that Bill didn't mind what sort of wedding it was, as long as they were married — and that was all right.

Then there was the business about the bridesmaid. Susan was still hopeful that Lynn Hardy from next door would still be able to do it, but Beryl wasn't so sure. Victor Hardy's attitude earlier that day when she had made a point of speaking to him while he was out the front of his house washing his car had been positively hostile. When Beryl had delicately broached the subject of the wedding and how she was still hoping Lynn could be bridesmaid, as had been planned all along, he had made his position abundantly clear. No, he had stated quite definitely, his daughter was to have nothing to do with the wedding. Nor with young Kevin, either, who, he had heard, was getting into some sort of trouble at school, and he didn't want his daughter mixed up with any of it. There was no use arguing with a man like that. He had made up his mind, and that was that. Pig-headed, Beryl had called him under her breath.

Beryl sipped her tea. It was already cold. With a grimace, she pushed the cup away from her. Susan was on night duty at the hospital. Kevin was up in his room. The telephone rang, and the sound of it jolted Beryl into full alertness. Apprehensively, she glanced at the clock on the mantelpiece. It was nine-thirty, a late time for anyone to ring. As she hurried to the phone, all sorts of alarming thoughts scurried through her mind. Who could it be, ringing up so late? An accident? Had something happened to David? Or was it the police about Johnny? She scooped up the receiver, fumbled, almost dropped it, then pressed it to her ear. The palms of her hands felt slippery. Her heart was beating fast.

"Hello?"

She heard the STD pips, then the voice coming through.

"Hello, Mum."

Beryl felt suddenly faint. The voice so familiar, and which she had been longing to hear. The line crackled and hummed, but the voice still came through quite strongly. The relief . . . He was still alive. "John!" she cried. "Where are you?"

"I can't tell you. I just called to let you know I'm okay. How are you?"

There was a tightness in her throat, and everything seemed to blur in front of her eyes. "I'm fine," she said huskily. "I miss you. We all do. When are you coming home?"

"Not for a while."

The wave of dizziness passed. "Listen to me, love," she said in a stronger voice. "You have to clear your name. The longer you leave it, the harder it'll be."

"No, Mum." John's voice seemed to rise and fall, carried along the airwaves from goodness knew where. But he was alive. "There's no way I could make the police believe me."

"But you're innocent," Beryl protested.

"I can't prove it," John pointed out.

Alive, alive . . . "You'll find a way. I know you will — and we'll all stand by you."

"I can't come back, Mum."

The tears pricking her eyes, the dam gates about to burst. "We . . . we love you, Johnny."

"I love you too, Mum." And it seemed that Johnny's voice was gradually breaking apart. "All of you." He paused. "I have to go now, Mum. Look after yourself."

"Don't go!" It was one last desperate cry. She had to hold onto him. He mustn't . . . "Not yet!"

But he had gone, and there was only the dial tone sounding persistently, annoyingly in her ear, to torment and mock her misery. Slowly she replaced the receiver, and tried to force herself not to let herself go. But it was impossible. It was all too much. The huge sobs cruelly wrenched her whole being — and they just came, and came, and came . . . tearing her apart.

29

John kept his promise to Fiona, and didn't call Angela — but that didn't stop him from brooding, from becoming restless and fidgety, jumping every time the phone rang, rushing to answer it, and his face registering bitter disappointment when he found it wasn't Angela. Fiona tried to brighten him up.

"Come on, kid," she said cheerfully. "No point sitting there brooding. You're doing the right thing."

"So you keep telling me," John said tiredly. "But I can't stop thinking about her."

"Do yourself a big, big favour," Fiona said gently, "and manage it somehow."

And that made John angry. He flared up at her. "What *you* want and what I want are two different things," he shouted, moving to the door. "I promised to go easy," he went on, "that's all. I'm *not* going to stop seeing her."

He still waited to hear from her, but the silence stretched interminably, and at last John, unable to stand the strain any more, picked up the phone and dialled the Hamiltons' number. Gordon Hamilton answered, and told him in the most friendly way that he had just missed Angela, that she had gone out with some friends, adding perhaps as a sop to his disappointment he sensed the boy must have felt, that he had the impression she wasn't looking forward to it all that much.

"She'll be home tomorrow morning if you'd like to call back," he said. "I know she was waiting for your call."

And that made it all so much better. Disappointment had been shot through with jealousy. Friends? What sort of friends? Boys? Spoilt kids with money who would soon make her forget him? But now here was her father telling him that she had been waiting for him to call. And there was the implication that she was missing him, perhaps even as much as he was missing her. He felt exultant.

He got through to her the following morning. She sounded very tired — and pleased. "Hi," she greeted him. "Sorry. I'm only half-awake."

John laughed. His relief was enormous. "What have you been up to?"

"A boring party. Only just got back." He could hear her yawning. "How are you?"

"I'm fine." A party that lasted all night? But his happiness at hearing her voice again was strong enough to overwhelm the faint twist of jealousy. He didn't own her, she could do anything she liked — couldn't she? "Look, I'm sorry I took so long to call."

"It's probably better you didn't." Sure, she sounded casual, but was it just wishful thinking for John to tell himself that perhaps she was being a little too casual? "I've been so busy, anyway."

"Oh." What did that mean? Perhaps she hadn't been missing him so much after all. Perhaps he had been deluding himself.

"But I'm glad you got around to it," Angela added quickly.

"That's good."

Of course she had missed him. He had just heard it in her voice. Unmistakeable. She had been quick to reassure him. No doubts any more. Everything sweet.

"You know, I'd like to return the favour," he said. "The dinner, I mean. So . . . why don't you let me take you out somewhere?"

"Where?" She was eager. "What do you mean?"

"Take you out to dinner," he replied. "I'd ask your Mum, but I don't know if she would handle it."

She was laughing, pleased, happy, no sign of tiredness now. "Where are we going?"

Her mood was infectious. John smiled. "Does that mean yes?"

"Of course it means yes," she said, and his heart leapt. "Come on, tell me. Where are we going?"

"To the most exclusive joint in Manly," he told her. "But bring your costume for a quick swim first."

The most exclusive joint in Manly proved to be one of the seafood places at the ocean end of the Corso, where John bought some fish and chips to take away. He had already bought a bottle of chilled white wine. He had arranged to meet her on the corner in the afternoon after she had caught up on a couple of hours' sleep, and the time had never moved so slowly for him. Finally, after an eternity, and with moments of great uncertainty whether she would come after all, she *had* come, and with the relief surging in him as powerfully as the breakers on the beach below, they had gone down the steps to the sand.

The sun was strong and the surf inviting. Angela looked absolutely fantastic in her brief bikini. Her flesh was firm and bronzed, and seemed to be pricked with light. They spread a blanket out on the sand, left their things and ran down to the surf. The water was cool and refreshing. They splashed each other and were tossed this way and that by the tumbling waves. They swam and lay in the sun.

"I told you it was exclusive," John said. "Just you and me. Are you hungry?"

There were quite a number of people on the beach. Stollers paused on the esplanade above them and looked out to sea. John opened the bottle of wine and poured some into two paper cups. The packet of fish and chips was open on the blanket between them.

"You're mad," Angela said. "Exclusive? You had me

believing you." She took the paper cup John held out to her.

"I know," John laughed. "You expected cosy corners and candlelight. But this is all I can afford." He gestured to the fish and chips. "Go on. Eat up, before they get cold."

"Why did you take so long to call?" Angela asked suddenly, her expression serious.

A container ship was anchored out at sea, waiting for clearance to enter the Heads. Seagulls circled above the sand. The sun was moving down behind the buildings, and people were packing up and leaving the beach.

"I wasn't sure if you were all that interested," John said awkwardly, slightly taken aback by the directness of her question. He looked back at Angela. She sat on the blanket, her legs drawn up, hugging them, watching him. He took in the length of firmly fleshed thigh, and smiled slowly. Some chick. "Besides, some things are better when you've had to wait for them," he said.

Angela's eyes softened. The surf thundered, the seagulls swooped and called, and above the stone wall that dropped down from the explanade, the shops were full, cameras clicked, and the ferries sounded their horns as they nudged in towards the wharf. But here, on the sand, was something else — something, John was certain, could be duplicated nowhere else. How could anyone ever, at any time be privy to these same feelings that were beginning to stir him beyond measure, these rising emotions? How could anyone *know* what it was like, this . . . this absolute certainty. Something outside themselves was directing every movement they made, bringing them together — otherwise how could he have dreamt about this girl in such detail as to eliminate any doubts he might have that it wasn't Angela who figured in those dreams so often, but a girl who happened to look like her?

"Maybe," Angela said with a faint smile, and John started. Then he remembered what he had said about some things being better if you waited for them.

The next few hours passed as if in a dream. There was

certainly an unreal quality about them, as if he was walking along and his feet weren't quite touching the ground — a floating quality. They walked hand in hand along the beach, the sand crunching softly beneath their bare feet, the salt drying on their skin. As they talked John pointed out the house where he lived with Fiona. Then they were running along the beach, splashing through the water that surged up beneath their feet and drew back again, pulling the sand away. Angela laughed as he caught up with her, as she stumbled, and he caught her in his arms and held her close to keep her from falling. Then he was kissing her, and he could taste the salt on her lips, feel her body moulding against his. Then she broke away, and he was chasing her again.

It was getting dark. They went to a beer garden, and then he walked with her back to her car. They were quiet, content in each other's company. There had been a time, back there on the beach, when he had kissed her and she had begun to return his kisses before suddenly breaking it off just when he thought it all might lead to something. But she had made it clear to him, by her attitude, by her expression, that that was something she didn't want — not yet, anyway — and he was content to leave it at that. It didn't matter, and there was the thought — perhaps a rationalisation — that it might have spoilt the mood they had built up between them. Maybe it was too soon. There was time. Delicious anticipation, and plenty of time to think about her.

Time? How much time? Suddenly, as he waved goodbye to her, and the little red sports car pulled away from the curb, the realisation of who he was and what he was came crowding back on him, bringing with it a mood of desolation. There wasn't much time, he was deluding himself, and at any moment now . . .maybe a squeal of tyres, a hand on his shoulder, an authoritative voice. He had to do something, and soon — he just couldn't let it go on like this. Maybe, without Angela, if he had never met her, it might have been different. But now something had to be sorted out.

He let himself into the house quietly, hoping Fiona was already in bed and wouldn't hear him. The one thing he didn't want right now was a session with her, where he would have to justify himself in the face of her disapproval — and frankly, he had no idea why she should be so dead set against Angela.

But despite all his caution, as he made his way across the darkened living room of her apartment, he bumped into a table. He froze.

"Johnny, is that you?" Fiona's voice came from the bedroom.

He cursed his clumsiness. There was nothing for it now. He put down the bag he was carrying, and crossing to the bedroom door, opened it. Fiona was sitting up in bed, reading a book. She looked up at him severely over the top of her spectacles.

"I take it you've had a fun night," she said, taking in his dishevelled appearance, his bare feet.

John was ready for her. Straight into the attack. "Before you start," he said seriously, "there are a few things you should know."

Fiona raised an eyebrow and folded her arms. She nodded to the side of the bed, but John preferred to remain standing. He told her so. Fiona shrugged. "Suit yourself. It's not an interrogation."

It sure wasn't. John would see to that. "For starters," he said, "Angela's nothing like you say. She might be from a rich family, but she's not stuck up."

A pained expression passed across Fiona's face. "That's not what I said."

"You implied it," John retorted. "She knows I'm broke and she couldn't care less. It's *me* she's interested in."

Fiona's lips stretched in a sardonic smile. "You're so hung up about the snobbery thing, you're forgetting the little matter of the police. Oh, I know it's only a minor detail. . ."

"We've been through all that," John said sharply. He

knew. He hadn't forgotten.

Fiona grimaced. "Exactly — and you're choosing to ignore it." She shook her head. "Worrying about whether she's a snob or not, for heaven's sake. I don't know." She stared up at John for a long, thoughtful moment. "What are you out for?" she asked abrasively. "A bit of fun?"

That was nasty. She was deliberately being nasty. "You know it's more serious than that," John said bitingly.

"Exactly." The woman in the bed nodded fiercely, as if something had just been vindicated to her. "And it's not fair to her. Don't you see? Under the circumstances."

Didn't she see? Didn't she understand? "I didn't kill Sam Selmer," he cried.

"I know that," she said calmly. "But I'm not the police. Stop and think about it — what you're getting yourself into. Or more importantly, what you're getting Angela Hamilton into."

"Yeah." Angela — she was the one he had to think about now. Something to do. Only one thing to do. It had been there, in his mind, from the time he had waved goodbye to Angela, lodged there, right at the back, but gradually breaking loose and making its way to the front. Now was the time. "I guess I'd better go and pack," he said flatly.

"What?" Fiona was startled.

"I'm going to Melbourne." There, that was it. It was out now.

"What the hell for?"

"You're right about the police," he said. "I'm no good to Angela till I sort this whole mess out."

Fiona was staring at him wide-eyed. "You're not thinking of giving yourself up?"

John shook his head. He wasn't thinking of that at all. "I'm going to prove I'm innocent," he told her. "Find out who really killed Sam."

"That's taking one hell of a risk." Fiona's voice was low, even, as if she were keeping it under firm control. "It's not fair on your family, either."

"They won't even know I'm there."

"You can't do it on your own."

"I've got a mate," John said simply. "I'll ask him to help. His name's Bill Todd, and he'll help me for sure."

30

As soon as he entered the house, David Palmer could see the strain Beryl was under. He had been away two days, and now that he was back, he sensed the change that had taken place. The atmosphere was so thick you could almost cut it with a knife. Beryl was edgy and snappy with him. He himself was in a bit of a mood, still smarting from the snub Vic Hardy next door had just given him as he had pulled up in front of the house.

It was unlike Beryl to be snappy, and it worried him. Sitting her down, he asked her as gently as he could, what was the matter. Gradually it had come out, about Susan's new plans for the wedding, which she now wanted to have at home; about Kevin getting into trouble at school for fighting; about Vic Hardy not letting his daughter be bridesmaid; and finally — and it was obvious that Beryl was close to breaking point — there was the call she'd had from John the night before. She twisted her hands together as she spoke.

"Where from?" he asked sharply.

"I don't know," Beryl replied. "It was STD. He just wanted me to know he was all right." She sniffed. "I didn't want to worry the kids, so I didn't tell them."

Suddenly, she gave a cry, and raced into the kitchen.

David could smell something burning. He followed her.

Her face crumpling, she was staring in dismay down at a blackened pan of burnt potatoes on the stove. The tears began to flow. David lifted the pan from the ring, and took her in his arms.

"I'm so unhappy, David," she sobbed. "So unhappy."

He patted her gently on the back. It would be a good thing for her to let it all come out at last.

That evening, after dinner, Beryl went to bed early, and David had a conference with Susan and Kevin in Kevin's room. He had already resolved the business over Lynn Hardy being Susan's bridesmaid. He had simply done that by going across to the Hardy house and having it out with Vic, who, in the end, had relented in his attitude, although reluctantly. So that was settled.

"We have to give her as much help as we can," he told Susan and Kevin. "The wedding and everything — she'll need everything we can give her."

"Sure." Kevin nodded solemnly. Susan, still in her nurse's uniform, stood with her arms folded.

"One other thing," David went on a little awkwardly. "Try and get to the phone as much as possible. She didn't tell you, but John called her last night. It really threw her. If there are any more calls from him, I'd like us to take them."

"He'll get an earful from me," Susan said vehemently, "that's for sure."

Kevin looked at her in surprise. "What do you mean?"

"I mean he's being so selfish," Susan said seriously, looking from him to her father. "He's too scared to face up to what he's done, so he stays hiding somewhere, making our lives a misery — making calls from God knows where whenever he gets depressed."

"What do you mean, 'what he's done'?" There was an angry light in Kevin's eyes.

"Of course he did it," Susan said with a patient sigh. "I don't think he meant to, but . . . well, look at the facts. The police saw him running away, after all."

David stepped in. They were getting into an argument, and that would only make things worse. "We're not here to talk about that," he said sharply, "and I don't want to hear any arguing about it — okay? That's all your mother'll need to really send her off the deep end." He glared at them both. "From now on we do everything we can to help her. Agreed?"

It was agreed.

31

He had gone. With the thought that he might have changed his mind — yet somehow sensing he hadn't, John being the determined sort of boy he was — Fiona opened the door of his room. She stared at the bed that had obviously not been slept in, the empty wardrobe, and knew for a fact that he had gone. There was a dull ache behind her temples. She had drunk the best part of half a bottle of whisky the previous night after John had stormed out of her room, and there was a thick taste in her mouth. She sat heavily on the edge of the bed, and tried to bring her scrambled thoughts together into some form of coherence. She heard voices — her own voice.

"It's not a game of cops and robbers. You're heading back to the worst place you could possibly be, on the off chance you'll be able to come up with an answer."

"I have to do something."

"What about money? You haven't got any and I'm certainly not subsidising your stupidity."

"I haven't asked for money."

So he had gone. The young fool. What on earth did he feel he could achieve? Nothing. He would be walking straight into the arms of the law. It was sheer and utter madness. Well . . . She tried to be philosophical about it.

He knew what he was doing, and it didn't concern her. She eased herself up from the bed, and there was a sudden stab of pain behind her eyes. Who was she kidding? Of course it was her concern. Carefully, she moved out of the room and crossed the hallway into the kitchen. A cup of tea would go down particularly well at this time. She put on the kettle and waited for it to boil. She felt hopelessly sad.

He could have been her own son — the son she'd never had. No, that was wrong. The son she *did* have, once. Little Scott, who hadn't had much of a chance. Three days, that was all. She had hoped, then, that he would amount to something, be successful like his father, the man she could never marry. There would have been something of the boy's father with him — something that would always remind her of him. It was why she had called the boy Scott, after his father, who never even knew that he had existed for even that flicker of time.

Then, many years later, there had been John. And there had been times, after David Palmer had left him with her and returned to Melbourne, when she had almost come to believe that this could be the same boy. Perhaps there had been some awful misunderstanding at the hospital, a mix-up, and that the boy they had told her was dead was not little Scott. It was a hopeless dream. She had been there when the twins were born — no amount of self-delusion could ever make her forget that.

There was a shrill whistling sound. The kettle was boiling. She stood up and crossed to it. John and Scott, Scott and John. What would Scott have looked like had he been allowed to grow up? Like his father? Possibly. She took the kettle off the stove. The phone rang. With a grunt of annoyance, Fiona replaced thbe kettle on the stove and moved to answer the phone that was ringing so shrilly, so insistently.

"Hello." She didn't recognise the voice. It was bright, quite pleasant. "It's Angela Hamilton here." Oh no. Fiona stiffened. She should have expected something like this to happen, should have been ready for it — but she wasn't.

The girl went on. "You're Aunt Fiona, aren't you? Scott's told me all about you."

Yes, he would, Fiona thought. Bubbling away, the two of them. Why *her*. . .? The odds against something like this happening were astronomical. Something for the record books. "Has he?"

"All good, I might add," the girl went on brightly, polished vowels, good schooling — Patricia had made sure of that. Two kids with upbringings that couldn't be more different. "Is he in? I'd like to talk to him."

Fiona still hadn't quite recovered her composure. She was a little flustered. "No. . .no, you can't," she stammered. "He's gone away."

"But I saw him last night," Angela said in disbelief. "He didn't say anything about going away."

"Well, that's what he's done." Fiona was fully recovered now. Her tone was curt.

"But. . .he would have told me." All the cheeriness had gone from the girl's voice. Now it sounded small, quite pathetic, and Fiona experienced a momentary pang.

"There's been a family problem," she said stiffly. "He had to go back to Brisbane."

"I see." There was an obvious effort to keep her voice steady. "Could you tell me when he'll be back?"

"I really don't know."

"He must have given you *some* idea." There was a break in the girl's voice, a small quaver. "He *is* coming back, isn't he?"

"I'm not in the habit of lying," Fiona told her tersely. "If I knew when he'd be back I would have told you. Now is that all? I'm very busy."

"Yes," Angela said weakly. "That's all."

Fiona put down the receiver firmly. It was tough, but she had to do it. Anything to discourage that girl from having anything more to do with the boy she knew as Scott Edwards. Somehow Fiona had a feeling she wouldn't be so easily put off. If she was anything like her mother she wouldn't be.

32

It was cold. Huddling in the shadows, John Palmer shivered. It had been a long wait, but Bill would have to come back some time. The chances were he had gone out with Susan, to the pictures or somewhere. John had tried to ring him earlier, but there had been no answer. So he had decided to wait outside the apartment building. It was the only thing he could do. He had nowhere else to go. He certainly couldn't go home — not until all this business had been sorted out and Sam Selmer's murderer had been found.

There were lights in some of the windows of the building that towered above him — but Bill Todd's flat remained in darkness. Light from a street lamp brushed across the leaves of the thick shrubbery which concealed John from the street. Occasionally a car passed along the street, its headlights swelling and briefly illuminating the trees that lined both sides of the street. Ghostly shapes, moving shadows. If anyone saw him, they would naturally assume he was a prowler, and call the cops. He kept very still behind the bushes, starting at every sound, shrinking back into the shadows and holding his breath every time someone approached. He had come so far, all the way back to Melbourne, hitching lifts all the way — so close, nothing must happen.

There was another car coming. He heard it turning into the street, slowing down, its headlights blasting through the darkness. It pulled up outside the flats. The engine didn't stop running, the headlights were left on. The driver's door opened and a heavily built man stepped out into the street. In the dim light, John saw a figure inside the car move across behind the wheel and roll down the window.

"Are you sure you won't need it tomorrow?"

John caught his breath. It was Susan's voice, unmistakeable. Bill had come back at last.

"Of course not. Just don't prang it, that's all."

"Don't you trust me?" Susan was laughing.

"Is there a safe way to answer that?" Bill was laughing, too. No problems for either of them. "I love you," Bill said.

"I love you, too."

Bill stepped back as Susan wound up the window, blew him a kiss and swung the car out from the curb. Bill stood on the road, watching its tail lights until they disappeared around a corner. Then he turned and headed towards the building. As he passed beneath the street light, John saw that he was grinning widely. Not a worry in the world. Quietly, John eased himself out from his hiding place. Bill had almost reached the entrance when John caught up with him and placed his hand on his shoulder. Bill jumped and swore. There was a look of horror on his face as he swung and stared at John.

"Jesus, what do you . . . ?"

"I've got to talk to you," John said quickly. "Important. Please."

Bill led the way into the building and up the stairs to his flat. "Hell, you gave me a fright," he said. "I thought I was going to get mugged or something."

Nor was he quickly recovering from his shock, it seemed. All the colour had drained from his face, and there was something in his eyes, the way they constantly avoided John's, his obvious nervousness as he moved restlessly about the lounge room of his flat, fiddled with things...

"I need help."

Bill glanced anxiously towards the hallway from which the bedrooms opened. "Keep it down. I don't want to wake Mum." He moved closer to John. "What do you want? Money?"

"I want to clear myself," John said in a lower voice, but no less fervently.

Bill's eyes flickered. "What could I do?" he murmured uneasily, turning away again.

"I've got to find out who killed Sam," John told him. "They think I did it, they're looking for me — so I can't move around, can I? So I... thought you could ask a few questions for me."

"What sort of questions?"

For Chrissake, surely he could see how urgent it all was. Why was he hedging, putting up obstacles? "There's got to be *some* sort of clue," he said, trying hard to keep his voice low. It wasn't easy; his exasperation was close to getting too much for him.

Bill was still moving around the room. "Don't look at me," he muttered. "I don't know anything — just as much as you do. Sam was on the phone and someone bashed his head in with a crowbar." He spread his hands in a gesture of helplessness. His face was drawn.

"You can find out things for me." John was thinking hard. What did he really hope to achieve by coming here? The long trip, the fear, the expectation of being caught at any moment, had to be worth it. "Like, did Sam have any enemies? Or even Mrs Selmer — maybe she did it." It was a thought, but maybe not a good one.

"No way," Bill said definitely.

John fought on. "It's no more crazy than *me* doing it." His voice was rising again. Bill held up his hand and nodded towards the hallway.

"I've got to know her pretty well," he said quietly, firmly. "She couldn't kill anyone."

Got to know her? What did that mean? John looked at Bill interrogatively. "She . . . she rehired me," Bill explained awkwardly. "I'm sort of doing all Sam's work now."

Hey, this was something. John brightened. "That's great." Bill looked surprised. John went on. "I mean, if you're there, on the spot, you can find out all sorts of things. Like . . ."

"No!" Bill's voice cut right across him with such contained force that John was taken aback. "Look, you're innocent — right?" Bill went on in a more reasonable tone. John nodded. Of course he was. "Well, let the police handle it. Give yourself up and co-operate with them. They're not going to convict you for something you didn't do." Not much they wouldn't. John snorted. He had heard about cases where innocent people had been put away for a long time, or even hanged. "The longer you keep running, the worse it's going to get," Bill pointed out.

John stared at him. He felt weak. After all the effort of getting here . . . Bill was a mate, he was going to marry Susan, which would make him family, and family should stick together.

"There's nothing I can do," Bill said adamantly.

Well, that was it then. No point hanging around here. Tired and disappointed, John moved towards the door. "I'd better go."

"Give yourself up," Bill said with an expression on his face that John was unable to fathom. But he was too tired to bother with expressions and atmosphere, or why Bill was looking so much on edge. Bill took a step forward. "Have you got somewhere to stay?"

That was funny. A place to stay. John shrugged. Nowhere to stay. No money. Thought Bill would be able to help him — or at least show some *interest* in helping him. He watched Bill reach into his hip pocket and bring out his wallet. Some banknotes were held out towards him. "Find yourself a place. Think it over."

John took the money. "Thanks."

Bill was more businesslike now. "Call me in the morning," he said. "Before work. Let me know where you are."

"Yeah." John was down. It was all catching up on him, and things looked more hopeless than ever. He was a fool to have come. He should have stayed right where he was, in Manly with Aunt Fiona, and maybe everything would have been all right after a while. With a sinking heart he thought of Angela Hamilton and wondered if he would ever see her again.

33

Angela looked at the girl who had opened the door and sensed an immediate hostility. She didn't know why. It was as if the girl had recognised her — there had been a little start of recognition, she was sure — but she was certain she had never seen her before. She forced a smile.

"Hi, I'm looking for Mrs McDonald. Is she in?"

The girl turned her head slightly. "Fiona," she called over her shoulder. "There's someone here to see you." She looked back at Angela. Her eyes were cold. She jerked her head towards the open door of the room behind her. "Go in and take a seat."

Angela moved past her and walked into the room. "Who is it?" Fiona was calling back just as she entered the room. She looked curiously up at Angela.

"Hello," Angela said. "I'm Angela Hamilton. We spoke on the phone.

There was a definite reaction. The woman facing her seemed to go rigid. She looked startled, and then it was as if a whole range of emotions passed in swift succession across her angular face. Among them Angela sensed curiosity, fear and hostility. What the others were, she didn't know.

"Look, please," she said with the sense of taking

something firmly in her grasp. "Won't you tell me where Scott is?"

The woman was staring at her intently as if trying to place her, or perhaps willing her features to remain indelibly pressed on her memory — a curious, intense regard that made Angela uneasy. This woman was nothing like the image she had built up of her. From the way Scott had described her, she had imagined Aunt Fiona to be kindly and soft-spoken. She seemed to be neither.

At last, Fiona shook her head. "No." Her gaze was unwavering.

"Why not?" Angela was hurt, but tried not to show it. What was going on here? Why was the woman looking at her like that? Why the hostility from the girl who had opened the door?

"I think it's better if you and Scott don't see each other any more," Fiona said tonelessly.

Angela was suddenly angry. This woman — *kindly* Aunt Fiona — had no right to talk to her like that, to interfere. "I think it's none of your business," she snapped.

Now Fiona was frowning. She looked worried. She seemed to be picking her words carefully. "You don't understand. There are some things you don't know about."

"So tell me," Angela cried. "*Why* don't you tell me?"

Fiona heaved a deep sigh and appeared to come to a decision. "All right. If you must know." She sat down on the sofa and pointed Angela to a chair. Angela shook her head. She would remain standing. She had come here for answers, and she was going to get them. "You've already met Jill."

"The girl who opened the door? She didn't seem very friendly — I'm sure I've never seen her before."

"She's seen you. She was with . . . Scott the day you fell off the horse."

"Oh." Of course she wouldn't remember.

"And you're right — she doesn't like you." Fiona was less hesitant now, as if after some preliminary fumbling in the darkness she had at last found the direction she wanted to go. "She's got a reason — and a very big one, too." A smile played at the corners of her lips. "You're a danger to her."

"So?"

"She's pregnant, you see. She's pregnant to Scott."

"*What?*" That sharp-featured girl who had opened the door to her? She and Scott . . .? It was as if someone — Aunt Fiona — had dashed a glass of ice-cold water in her face, the shock of it sluicing away any pretence of control or reserve. And without them, there was nothing much else. The things he had said to her . . . There had been no mention of a girl called Jill. She didn't know what to say. All she could do was gape at the grim-faced woman opposite.

"My guess is that he wanted to have one last fling," Fiona went on sombrely. "Deep down he knows he's going to have to stand by Jill, but he's very young." She smiled briefly. "I think he just wanted to have a couple of weeks where he could blot out his responsibilities."

It was hard to keep herself under control, not to cry out and scream betrayal. But he hadn't *promised* her anything. He had kissed her but hadn't told her he loved her. They had held hands and everything seemed to be perfect. "That's all you think it was?" she asked weakly.

"I'm sorry," Fiona murmured, looking away.

"Is he going to marry her?" Nothing like this had ever happened to her before. She had never felt so shatttered in her life — and with that part of her that was still able to reason, she wondered why. It was true she hardly knew him, but there had been such an *empathy* between them, a knowledge that had gone well beyond the shortness of the time they had known each other. It was something she hadn't been able to understand. She still didn't understand it.

"I'm not sure," Fiona replied, her narrow shoulders lifting in the slightest of shrugs. "That's something they'll have to work out together."

"They haven't done too much of that so far, have they?" Sure it sounded bitchy, but Angela didn't care about that. She had been very badly hurt.

The sharp lines of Fiona's face had softened. Her tone was gentle. She leaned forward in her seat. "Angela, I know it may not seem that way from your point of view, but Scott *is* very fond of Jill."

"Does he love her?" It was something she had to know, the most important question of all.

"I don't know," Fiona said mildly. "That's something else he has to sort out. In his own mind."

"Pretty soon, I'd say, wouldn't you?"

Fiona looked at her steadily. "You're hurt," she said, "and you've got every right to be. I'm only sorry you had to find out this way."

And she did look sorry, and there might have been a time when Angela would have responded to that. But she had her pride — or what was left of it; so much of it was hanging in tatters — and she needed to salvage as much as she could. She drew herself up. Her expression was scornful.

"Wrong on two counts," she said coldly. "I'm not hurt, and quite frankly, I don't think you're in the least bit sorry." She moved to the door. "But you've done me one favour. Now I know exactly what he's like." She opened the door and turned back into the room to face the woman who was sitting so rigidly, so stonily on the couch watching her. "I won't be bothering him again," she said, and closed the door quickly behind her as the cracks began to appear on the calm facade she had deliberately and with such effort forced on herself.

34

There she was, right on time, good old Mum, coming away from the markets as she did every morning, a solid figure implacably making her way along the busy street, laden down with her shopping, heading home. John followed her from a distance, never letting her out of his sight for a moment. People moved around them, busy, preoccupied. Mum plodded on. She always came to the markets instead of shopping at the brand new supermarket that had been built closer to home. Old habits die hard, she said when anybody teased her about it. Besides, the veggies were always fresher, the service better — and anyway, she liked going there. So . . . here she was. John followed her along the busy street, waiting for an opportunity get her alone.

He was filling in time. He had spent the night in a seedy little private hotel in North Melbourne where a neon light had flashed all night outside his window and he hadn't been able to sleep. He had called Bill, catching him just as he was leaving for work. Bill had sounded very thoughtful, had asked him where he was staying, got the name of the hotel and the room number, then told him to wait there, he would do some fishing around at work and come around to the hotel around lunch-time. "Whatever you do," he had said, "don't leave your room. It's not worth the risk."

But John hadn't relished the idea of waiting the two or three hours before Bill showed up, besides, there was something he wanted to do. He had gone to the markets and waited, his eyes strained for a glimpse of his mother, hoping she hadn't had a sudden change of heart in the past few weeks and decided it might be more convenient for her to do her shopping at the supermarket after all.

She was turning off into a quiet side street. Here was his chance. He hurried forward, rounded the corner. There was no one else in the street.

"Mum!"

It was as if she had just been struck by a heavy object in the small of her back. She started, stiffened, then slowly, perhaps willing herself not to believe what she had just heard in case it turned out to be an illusion, she turned. John was running forward. Her face was mirroring a run of emotions, disbelief, happiness and misery.

"Johnny!" she exclaimed, putting down her bags and holding her arms out to him. "Johnny!" She held him in her arms, tightly, hugging him, kissing him, and she felt just the way she had always felt, smelt the way she had always smelt, comfortable, reassuring, home and happiness. He could bury himself in the warmth of her.

"Oh, Mum." He was almost sobbing. "I'm sorry."

Then she was pulling away from him, looking up and down the street. "What are you doing here?" she asked fearfully.

"I followed you from the market."

"I mean here in Melbourne." There were lines in her face he hadn't seen before. There was deep concern in her eyes.

"I've come back to sort things out."

She gasped and one hand fluttered ineffectually at her throat. "You're going to the police?"

He shook his head. "I want to do it myself," he told her. She was looking up at him in disbelief. "I'm all right," he said. "Honest. I've got friends who are helping me." It was something to say to her. It would make her feel better to know he wasn't alone. He tried to sound confident.

"Here?" she asked.

"Yeah. Where I've been staying since I ran away."

"Who?"

"I'll explain when it's all over — okay?" He had been here too long. He should be making his way back to the hotel. He didn't want to miss Bill. "I haven't got the time now." His mother was looking at him uncomprehendingly. John hugged her. "I've got to go. I shouldn't even be here."

"No!" Her eyes were brimming with tears.

John forced himself to be resolute. "I've got to go, Mum. I've got to get back to where I'm staying."

"You'll keep in touch?" Her fingers plucked at him. There was desperation in her voice.

John nodded heavily. There was a catch in his throat. His mother's tears were overflowing. "I love you, Mum," he said brokenly, then before she could say anything, plead with him, do something to tear away the gossamer fabric of his determination, he swung away and moved quickly back up the side street the way he had come. He didn't look back.

He moved miserably through the busy streets. People jostled him, bumped him, but he was hardly aware of them. He walked instinctively, and his mother's face stayed with him. He shouldn't have done it. He shouldn't have given in to the impulse to see her again, even if only for a few moments — but that impulse had been too strong for him to resist. It hadn't been fair on her. If he hadn't waited for her at the markets and followed her — she would have continued to go about her business, sad but capable, accustoming herself to the situation. Now all he had done was upset her.

He was coming close to the hotel. It was almost twelve. A tram glided past him. In the distance, he could hear a siren. It was coming closer — and suddenly, he was reminded of that other time when he had heard an approaching siren. He felt inexplicably frightened. There was the sense of things repeating themselves. That other time — the darkened warehouse, heavy silence, blood on the walls. The siren was just behind him. He veered across the footpath to the wall of the building as the police car, its light flashing, sped past him, and with an anguished screech of tyres, took the corner widely into the street where the hotel was. Then the siren stopped. Cautiously now, John moved to the corner.

The police car was standing outside the hotel. Four uniformed men had climbed out of it. One of them was issuing instructions. Two men walked into the main entrance of the hotel, while another moved down the narrow alleyway alongside to the rear of the building. The fourth man, the one who had given the orders, remained beside the car.

The street was quiet. John stood at the corner and watched. Another few minutes and he would have been inside the building, in his room, waiting for Bill Todd to show. There would have been no way out for him. He would have been trapped. There was always the possibility that these cops weren't looking for him, but were here on another matter altogether — but somehow, he didn't think so. He could almost see those two coppers who had gone in through the main entrance lumbering up the stairs and stopping outside his room — number 23 — then, with their guns drawn, standing on either side of the door and yelling at him to open up, the sharp splintering sound of wood as the door was kicked open . . .

He shouldn't be staying. He should be getting away from here, now, while he had the chance, before anyone spotted him. But it was as if he stood rooted to that corner, staring diagonally across the street at that rundown little hotel where he had spent a sleepless night, and which now had a patrol car standing outside it while the cops were inside looking for him.

Except one cop, who stood beside the car, his hands behind his back, perfectly casual in appearance, but from the quick movements of his head as he glanced up and down the street, alert and watchful.

Then the cop's eyes had fixed on John, still hesitating on the corner opposite. Involuntarily, John took a step backwards. If he hadn't done that, he knew at the very moment of doing it, it was possible the copper would have dismissed him as a curious bystander. Just possible. But in that quick backward step, there was evasion, guilt. The policeman stiffened.

"All right, you!" he called sharply.

This was it. John panicked. He had been seen, possibly even recognised. Swinging away from the corner, he began to run back the way he had come. He heard shouting behind him. He ran faster, cutting across the street into a laneway, realising with horror that it was a dead-end with a low wall at the end of it. There was no way of turning back because he could hear the sounds of pursuit behind him. He launched himself at the wall, sprang at it, his feet leaving the ground, his arms outstretched. His fingers grabbed hold of the wall, and he was hoisting himself, swinging his legs up and over, dropping down onto rough ground on the other side, stumbling, righting himself, then sprinting away from the wall. More shouts behind him.

He was in a building site. There were mounds of rubble, trenches had been dug for the foundations — but that was as far as it had got. There was no one working on the site. On the other side of it was a high wooden fence with a door set into it. John headed for the door. He didn't dare look back. Every particle of his strength was concentrated on getting to that gate in the fence in front of him. His progress seemed to be painfully slow. The wall didn't appear to be getting any closer as he scrambled and slid over the piles of rubble. There was a dull ache in his side. He gulped the precious air down into his bursting lungs. There was a roaring sound in his ears.

Then he had reached the door in the fence, pushing it open and stepping out into a street. The pavement was crowded with people. Slowing down to a brisk walk, he quickly lost himself in the crowd.

35

"I know you don't want me to go on, so I'll say it only once — but I did tell you, didn't I?"

Of course she was right. She had told him when he had rung her that by running away he had only made things worse for himself. He had had to agree with that. But he had panicked. On the phone her voice had been brisk and deliberate. She had given him the address of some friends of hers in East Bentleigh, and told him to wait for her there. Her friends wouldn't ask any questions — and they hadn't. Fiona had told him she would probably arrive in Melbourne on the first flight the following day. Now here she was. They were sitting out in the backyard of the small suburban house. The sun was shining, birds were singing, and Fiona was dressed in grey.

"The thing to concentrate on now," she said, "is to get you back to Sydney. I've hired a car. We'll drive back. There shouldn't be any problems."

"Won't there be roadblocks or something?"

Fiona gave him a scornful smile. "You're not exactly Al Capone, darling."

Some put-down. John remained silent and stared glumly at the black and white cat that was sunning itself on the back steps.

"Well, I don't expect to be overwhelmed with thanks," Fiona remarked drily, "but a word or two wouldn't go astray."

She had got him wrong. Of course he was grateful. He had been thinking about something else. He had spent most of yesterday and last night thinking about it. The coppers had known exactly where to find him.

"Sorry," he murmured. "It's that I can't work out who would've dobbed me in."

"It seems pretty obvious to me," Fiona said gruffly, "judging by what you've already told me."

He looked up at her. "The bloke at the hotel?" It could have been; the guy had given him a pretty searching look when he booked in.

"I doubt it." Fiona shook her head. "No, I think it's more obvious than that."

"What?" John was watching her closely. He was puzzled. Who else? How could it be more obvious?

"Who knew you were here? Who saw you?"

"Mum. I saw Mum. And Bill Todd." They were the only two."

Fiona was leaning towards him. Her eyes were gleaming, and she reminded John of a bird of prey about to pounce. "And who knew where you were staying?"

Ah . . . there was only Bill. Bill had asked him where he was staying. Bill was coming around to see him. But it was impossible . . . Not Bill. Bill wouldn't . . . "Bill," he said. "But he wouldn't have."

"Why not?" She was closing in on him, springing the trap.

Well, it was obvious, wasn't it? "Because he's . . . we've been mates for years. Why would he?"

"I don't know," Fiona said with a shrug. "Maybe it doesn't make a great deal of sense — but it fits, doesn't it? Bill waits for you to ring up and tell him where you are — and bingo, two seconds later, the cops turn up."

John let it pass. It didn't matter how much later it was. He thought hard. There had to be *some* argument against it — something simple and obvious.

"No, Bill wouldn't do that," he said. It was the best he could do. "I know him." It did sound a bit feeble.

"So you think it was your mother?" John said nothing. A remark like that didn't warrant any sort of acknowledgement. "Which leaves . . . ?"

"The bloke at the hotel."

"Why would he?" Fiona said reasonably. "Look, even if he did read the police lists, or something, he wouldn't recognise you. You don't look like John Palmer. Remember? You're Scott Edwards. A completely different person."

"Well, I don't know who it was," John muttered sullenly.

"Your mate," Fiona said quietly. "Bill Todd."

"No, he wouldn't do it," John exclaimed, slamming his fist into the open palm of his other hand. There *had* to be a simple explanation. He wished it would come to him. "He just hasn't got any reason to do something like that."

36

John Palmer had made the morning newspapers, and Bill Todd didn't want to know about it. He didn't want his mother to go on talking about it. He was just about to leave the flat for work. The remains of his breakfast still lay on the kitchen table. He hadn't been hungry and had only pecked at his food. His mother was sitting at the table with the newspaper open in front of her.

"It says he's changed his appearance," she observed.

"So?" Bill looked down at his mother. She was looking very grey these days, and careworn. She'd had a hard slog of it. "Wouldn't you try to make yourself look different?"

He was terse. He couldn't help it. . . the tension, the strain. Maybe he needn't have called the police about John; there might have been some other way, but none had come to him. His action had been quick and impulsive. It mighn't have been too bad if they had caught John at that hotel. Sooner or later everything would be sorted out. The cops would *have* to see he was innocent, and let him go. Nothing surer. But in the meantime, there was Susan, the wedding — nothing could jeopardise that. There was no way he would let himself lose Susan. And there was his mother, too. All those years of battling after his father died. She deserved something better.

"I only asked if you had read it." Her gaze was mild and watery.

"And I said I did."

She stared up at him for some moments. There seemed to be something on her mind. Then, suddenly, she said, "He was here, wasn't he?"

She might have slapped his face. He reeled inwardly. "Who?"

"John."

He laughed, but it was a very unconvincing sound. "Oh, come off it." He feld cold and clammy, his insides knotting.

"Two nights ago." Her voice was soft, not even accusing, but it might have been the voice of Justice herself. She was wearing a flowered dressing gown.

"No!" Bill cried. "Not John."

"I heard his voice," she said emphatically.

"You couldn't have."

She was certain. Bill was rattled. "Bill, I heard him," she said evenly. "He was talking to you."

Despite himself, Bill raised his voice. It had an uneven edge to it. "But he *wasn't* here." Why didn't she believe him? Why did she have to go on and on about it?

"I heard someone." She was implacable.

"All right, you heard someone." There was exasperation mingled with fear. He had thought she was fast asleep when John had come to the flat that night. "Okay, there *was* someone here, but it wasn't John."

He could see she didn't believe him. She was looking at him suspiciously, as she always did when she didn't believe him — and that had been often enough.

"Well, what's wrong now?" he demanded.

Mrs Todd's expression didn't change. She wasn't stung or intimidated by the aggressiveness in her son's voice. "I don't like the way you're being so secretive," she said. "There's something you're not telling me."

Bill gestured impatiently. He should be on his way to work by now, but he felt he had to see this thing through. "All right, if you must know," he snapped, "it was Andrew

Blaxland — the guy who was here. From work. He's a mate of mine, and . . ."

"I'm not talking about that," she broke in.

Bill frowned. "What *are* you talking about?"

"Before that," she said, not taking her eyes off him as he hovered by the door. "You've never explained why you wanted me to tell people you were here when you weren't. When Sam Selmer was killed. I don't like being made to tell lies."

He knew he wasn't handling the situation very well. He hadn't worked out an alibi, and now that she was offering him a direct challenge, it wasn't the time to start thinking about one. He had that much sense at least.

"Look, it's no big deal." A minor thing, nothing for anyone to worry about. "The important thing is that I wasn't at the factory. I don't want people to *think* I could have been." He spread his hands in a gesture of inquiry. "What's so complicated about that?"

Mrs Todd was slowly shaking her head. She was still suspicious. "But you haven't ever told me where you were."

It had gone on long enough. It was time to bring it to an end. He tried to sound reassuring. "Look, there's nothing to worry about," he said, opening the door. "You just have to believe me, that's all. I don't want to talk about it any more. As far as I'm concerned, that's it, finish."

Quickly, before she had a chance to say anything more, he stepped out into the hallway and closed the door behind him.

37

Something was niggling at John. Since they had arrived back at Manly the night before, it had been worrying him — something that didn't gel. Last night he had been exhausted after the long drive from Melbourne and had turned in more or less immediately. For the first time in what seemed ages he had had a good night's sleep, deep and dreamless, and when he awoke he felt alive again and able to cope with anything that might be thrown his way.

For a long while, he lay on his back, his hands clasped behind his head, staring up at the ceiling, thinking, going over the events of the past two days in his mind, reliving them. In a sense they seemed so distant now as to be hardly real. A dream. There was definitely a dream-like quality about everything that had happened.

He remembered things — little things, like Bill's evasiveness when he was speaking to him in his flat, and how later, when he had rung him, he had sounded so confident. But in the flat . . . Bill had said something, and John hadn't thought much about it at the time. It was only since Fiona had been so definite about Bill that he had begun to think about him more, and wonder if Fiona hadn't been right after all. He looked for telltale signs, but there was nothing absolutely conclusive, nothing to support Fiona's certainty. Except . . .

Throwing back the blankets, he leapt out of bed and quickly threw on his clothes. He had a hunch. There was a possibility. He moved quickly into the living room, where he paused and thought for a few moments. He knew Fiona kept a folder of press clippings about Sam Selmer's murder. She had showed it to him when she had cut out and added the more recent stories about the "Crowbar Killer" being sighted in Melbourne two days ago. He remembered that she had put the folder away in one of the sideboard drawers. The top one, he thought, and opened it. It wasn't there. He found the folder in the third drawer he opened. With mounting excitement, he riffled through it.

Five minutes later he was in Fiona's room. She was still asleep, but he made no attempt to be quiet. He was really excited now.

"Aunt Fiona." Crossing to the side of the bed, he gently shook her. "Aunt Fiona, wake up."

She opened her eyes and blinked sleepily up at him. She groaned and opened her eyes wider. "What's wrong?"

"I need to talk to you." He couldn't contain his excitement. It was bubbling over.

Fiona was frowning. She regarded him coldly. "Now?"

"It's important," John persisted.

Fiona groaned again. "Can't you tell me in the morning?" she murmured thickly. "What time is it?"

John ignored her. He had news to tell. "You were right," he said. "It must have been Bill."

Fiona struggled up into a sitting position. "Bravo."

John went on. "What had me confused was that I couldn't see *why* he'd dob me in."

"What's different now?" Fiona asked drily.

"I figured it out." His triumph was like a thin layer of murky foam floating on the top of his disillusion. "I know why he did it."

Reluctantly, at his urging, she got out of bed and went into the kitchen to make some coffee for them both. John talked to her. He told her what he had discovered.

"And that's what had been going round and round in my head," he said. "I remember Bill said something about Sam Selmer being on the phone when he was attacked. I didn't take any notice at first, because when *I* got to Sam's office he was lying on the ground and the phone *was* off the hook. There's only one way Bill could've known that. He had to be *there* while Sam was on the phone. And if Sam was on the phone when he was attacked, then Bill must have been the attacker." It was the only answer.

Fiona nodded to the folder of clippings. "It's not mentioned in any of these?" she asked.

That was precisely it. John shook his head. "And if it wasn't in the papers, I don't reckon it would've been on TV." Then, suddenly, he thought of something else. His face fell. Something he had overlooked. "Damn," he muttered. "I just thought of another way. The police might have told him."

Fiona finished her coffee. "Or Mrs Selmer might have told him," she said matter-of-factly. "Or maybe there's a clipping I didn't get. Or maybe it *was* on TV. Who knows?" She paused. John felt deflated. Now he would have to start all over again. "But I'd say you're right," Fiona went on, and John looked at her in surprise. "When you went to Melbourne you thought you were going to your best mate. So tell me — how did you get to the point where you thought he could be a murderer?"

John shrugged. "How?"

"I'm asking you." John said nothing. "All right. Was Bill mad at Sam Selmer, too?"

"John nodded. "More than me," he said thoughtfully. That was true. He had much more to lose than John did.

"Right." Fiona sounded as if she were getting somewhere at last. "Has he got a bad temper?"

Had he ever. "I saw him go up once," he said. "It was like a volcano." He continued slowly, going over things in his mind, remembering, musing aloud. "He was acting real strange when I got down there. The way he looked at me . . . something in his voice . . . I don't know . . . like he was scared of me. And not because of the cops. That wouldn't worry him." He had been in trouble with the cops before. He knew how to handle them.

Fiona had her own definite views on the subject. "I'd say he felt as guilty as hell," she said flatly, "and the last thing he wanted was to have you nosing around. That's why he dobbed you in."

There was nothing left of John's former excitement. Now he felt utterly miserable. "I thought he was my mate," he muttered.

"Darling, he's running scared," Fiona stated. "Unfortunately you haven't a leg to stand on. It's all supposition."

She was right. They were just theorising. Nothing that could be proved. Then something else occurred to him. "Susan," he said. He saw the puzzled look on Fiona's face. "They're getting married." His mind was racing. "But they can't. I've got to do something about it."

Driven by a new urgency, he pushed back his chair and crossed to the telephone. Fiona watched him impassively as he dialled STD to Melbourne and silently prayed it would be Susan who answered the phone. He didn't want to speak to anyone else. It was very important.

He was lucky. It *was* Susan who answered. Her voice hardened when John announced himself. "What do you want?" she demanded. Her voice was very clear. "You don't know the trouble. . . the police have been here. Mum's very upset."

"I've got something important to tell you. Is anyone else up?"

"What do you *want?*"

"I want you to call off the wedding."

"*What?*"

"I want you to call off the wedding."

There was silence at the other end. The connection was still open. She hadn't hung up on him. "Are you there?" John asked.

Her voice came back, very brittle. "You're mad."

He had known it wouldn't be easy, but he had to go on

with it. He had to let her know. "Susie, you've got to listen to me."

"You're not making any sense." Now there was alarm in her voice, a twist of fear. "Why on earth should I call off the wedding . . . ?"

"You're not going to like it," he said, riding over her. He *had* to get through to her, to make her understand. "But I know it was Bill who dobbed me in to the cops the other day — and I know why he did it. He's trying to cover up for what he did, because . . ." and here he went, straight into it, no punches pulled ". . . he killed Sam."

The silence at the other end was longer. It stretched. John tried to visualise her standing there at the phone, stunned, shattered. "Did you hear me? I said Bill killed Sam. You mustn't marry him."

There was another pause, then, "Go away," Susan said tightly, and he could hear the controlled anger in her voice.

"I'm serious." He was becoming desperate. She *had* to listen to him. But knowing Susan . . . "Promise you won't marry him."

At the other end of the line, in Melbourne, Susan seemed to be gathering up all her strength. She spoke slowly, clearly, her anger threatening to break through at any moment. "I want you to get off the phone and leave us all alone."

Then there was a click and the line was dead. Thoughtfully, John replaced the receiver. It hadn't worked this way. There had to be another way. He dropped into a chair.

"She wouldn't listen to you, eh?" Fiona remarked.

John sighed heavily. Problems, problems all the way. "What am I going to do?" He thought for a few moments, trying to put it all together. Fiona watched him. "The way I see it," he said finally. "I've got three choices. I can go to the police . . ."

"As a last resort, I hope," Fiona observed with a smile.

John smiled back at her. "I'm not stupid. Yeah, last resort. The other thing I can do is ring Bill and have it out with him. Or I can ring Mum and Dad."

"You know them better than I do," Fiona said quietly. "What's your best shot?"

Yeah, something that needed to be thought about, and thought about very carefully. Go over the options, examine them. He thought aloud. "Bill? I don't know. He's not a murderer. No, hold it. I mean, okay . . . I *know* he killed Sam — but he's not a murderer. You get what I mean?"

Fiona got what he meant. She nodded. "He must be scared sick then," she said.

"Right," John said a little more confidently. A plan of action was beginning to form. "If I give it a bit of time . . . I mean, it's obvious that Susan's going to get onto him about it. Tell him what I said. That'll throw him. So if I called him . . . at work . . . maybe I could talk him into doing the right thing."

Fiona was regarding him levelly. Outside this cluttered, friendly room, life was going on as normal. The horn sounded on an incoming ferry. "Do you think he really loves Susan?" she asked quietly.

John laughed shortly. That was the one thing he couldn't be more certain about. "He's wrapped."

"Then I'd call him and play on it," Fiona suggested mildly. "How can he marry her after what he's done? That sort of thing." She waved one hand carelessly. "Unless, of course, it's better to work through your parents."

John thought about this, then shook his head. It wouldn't be any good. The memory of his father's attitude was still very clear. "Dad's reaction would be just the same as Susan's," he said. "He's never stood by me — not ever — so why should he start now?"

"And your mother?"

"She'd want to," John replied. "But with Dad and Susan it'd be two against one. It's not fair to dump that on her."

"So Bill it is then?"

"Bill it is."

And Bill it was. John waited an hour. Fiona made tea. When he was ready, John smiled at Fiona and crossed his fingers. Fiona made a circle of her thumb and forefinger. John dialled the Selmer Warehouse number.

As soon as he realised who was calling, Bill Todd became aggressive. "She doesn't believe you," he said when John asked him if Susan had been in touch with him about John's call.

"You can't marry her, Bill," John said quickly, getting in as much as he could before Bill took it into his head to hang up on him. "Not after what you've done."

Bill laughed. It was a very short, hollow sound, more like a bark. "You're crazy." His voice was uneven, nervous. Of course he's guilty, John thought with grim satisfaction, he's brazening it out. "I don't know where you got the idea I killed Sam, but you're wrong."

Now for the killer punch. John delivered it. "So how did you know he was on the phone when he was killed?"

The silence was brief and telling. "What . . . what are you talking about?"

John had seen Bill lose his temper, had seen him in a rage when he was capable of doing anything. He had forgotten what caused it, but it had been a frightening thing to see. "When I was in Melbourne you said that Sam was on the phone when he was killed. How do you know that?"

"I must have read it," Bill said quickly — too quickly. John was tuned in to his mood, to the bluster, the rising panic.

"It wasn't in the papers," he said.

Bill was still trying, casting around. "I don't know. Someone must have told me."

John caught Fiona's eye as she looked up from the magazine she was glancing through. "Listen to yourself, mate," he said sternly to Bill. "You're packing it. You *did* do it, didn't you?"

Bill ignored the question. "Wouldn't *you* be packing it if some crazy guy started calling you a murderer the day before your wedding?" It's so unfair, he seemed to be saying, people ganging up on me . . . "Anyway, I've got an alibi. I was with my Mum when it happened."

Some alibi. John grimaced. "I know her, Bill." In all the times he had been in trouble in the past she had stood by him, had covered up for him. Her only son, all she had. "She'd say anything you wanted her to — you know that."

This got to Bill. He was stung. "I told you what to do," he said angrily. "If you're innocent, go to the police. There's no way you'll be convicted — not if you're innocent."

"Is that what you thought when you dobbed me in?" John asked quietly, turning the knife.

Bill sounded as if he was having a hell of a battle keeping his temper in check. "I'm hanging up, John," he said thickly. "And I'm calling the police. You try to get in touch again — with me or your family, they'll trace it."

They were getting away from the point. There was more John had to say, an appeal he had to make. "Hey, just listen for a minute," he cried. "If you love Susan, you can't marry her. The truth will come out. It's got to — and where's that going to leave her?"

There was no answer, only the slamming down of the receiver at the other end. John hung up.

"Are you calling back?" Fiona asked him. She looked and sounded concerned.

John didn't answer her. All he wanted right now was to be alone.

38

The wedding passed off uneventfully enough. There were presents, speeches and telegrams, and the cake was an artistic masterpice. David's father had come down from Queensland, and the friction between them was more or less pushed to the background for the actual occasion. Beryl had worked hard, was tired, but it had been worth it. It had been a nice wedding, simple enough, and having it at home rather than in church had seemed to give it an added intimacy. So . . . things had worked out, after all. Lynn Hardy from next door had looked very pretty in the bridesmaid's gown Beryl had made up for her. Kevin had thought so, too, from the way his eyes had lit up when he saw her. They were very close, those two. It looked as though something was developing between them — which would be all right as long as it didn't get out of hand. But it wasn't a time to worry about that now. Bill and Susan were married at last; their whole life stretched before them.

And yet it might not have gone off so smoothly. Those reporters on the front lawn, for instance. Bill had been furious. He had grabbed one of them by the shirt when he had come up to him as he stepped out of the car with his mother, and started asking questions. Bill had sworn at him, threatened him, and it was only Nora Todd's quiet, persistent urging that prevented any damage being done. And then there was Nora's manner. This was something that had nagged at Beryl a little. She had seemed very quiet, withdrawn, as if there was something bothering her. She didn't look happy. It was her son's wedding, and God knew how fond she was of Susan, so she should have been happier than she was. No, there was something definitely worrying her. Beryl had tried to speak to her, to draw her out, but Nora had been uncommunicative. Once or twice, Beryl had caught her casting an apprehensive glance in Bill's direction.

Then Bill had made a speech, awkward and fumbling, with lots of hum's and ha's, but there had been one moment when he hadn't been lost for words, when he had opened up his heart, and looking directly at his mother, had thanked her for all she had done for him. From the expressions on both their faces it had been obvious — to Beryl, anyway — that a deep unspoken communication was passing between them beneath the words of sincere praise he was offering her. An impression, as if he were silently imploring her. Then the moment had passed and David's father was loudly calling for a toast to the bride and groom.

And there was another cloud that marred the completion of the day — and that was John. Wherever he was, he would be thinking about the wedding, thinking about Bill and Susan. Poor John — if only he would give himself up soon, so this whole tragic mess about Sam Selmer could be cleared up once and for all.

Now the party was almost over. Beryl looked around the sitting room, at all the debris, the empty glasses and overflowing ashtrays, the drained champagne bottles, the crumbling remains of the cake. There was a lot of cleaning up to do, but there was plenty of time. David and Kevin would help her. Lynn, too, probably.

Bill and Susan had already been driven off to the hotel where they would spend their honeymoon. Beryl moved back out into the hallway and saw Nora Todd standing near the door. She had her coat on and was just about to leave. Her face looked more deeply lined than ever. Her mouth was turned down at the corners. Voices drifted out from the other rooms. Outside, a car started up. Beryl smiled at Nora.

"Well, that's that then. All over bar the cleaning up. Are you sure you won't stay for a cup of coffee, Nora?"

Nora shook her head. "No, thanks."

"It's early yet. No need to go home. Anyway, I guess you'll be finding it pretty lonely now."

Nora managed a a bleak smile. There was definitely something wrong. Beryl pressed her. "Come on now," she said heartily. "Cheer up. You haven't really lost a son. You'll still see a lot of him. And there's the grandchildren to look forward to."

'Oh." Nora's face began to crumple. She looked to be on the verge of tears. Quickly turning away, she opened the front door,. "You don't understand," she said in a broken voice as she hurried outside.

Understand what? Puzzled, Beryl stared after her as she walked, a tiny unhappy figure, down the path to the front gate.

39

Patricia Hamilton decided to throw a party. She had a special motive, of course. The thought had come to her when they all came home late one night after a glittering charity dinner at the Wentworth. After Angela and Wayne had gone to bed, she and Gordon had a nightcap, and it was then that she brought up the subject with him. Gordon looked at her dubiously.

"What are you cooking up?" he asked.

"Nothing," she replied. "Truly." She looked away from him. What was the use? She might as well tell him. "I was just thinking," she went on. "Simon's such a nice boy — and you must have noticed how he and Angela were together all night. And frankly, I'd like them to see more of each other . . ."

Gordon smiled sardonically. "Simon Armstrong? I didn't think she even *liked* him. In fact, I'm sure she thinks he's a bore.

Perhaps, but Patricia didn't agree. And certainly, if they saw more of each other, she might come to be actually fond of him, and that would take her mind off that Scott Edwards boy who had been so clumsy at dinner that night. And she *had* looked happy with Simon.

"I think they'd be perfect together," she said. He was

acceptable, his family had money, and even if his mother *was* something of a tartar, that was something they should be able to weather without too much difficulty.

"I don't know," Gordon said, finishing his port. "It could all be an act, of course."

Patricia looked at him sharply. "Has she said anything?"

Gordon shrugged. "I know my daughter," he said evasively.

Patricia stared at him coldly. *His* daughter? Yes, she guessed Angela was, really. Gordon couldn't have been more of a father to her than if she were actually his own. Of course Angela had been talking to him, telling him all her problems. Patricia experienced a faint surge of jealousy. It had always been like that. But she didn't say anything more. She was tired. It had been a long night.

In the morning, at breakfast, when she mentioned the idea of having a party, Angela didn't seem to be particularly excited about it. After breakfast Patricia drew up a guest list. At the top of the list were Simon Amrstrong and his mother. She had just finished it when Angela came down the stairs carrying a beach bag and a towel. Patricia looked up from the couch on which she was sitting and gave her a warm smile.

"Where are you off to?"

"Three guesses."

"If I get it right, will you take a look at my list?"

"List?"

"The guest list for the party. I *told* you at breakfast." She held the sheet of paper out to Angela who was hesitating in the doorway. "There might be somebody I missed — or someone you want crossed off. It's only tentative at this stage."

Angela shrugged indifferently. "It's up to you," she said, then moved across the hall to the front door.

Patricia was disappointed. She wished Angela would show more interest. It would be *her* party after all, her friends, Simon, nice people. She heard a step. Gordon had just reached the foot of the stairs. The front door closed behind Angela. Patricia gestured towards it with her pen.

"Her party, and she doesn't show a scrap of interest," she said reprovingly.

Gordon shrugged. He was adjusting his tie. "She's just had her birthday party," he reminded her. "Maybe she doesn't *want* another one." He stopped fiddling with his tie. "There are other things on her mind, too."

Patricia raised her eyebrows. "Such as?"

He smiled. "My bet is she's heading straight for Manly."

"Why would she want to go there?"

Gordon's smile broadened. "Scott Edwards country," he said.

He was being provocative. Patricia didn't like that smile. He was enjoying himself at her expense. He knew what she thought about Scott Edwards. Turning the knife. "She's finished with him."

"You might think she has," Gordon said with that infuriating smile that made Patricia feel she could throw something at him. "But you can never be too sure about anything as far as young people are concerned."

40

The salt breeze was warm on her face as Angela drove into Manly. The surf was high and the board riders were slicing in across the rising foam-capped walls of dark green water. There were plenty of swimmers and the beach was crowded. Angela was lucky to find a parking space near the South Steyne end.

She walked slowly along the front, looking down at the people on the beach, looking out for one familiar figure, and hoping, hoping that he would have come down to the beach today. It was the day for it — a perfect day for the beach, a warm sunny day. Scott was bound to be somewhere down on that broad sweep of sand. She passd handicraft stalls, and avoided a couple of running, sand-covered children. She wanted to see Scott. She wanted to talk to him, have things out with him. She was apprehensive. She didn't know what sort of reception he would give her if she did happen to run into him. But that couldn't be helped. She had to know where she stood.

She stopped by the wall and looked idly out at the waves and the board riders, at the clusters of swimmers. She had intended to go for a swim herself, whether or not she ran into Scott, but now she had lost interest. She had come to the beach to look for Scott rather than go back to the boarding house and face that awful woman again, or that thorough bitch of a girl who had been so cold towards her and who was apparently bearing Scott's child — not, she supposed, that that was such a bad thing in itself. Things like that happened all the time, although she might have thought that a girl like Jill would be on the Pill at least . . . No, what did bother her was that Scott had kept it from her. He might have told her. She might have understood. She liked to think she would have understood. No point in throwing a scene. That would have only driven him away. But now . . .

There were two people running up the sand from the water. She saw them out of the corner of her eye, then gave them a casual glance. A boy and girl, running and laughing, the boy chasing the girl, and there was something. . .something familiar about them, about the boy, bronzed and fair-haired and running like an athlete, that riveted her attention. They were sprinting up the sand towards her, Scott and Jill, their hair wet and streaming, kicking up sand, and then Scott swooping to pick up a towel and flicking it at Jill who ducked out of the way. With some dismay, Angela saw how happy they looked, how much in accord they seemed, a natural pair — and Jill certainly didn't *look* pregnant. She looked beautiful, and slim, very tanned and her swimsuit very brief.

Angela stood there by the wall and watched them bitterly. Obviously they were very fond of each other — and there was no room for her. Scott had only been stringing her along. It hurt — it really did.

Then, just as she was about to turn away from the wall, she realised that Scott had seen her. He was standing still, the towel hanging loosely from his hand, staring up at her. Jill was talking to him a puzzled expression on her face, but he didn't seem to be hearing her. Abruptly, Angela turned away from the wall and walked as fast as she could back to the car.

Scott caught up with her as she was climbing into the car. He was still wet. He grinned at her. "Hi. Good to see you."

Oh yeah, sure. Putting on the charm again — after what she had just seen. Angela made a sound that was meant to be cynical. Scott assumed an expression of the utmost seriousness. It was really laughable — and sad.

"Look, if you're mad at me because I didn't call . . ."

Angela pulled the seat belt across her with a quick, savage movement. "It's no use," she interrupted him. "I know all about you and Jill." The seat belt buckle clicked into place. "I . . . I just didn't expect to see you all over her, that's all." She turned the key in the ignition. The engine purred comfortably.

"Hang on." Scott reached in and switched the engine off.

"Do you mind?" She was indignant. Bloody cheek.

"What's this about me and Jill?" he challenged. He was frowning. His eyebrows almost met when he frowned.

"Fiona told me all about it." He was looking at her blankly, as if he had no idea what she was talking about — and that, too, was a laugh. What sort of actor did he think he was? A good one, that was for sure. He had pulled the wool over her eyes once. "About Jill's baby. *Your* baby."

"*What?*" It was as if she had actually struck him — that was how good an actor he was. His expression was one of pure disbelief. She had made her point, had delivered her king-hit, and now it was time to leave. "You . . . you're crazy," he spluttered. "I don't know what you're talking about."

Angela glared at him, and switched the engine on again. This time he didn't stop her. He just stood there, watching her with a dumbfounded look on his face as she backed the little sports car out onto the street, narrowly missing a passing cab, and accompanied by the furious blasting of its horn, swung and drove back the way she had come. So much for her day at the beach. Nevertheless, she did feel a sort of grim satisfaction.

But by the time she reached home that mood had passed. Now she was depressed, and indignant. Scott's treachery had struck her more deeply than she had thought. She stormed into the house. She needed to talk to somebody, spill it all out.

But not to her mother who was standing in the hallway with a look of concern on her face. Not to her tall, elegant mother who tried to stop her as she brushed past her, whose voice was querulous as she called after her. No, it was her father she needed to talk to right now, someone who would understand, sympathise with her, somehow put things into perspective and make them sound not nearly as bad as they seemed.

He met her in the living room. There he was, solid, reassuring, a comfortable smell of pipe tobacco. "I heard you coming," he said.

She threw herself into his arms. It was too much. She couldn't hold it back any longer — her unhappiness, her anger, her bitterness, the huge sense of loss. "Scott's with *her,*" she wailed.

He patted her gently on the back. "Jill?" he asked.

She had already told him what she had heard from Fiona. The tears were coming. The words choked up in her throat. "You should have seen her." The memory of the tanned girl in her skimpy swimsuit, running and laughing. "I'll bet she let herself get . . ." Oh, she could see them, moments of tender lovemaking.

"What's going on?" Patricia queried, coming up behind them.

Angela pulled herself away from her father. "She's having his baby." She hurled the answer at the woman who had just come into the room.

"Who's Jill?" Patricia was glaring at her husband, who gave her a warning look. Patricia rounded on her daughter, her eyes flashing angrily. "Whoever it is, it serves her right." She pointed one beautifully manicured finger at Angela. "*You* can thank your lucky stars you're not in the same boat."

"For God's sake, Patricia," Gordon said harshly. "Have a heart."

Patricia stiffened. Her eyes were cold. Gordon put his arm around Angela and began to lead her out of the living room towards the study.

"What did you expect?" he said gently. "You asked for it, going down there like that. When you think it over, you'll realise you're not being fair on either of them."

"Would someone *please* tell me what's going on?" Patricia cried out in exasperation.

"Later," Gordon said evenly. "Okay?"

In the study, Gordon closed the door behind them. "Thanks," Angela said, dropping into the chair in front of the desk. "It's bad enough *without* mother."

It was a friendly room, books, papers, the pipestand, objects she had grown up with, that had been there all the time. A haven. Gordon moved around behind the desk and sat down on the high-backed leather chair. He folded his hands on the desk and leaned forward.

"Why did you go down there?"

Angela was feeling better already — just a little. "Just dumb, I guess." That sounded really brave, pushing out the quiet humour to cover her hurt and confusion. "I wanted to sort things out with him."

Gordon's gaze on her was steady. "And?"

And? It was obvious, wasn't it? "You don't think I could talk to him with *her* there, do you?"

How many times they had talked in this room. It was here that she had told him all her problems, where she had told him about Scott and Jill.

"It would be better if you stayed away," Gordon said in that quiet drawl of his. "Scott *is* trying to do the right thing."

"Yeah?" Well, she wasn't so sure about that. "The right thing for who?"

It wasn't quite what she had expected to hear. She stood up and moved across to the door. "I'll have to tell your mother all about it," Gordon said behind her.

"Go for your life," she said bitterly, wrenching the door open and stepping out into the hall.

41

John was having it out with Fiona. The fury was still with him, although the main part of it had been spent. He was no longer shouting at her, demanding to know why she had done such a vicious, terrible thing to him — and even when he had been shouting at her, she had sat there, implacable as a rock, just waiting for the momentum to die down so she could get a word in. Not that she had said much, apart from admitting that, yes, she had told Angela that Jill was expecting his baby, but she had done it for his own good. He would see that in time, maybe he would even thank her.

But John wasn't seeing reason at all. All he could see was that he had been betrayed, stabbed in the back, by someone he had trusted above anyone else. The whole ground had opened up beneath his feet; now he had nothing to stand on.

"I'll ring Angela," he snapped. "I'll tell her it's a lie."

"What will that achieve?" Fiona's voice was one of sweet reason. "You've got an out now. You don't ever have to see her again."

When he had seen Angela at the beach, it had been like a vision he had been long awaiting but had despaired of ever seeing — but it was as if she had suddenly materialised out of nowhere while he was fooling about on the sand with Jill. Then, as he was staring up at her, she had turned and walked away. He had sprinted up the sand after her. It had been important to see her before she disappeared, to explain . . .

"I want to clear this whole thing up," he said to Fiona who was setting the table for dinner. There was a stew simmering on the stove. He had had to wait until she came home before he could challenge her. It had been a long, agonising wait. Jill had tried to calm him down, then realising it was hopeless, had gone to her room.

"You're making a huge mistake," Fiona said.

"You're a liar, Aunt Fiona." He was raising his voice again. "That's what I can't hack. That you lied to me. It was none of your damned business.'

Fiona looked up at him. She winced, then turning away, moved out to the kitchen. John followed her. Maybe he was being a bit hard on her, but he couldn't help it. That moment . . . that moment when Angela had looked at him so coldly and accused him of being the father of Jill's baby . . . What baby? He didn't even know Jill was having a baby. He was sure she wasn't, but to say something like that, when it was obviously not true, when he knew hardly anything about Jill at all, except that she was a nice kid who brought him a cup of coffee in the mornings . . . "She thinks I'm a heel," he said in a more placatory tone as he came into the kitchen.

Fiona was rummaging in the cutlery drawer. She had been to town. She was still dressed up. "Do you seriously believe she spends her life worrying about what you get up to?" she asked, and there was a faint curl to her upper lip.

"She might," John replied with a shrug. Why shouldn't she? Why had she come all the way across to Manly?

Fiona slammed the drawer shut, and carried the knives and forks out into the other room. "How do you think it makes me feel?" John called after her.

"That's the least of your worries." There was a clatter of cutlery from the other room. John picked up his jacket from the kitchen chair over which it was draped. Fiona reappeared in the doorway. She saw him putting on the jacket. "You're not going to see her . . . ?"

"Yeah." John stared defiantly back at her. There was nothing she could do about it, nothing she could say. "And I'm going to tell her I love her." That was what he *would* do. He had just thought of it. He should have thought of it a long time ago. "We'll sort out whatever has to be sorted out together."

"Johnny." There was a new element in her voice, a gravity, even urgency.

Ignoring it, John moved quickly to the door. Now that he had made up his mind, it was as if there was hardly any time left in which to do it. "If you don't like it," he said gruffly, "stiff . . ."

"Please, Johnny." She had followed him to the door. He opened the door. She grabbed his sleeve.

"Save your breath," he snarled.

"No, Johnny." She was insistent, very serious, something important she had to tell him. She held on to his sleeve. He wheeled back to face her, and was startled to see the tears in her eyes, the way her face seemed to have lost its angularity, even definition, as if it were slowly dissolving. "You can call me a busybody," she said in a muted, blurred voice. "And a liar. And maybe I am. But there's something you don't know."

Abruptly she let go of his arm, and wiping an eye with the corner of her sleeve, turned back into the room. "Shut the door," she said.

Intrigued almost in spite of himself because he really had made up his mind not to listen to anything more this woman — dear Aunt Fiona — might have to tell him, John closed the door and faced Fiona who was standing stiffly in the middle of the room beside the table. One hand was clenched into a fist and was resting on the table, a network of blue veins standing out from the stretched skin. She seemed to be under some sort of tension, under the influence of strong conflicting emotions that buffeted her this way and that — and when she did speak, it seemed to be with a massive effort that threatened to defeat her.

"I've done everything I can to avoid it," she said brokenly. "But . . . believe me, I'm telling the truth now." John stared at her, his breath caught up near his throat somewhere. The tone of her voice, the way she stood, prepared him to hear something he knew he wouldn't want to hear. Pulling out a chair from the table, he lowered himself into it. Fiona took a deep breath and went on. "The reason you can't get involved with Angela Hamilton," she said with the air of one who was cutting everything loose, "is because she's your sister."

For one stunned, bewildered moment John believed her. Then he didn't believe her. He had never heard anything so transparent in his life before — and she had looked so serious when she was telling him; looked so serious now, but what a rotten thing to tell him. How low could anyone get? His anger rose. His cheeks were warm and tingling.

"I didn't want to tell you," Fiona said with finality.

"No!" John shouted, springing to his feet.

"It's true," Fiona said quietly but firmly.

John's body was taut. There was a rushing sound inside his head. He could hear himself shouting. "That's not even a *good* lie! For God's sake . . . my *sister?* Do you expect me to believe something like that . . . that sort of rubbish? No, no!" He shook his head violently. He waved an outstretched finger at her. She didn't flinch. "If you want to split us up, you'll have to do better than *that!*"

"I've got proof." Her voice was tired but matter-of-fact. John watched her as she crossed to the bureau and took a photograph album out from one of the drawers. What now? What proof? What if she was right? But she *couldn't* be right. It was just something she'd made up, on the spur of the moment, that was why it was all so far-fetched. So . . . what proof? He stared at Fiona as she opened the album, flicked through its pages, then slipped out a picture and handed it to him.

He took it gingerly from her, as if it might disintegrate between his fingers, and carried it back to the chair. He sat down and with a sense of trepidation, looked closely at the picture.

Faces and images in black and white, swimming in and out of focus, two grown-ups, each of them holding a baby in their arms, standing on the front steps of a building, obviously the one where he now was, the boarding house. And the picture must have been taken quite some time ago. He recognised his father, much younger and thinner, his hair much shorter — and the woman standing next to him on the steps, no mistaking her, the same high cheekbones and wide eyes, although her hair was dark in the picture and fell all the way down to her shoulders. Patricia Hamilton — Angela's mother, standing there with his father, each of them holding a baby in their arms. It was a lot to take in, to absorb. His mouth was dry. He stared at the picture, numb. Fiona sat down next to him.

"Patricia and your father came here one night," she said quietly. "Twenty years ago. She was pregnant." John stared at the photograph, riveted, unable to take his eyes from it. "She gave birth to twins," Fiona went on in that same level voice. "You and your sister — Angela." Her hand fluttered briefly over his. "You mustn't blame anyone for what happened." John looked up at her, his face set, a tumult of emotions inside. "A week after you were born, she left and took your sister — Angela — with her. Your father didn't see either of them again."

So . . . John felt weak. A day full of shocks, one after the other. "Didn't he go after them?" he asked thickly.

"No."

Why not? Anyone else . . . "Didn't he even *try?*"

Fiona shook her head. "No point. He felt that whatever it was that had brought them together . . . well, it was gone."

The enormity of it — what could have happened — was beginning to sink in. He and Angela — his *sister.* Jesus! It could have happened at any time, the powerful surge of their emotions, the moonlight, the whispering surf, the girl on the horse . . .

"You *let* me!" he cried indignantly. "You *knew* how I felt about her. Why didn't you tell me before?"

"I was scared," Fiona replied sombrely, and she looked it. "In your position, you can't afford to let anyone know who you really are. Until you clear yourself you've got to forget about them."

"*No!*" That he *wouldn't* do. Suddenly he had a mother — and a sister — a twin sister. Patricia Hamilton regarding him so coolly, with barely concealed dislike.

"You'll put yourself in gaol," Fiona warned him.

Probably, but this was more important than that — a thousand times more important. "I don't care. I've got to get to know her." He looked again at the picture, at the woman with the impeccable table manners. "I want to know why she walked out."

And maybe even then a plan was beginning to form in his mind.

42

"What kind of a job?"

"Anything. Whatever's going."

"Why come to me?" Gordon Hamilton asked. They were sitting in his study. John Palmer was feeling uncomfortable. He was wearing a suit and tie and this added to his discomfiture.

"I got the feeling you liked me," John said hesitantly. "I hoped you might give me a chance."

The late morning sun was slanting in through the study window. Beyond the window were fields and fences. Gordon Hamilton leaned back in his swivel chair, and by putting his hands together, made a steeple of his fingers. "Despite the fact you have no references," he observed.

Gordon Hamilton was one of those guys John felt he could trust. He was sympathetic, always listened to what you had to say. A straight sort of guy, didn't smile much. The thing was, though, John had always regarded him as Angela's father, and perhaps because of that his feelings towards him had been coloured. But now, it was different, John knew so much more, and if Gordon Hamilton wasn't Angela's father he was still a nice guy, perhaps even more of a nice guy than John had thought. Yes, it was funny to be in this house now, knowing what he knew. He had gradually come to terms with what Fiona had told him, but there was still an element of unreality about it, more so now that he was actually in the house with its elegant, muted, harmonious furnishings and the air of not being lived in — or lived in very gingerly so as not to mar that carefully cultivated harmony.

"I'll work hard," John promised him. He was sitting forward on his chair. "I'll work a week with no pay if you want. See how I go."

Fiona had tried to talk him out of it. She had tried to dissuade him from calling Gordon Hamilton. No use, she had said, but John had been adamant. Patricia Hamilton was his *mother,* damn it, she had walked out on him and his father when he was just a week old, and he wanted to know why. He had thought a lot about it. He wanted to know all about the Hamiltons, and there was one way he could do this. No, he had told Fiona, when she brought up the reservation, he wouldn't shoot his big mouth off and tell them what he knew before he had a chance to find out all he could about them. That was if Gordon Hamilton gave him a job, of course.

Gordon Hamilton sat behind his desk, his fingers still steepled, staring at something behind John's head. "If you think I'm trying to use my friendship with Angela," John said, "you're wrong. I guess you know things aren't too good between us?"

Gordon Hamilton's eyes settled on John again. He nodded. "You're certainly keen," he remarked.

John held the older man's gaze. He wanted him to see how earnest he was. "I just want a chance. If I don't work out, then get rid of me."

Gordon Hamilton smiled tightly. "I will."

John wasn't sure what he meant. "You'll give me the job?"

"Not so fast." Gordon Hamilton held up one hand in a restraining gesture. "You might not like what I have to offer." His eyes drifted across to the window. It was a fine day outside. "I need a stablehand at the stud. It's not a particularly pleasant job."

Hearing this, the tension began to leave John. In its place was a spreading glow. He could have yelped his delight, but all he did was grin broadly. "I'll take it."

Gordon Hamilton was still looking out the window. There seemed to be something wistful in his attitude, as if he wished he were somewhere else. "You start tomorrow," he said. "One week's trial. With pay."

John stood up. The glow inside him was really rich. "Thanks, Mister Hamilton." Gordon also stood. John held out his hand. Gordon shook it. His grip was firm and dry.

"There *is* one proviso," Gordon Hamilton said grimly. "Whatever happened between you and Angela . . . that's between the two of you. But if you do or say anything to upset her, don't bother staying around for explanations. Is that understood?"

It was. "Fair enough," John said seriously. "Thanks again."

As he closed the study door behind him and was moving to the front door, it opened and there was Patricia Hamilton stepping into the hallway, closing the door behind her.

John stood where he was and stared at her. There was no denying that she was beautiful — but that she was his *mother,* it was just too much for him to take in, now that he was seeing her in the flesh for the first time since Fiona had dropped her bombshell. The doubts and uncertainties were returning. This glamorous but glacial woman who was coming into the house — she and his father, it was just impossible to imagine, arriving at Fiona's place in Manly all those years ago. It was even difficult to imagine that she could have allowed herself at any time to become pregnant. But . . . How should he really regard her? His mother — and of course she didn't know who *he* was.

"What are you doing here?" She was looking at him in surprise and extreme distaste. "If you're here to see

Angela, she's out." There was no mistaking her tone. She wasn't pleased to see him — and she obviously didn't want to see him again. Which was absolutely bloody charming.

She was moving towards him. John stared at her. "No, I. . .I came to see Mister Hamilton," he stammered.

"Oh?" She arched one eyebrow. Could this be the same woman who had allowed her passion to override her judgement for one time at least — this woman who was so icy and so much in control of herself. "What for?"

"A job," he told her. "I start at the stud in the morning."

She stared at him blankly. John held her stare for a moment, then moved past her to the front door. "I'll be seeing you, Mrs Hamilton," he muttered.

As he stepped outside and could no longer feel her eyes on his back, he realised he might have set himself a hopeless task. There was no way he could get to know that woman, scratch that highly impregnable veneer to find out what lay beneath. She was an enigma — and would continue to be so. He moved slowly down the path. The gravel crunched lightly beneath his feet. At least he had landed the job — and that was something. He would have to play things by ear from here on in.

43

There were varying reactions in the Hamilton household when it was learned that Gordon Hamilton had given Scott Edwards a job at the stud — and none of them were favourable. Patricia was furious and told Wayne that she believed Scott was hired to keep an eye on him. Things hadn't been going too well out at the stud lately, a couple of important sales had fallen through because of Wayne's incompetence, and preoccupation with his social activities — and Gordon had already had it out with him. He had told Wayne that he had had enough; it was obvious his trust in him had been misplaced and that he was going to put on a new manager to make sure the business went smoothly in future. Patricia had managed to talk him out of it, but now, with this unexpected development of Scott being taken on to work at the stud, it seemed he still had his reservations. Patricia felt she had been thwarted — and that was the time when she was the most dangerous. Wayne had thought she was being melodramatic, but with a show of bravado told her that all he needed was a week to get rid of Scott Edwards. But it mightn't even come to that. Angela might do it for them.

When she heard the news Angela was livid. She confronted her father in his study.

"You *know* I can't stand him!" she cried.

Gordon Hamilton tried to reason with her. She was obviously upset. Her cheeks were suffused with small red patches. Her eyes mirrored her anger. She didn't often lose her temper. Now she had lost it.

"He's an employee," Gordon pointed out mildly. "You're not expected to *socialise* with him. He needs a job, so I gave him one. It's as simple as that."

"You *shouldn't* have!" Angela cried, flinging her arms wide.

"Why?" Gordon raised his eyebrows. "Because he hurt your pride?" He smiled reassuringly. "You'll get over it. I respect him for accepting his responsibilities. He got a girl pregnant, and now he's standing by her."

But Angela wasn't mollified. "Don't you care about *me?*" she demanded.

"Of course I do," Gordon replied. "But Scott had the guts to come all the way out here and ask me for work . . ."

"The nerve, you mean," Angela broke sharply across him.

"Guts, nerve." Gordon shrugged. "Doesn't matter what you call it. I've made my decision, and I think it's the right one."

"There are other places, other jobs," Angela persisted. "You don't have to employ him."

Gordon frowned. "I've given my word."

"And that's more important than hurting me?"

"Yes. Because you're being childish."

Angela pouted sulkily. "I'm being taught a lesson — is that it?"

"Scott keeps the job unless he gives me a reason to get rid of him," Gordon told her firmly. "You can't always have it your own way, sweetheart."

And that was the whole trouble. Looking at the closed expression on her father's face, Angela knew for a fact that this time at least she was not going to have her own way — and that really galled her. She swung angrily away. It was no use arguing with him any more. There were times when he could be quite as stubborn as she was.

44

"I wonder who *is* helping him?" Beryl Palmer asked suddenly.

David Palmer had just come in from the kitchen with a can of beer and flopped into the chair in front of the TV. He looked up from the blank screen.

"What's that, love?"

"John — I wonder who's helping him. When I saw him that day, he said he had someone helping him."

David didn't want to talk about it. He sipped his beer. "I think I know who it could be," Beryl said. "There's no way it would be your dad. And my parents haven't heard from him."

David sighed in exasperation, then hauling himself out of the chair, crossed to the TV set to turn it on.

"David, we have to face it," Beryl said behind him. Her voice was sharper, more determined. "You're going up to Sydney tomorrow — so why don't you take a chance and call on Fiona Thompson?"

David, about to turn on the TV, started. Fiona — it was ages since he had last heard that name. Fiona Thompson, in Manly, half a lifetime ago, who had helped deliver the twins while David, a bundle of nerves, had waited in the other room. Hearing Beryl drop her name like that had come as a shock. He straightened.

"What?"

"It stands to reason," Beryl said earnestly. "He lived with her for five years. He might have gone there."

David shook his head. He didn't want to believe it. "He was a kid when he left. He hasn't mentioned her for years. I doubt if he even remembers where she lived."

"It's worth a try."

He thought about it. No use opening up old memories, old wounds. "No, Beryl," he said finally. "I'm not doing it."

Beryl studied him levelly. "I know you don't want to see her, but if it means tracking John down . . ."

"I said I'm not doing it," David snapped.

Beryl slowly shook her head. "You can be so stubborn," she said in an annoyed voice. "It's not as though you'll have to stay. All you have to do is just ask. You'll be able to tell whether she's covering up or not."

For Christ's sake, wouldn't she stop? Hadn't he just made himself perfectly clear? He raised his voice. He was almost shouting at her. "I don't want to discuss Fiona Thompson — *or* John."

"You can't keep pushing things under the carpet, David." Beryl's voice was also raised.

David opened his mouth to retort, when there was a sound in the kitchen, and Kevin appeared in the doorway. He was just home from school. They hadn't heard him come in. He looked questioningly from his father to his mother.

"What are you two arguing about?" he asked.

"Nothing," Beryl replied and moved out to start getting the dinner ready.

Dinner was a rather restrained affair. The three of them sat quietly at the table, occupied by their own thoughts. It was a strain, and finally Kevin could stand it no longer. He put down his knife and fork with a loud clatter.

"This is crazy!" he exclaimed.

His parents looked up from their plates at him in

surprise.

"What?" David grunted, his fork arrested halfway between his plate and his mouth.

"I've been behaving like an adult, haven't I?" Kevin queried in an aggrieved voice.

There was something bugging the kid. David was puzzled. "Yes — yes, I suppose you have."

"Then how about treating me like one for a change?" the boy asked. The food on his plate was only half-eaten. David gestured with his fork. He swallowed the food that was in his mouth.

"Now hold your horses . . ."

"Oh come on, Dad," Kevin said in disgust. "I'm sick and tired of not knowing what's going on around the place."

David looked across the table at Beryl. She gave him a slight, barely perceptible nod. Kevin watched them both. Beryl sighed. "It had to happen," she said in a small voice.

David was feeling uncomfortable. She was probably right, but that didn't make it any easier. Beryl pushed her chair back and stood up. "I've got some sewing to finish," she announced quietly. "Leave the dishes. I'll do those later."

David put down his knife and fork, his appetite suddenly vanished. He gulped, and avoided looking at his son, his second son, his and Beryl's son. Of course the kid had to find out sooner or later, but David had kept putting it off, maybe hoping somehow, in some way, he would actually be spared the duty, that it would be taken out of his hands. There was plenty of time, he had thought, and now, suddenly, there was no more time. He looked down at his plate. Beryl wasn't even here to give him moral support. It was a task he had to face by himself. He cleared his throat.

"Your . . . ah . . . mother wasn't the first woman I lived with," he murmured. A bit abrupt, he thought, but it was out now.

Kevin was watching him intently from across the table. David could hear Beryl moving about in the other room.

"John's mother?" Kevin asked.

David nodded. His eyes met Kevin's briefly, then he looked away again. "Yes, I was . . . um . . . only about your age . . . a bit older . . . she was a year younger."

Kevin said nothing. He didn't interrupt, or ask questions. He wasn't helping. David stumbled on. "My Dad . . . and Mum . . . they didn't think we should get married."

Now Kevin did ask a question. "You wanted to?"

"Yes, I wanted to."

"Did you love her?"

What was the use? He had said just about all he had intended to say. Did he love Patricia? Of course he did. At the time. He was certain of it. They had run away together from Melbourne to Sydney. "At the time — yes," he said, embarrassed, aware of the warmth rising to his cheeks. "That's about it. John was born, and I met your mother."

"There has to be more to it than that," Kevin said quietly. "Who's Fiona?"

David cleared his throat again. Maybe it was better when the kid wasn't asking questions. "A woman who helped me look after John."

"And she's in Sydney?"

"Yes," David replied, then felt the need to expand some more. He was gathering confidence. He leaned forward, his arms resting on the table. "You see, son, I couldn't have looked after John by myself. Fiona looked after him. And then I met your mother — and Susan was born, then you . . ." He was faltering again. "Then . . . well, John came down here when he was five . . ." He managed a wan smile. "And I guess that's about it."

"So you think he might be in Sydney with this Fiona woman?" It wasn't so much a question as a statement of fact.

"I don't know," David said, and he really didn't. "Your mother seems to think so."

There was a long pause. From his expression, Kevin appeared to be formulating his thoughts, as if he had something very important he wanted to say, and unless he picked his words carefully, there was the very real danger of them going over his father's head. But when it did come out, it was simple enough.

"Do you love Mum?"

David was appalled. Could there be any doubt of that? The question cut right into him. "Of course I do," he said fervently. "That...all that other business happened a long time ago, son. You might think you're an adult, but ...you'll learn. Time changes things."

"Yeah." Kevin nodded thoughtfully. "What happened to John's mum?"

David gave him a startled look. What *had* happened? "Don't know," he muttered. "I never saw her again." That was enough. It was time to put an end to it. He stood up and began to collect the dishes. "How about we start the dishes?" he suggested in a brighter voice.

Kevin also stood up. "What was she like?" he asked.

"I loved her," David told him.

Yes, it was as simple as that.

45

Patricia Hamilton was going through a period of immense frustration, and it was all Angela's fault. She just wasn't co-operating. She was being stubborn and wilful. It was really such a nuisance.

It was Angela's attitude towards young Simon Armstrong that was the core of the problem. He was such a nice boy, and well connected, the ideal sort for Angela to marry — and what had Angela told her? She didn't *love* Simon, for heaven's sake!

Now what did that have to do with anything? Love? It was nonsense, wishy-washy, romantic twaddle, something that really only existed in the pages of one of those Mills and Boon romances. It was so unreal; it just didn't exist like that. But. . .and here she had to stop and reflect. She had to admit to herself that she had been in love once — head over heels, helplessly.

She had always thought she would marry someone rich — a doctor or a lawyer were the most obvious choices to a girl who already knew that life had a great deal more to offer than a poky little house in West St Kilda. Love, she had thought at that time, was something that could be controlled with reasonable ease. But then one night, she had met David Palmer at a youth club dance, and there was no way she could even describe, let alone have any control over, her feelings. David Palmer — the guy every girl wanted, a heart-throb, and he hadn't even noticed her at first. But finally he did ask her for a dance and that was when the whole world turned over. And it didn't matter that he had also come from a reasonably poor family or that he had no aspirations to become a doctor or a lawyer.

They had seen each other secretly after that, because she knew her parents wouldn't approve. There was the question of their religious differences, for a start. So she used to sneak out of the house at night and meet him. Nothing had happened during those meetings; they had just talked, and it had all been perfectly innocent. Then she had been found out, and there had been an awful row with her parents. They had called her every name under the sun, and accused her of having sex with the boy, and that had really stung. It had been so unfair and she was bitter. If that was what they believed about her, then why not give them real cause? And that was what she had done. She had done it deliberately, defiantly, had allowed David to make love to her. She had fallen pregnant immediately.

She had made one big mistake. She wouldn't make another one — and more importantly wouldn't allow her daughter, David Palmer's daughter, to make one.

"You're proposed to, *finally,* by the son of one of the best families in the State, and you have the audacity to throw it back in his face." She was really livid. Angela stared back at her, blank-faced.

"Mother, I don't love him."

So there it was — that impossible word. Patricia bared her teeth in an unpleasant smile. "Oh, don't be naive. Love has nothing to do with it." The girl was still watching her stonily, and this added to Patricia's annoyance. "I've spent years cultivating the right people," she went on. "Making damned sure you had the chance of marrying someone who would give you everything you wanted — and what do I get in return? 'I don't love him'."

Angela sighed. Then she smiled, and perhaps she really was trying to make light of it. "If he means that much to you, why don't *you* go after him?"

It was then, in a rage, that Patricia slapped her face.

46

Manly hadn't changed much, and Fiona's house hadn't changed at all. It was exactly as he remembered it. Perhaps it had had a few coats of paint since the time he had left, but that was about it. As he stood outside, the memories came rushing back with a sharpness that was almost painful. It was here that he and Patricia had come when they first arrived in Sydney. It was here that John had been born — John and his sister, a girl whose name he didn't know. It was here he had come back that time to find Patricia had gone, taking the girl with her and leaving him the boy. Their lives had changed in ways that couldn't be envisaged, but the house hadn't changed. It stood sturdy, like a rock, impervious to all the comings and goings. Slowly, David Palmer climbed the steps to the open front door. He wondered if Fiona had changed. It had been a long time.

There was a girl in the hallway. In her hand was a paintbrush and she stood with her head a little to one side, looking critically through the open door of one of the rooms. There was paint on her hands and specks of it in her hair. She was talking to someone inside the room. She looked around as David came into the hallway.

"Hi there," she said pleasantly. She was quite pretty. "Can I help you?"

"I'm looking for Fiona Thompson," he told her.

She indicated a door with her brush. "It's that one there."

Yes, sure it was. The same door. "Thanks," he said, moving to the door. The girl disappeared into the room she had been painting. David knocked on Fiona's door. He heard soft sounds behind the door, and a moment later it opened.

Fiona's surprise when she recognised him was very real. She looked shocked, in fact, as she stared hard at him. Then the surprise seemed to give way to apprehension. She looked quickly up and down the hallway. "David." She whispered his name.

There was something worrying her. She wasn't pleased to see him. "I'm sorry," he said. "I suppose I should've rung."

"No. . .ah. . ." Her eyes flicked up and down the hall again. David looked at her. She hadn't really changed at all. She gave him a shaky smile. "You gave me a surprise, that's all. Fifteen years is a long time." She opened the door wider and made room for him to enter. "You'd better come inside," she said.

Just as they came into the room, which David noted hadn't really changed much either, the phone rang. Fiona moved across to answer it. A small frown appeared briefly, then she covered the mouthpiece with her hand.

"Won't be a second," she told David. "Make yourself comfortable."

David moved around the room, looking at objects and pictures, most of which reinforced his memories of the place. Fifteen years, hardly anything changed. Behind him, Fiona was speaking quietly.

"Hello? Yes, I'm still here. . . I'm sorry I missed you like that. . .no, I'll probably be tied up here for a while. . .oh yes, don't worry. . . I'll be in touch as soon as I can. . .all right, 'bye."

She hung up. David was still moving around the room. He wasn't relaxed. He was feeling uncomfortable. It had been a long haul up from Melbourne with only a stop for

breakfast at Albury. He returned Fiona's smile.
"Still as popular as ever," he remarked.
"Tired little old thing like me?"
"Tired little old thing like you."
It was lighthearted enough, but neither of them were at their ease. Fiona crossed the room, her arms outstretched, and hugged him. "It's good to see you," she said lightly. "I thought you'd forgotten me."
"I could never do that," he said soberly.
Releasing him, Fiona stepped back and studied him quizzically for a few moments. It was as if she sensed he had come with a very definite purpose in mind and was in no way happy about it. She frowned.
"There's something wrong, isn't there?" she asked in a quiet, serious voice.
David moved away from her. He avoided looking at her. "I'll say," he muttered. He came straight to the point. "It's John. He's wanted by the police for murder. He . . . ran away before he could be charged."
Was she really as surprised as she looked? "Little Johnny?" she exclaimed.
"He's not 'little Johnny' any more," David reminded her. "Actually that's . . . sort of . . . the reason I came to see you."
"What do you mean?" She was looking at him unflinchingly, and David thought that maybe he had come here on a wild goose chase after all.
"He wouldn't have had anywhere to hide," he said. "I thought he might have come to you."
Fiona shook her head slowly. "No," she said. Her face softened. "Oh, David, what a terrible thing to happen."
David nodded. "Beryl — that's my wife — she's pretty cut up about it. I suppose we all are."
"Are you staying in Sydney overnight?" Fiona asked, seeming to come to some sort of decision."
"I'm not sure." David replied with a shrug. The depression was weighing him down. He had really thought he would find something here. "I've got a load already. So it'd probably be best if I head straight back."

Fiona appeared to be possessed of new resolve. Her eyes were shining. "Don't you dare," she said forcefully. "I haven't seen you in all this time, and you're not running out on me now." She moved towards the kitchen. "We're going to sit down and have a drink, and a good mag, and then you're going to stay the night." She smiled at him warmly. "Deal?"

David nodded and smiled back at her. "Deal." In some ways he felt relieved. He didn't really want to go — not yet. The flat was so familiar to him, so much a part of his childhood, and now that his question about John had been answered — and he was quite satisfied Fiona was telling the truth, as much as she loved the boy and would have done practically anything to protect him — he felt more relaxed, more comforted than he had been for a long time. He stood in the living room and listened to Fiona moving about in the kitchen. He heard the fridge door open, then Fiona's muttered exclamation.

"Wouldn't you know it," she called. "I'm right out of beer."

"Doesn't matter," David called back. "Cup of tea'll do just fine."

"It will not," Fiona said determinedly. "I've offered you a drink, and that's what you're going to have."

David laughed. Fiona never changed. Once she got her teeth into something, an idea. . . "No, seriously, it's no problem."

Fiona emerged from the kitchen. "It is to me," she said. "Look, tell you what, you be a love and go out and get some. I'll fix up the spare room for you."

"I don't want to be any trouble."

Linking her arm with his, Fiona turned him around and steered him towards the door. "That's not what you said twenty years ago," she said good-humouredly. "Now go on, hurry up. And none of your Melbourne beer either."

David grinned at her. He was feeling much better. "You'll take whatever you get." He stepped out into the hallway and gave her a careless wave. "Won't be long," he said.

47

There was much to be done now that David was out of the way. He would be back in a few minutes. Fiona moved quickly.

John had been in Jill's room, watching her painting around the edges of the wall, joking with her, commenting on the mess she had made of herself and the newspapers she had spread out across the floor. Then she had stepped out into the hallway to examine her handiwork, and he had heard her speaking to someone out there.

"I'm looking for Fiona Thompson."

The sound of his father's voice had jolted right through John. It was the last thing he had expected to hear, and coming so abruptly . . . He had felt weak, dizzy, had flung himself behind the door and forced himself not to panic. His heart had pounded, a cold sweat had formed on his forehead, and his knees threatened to give way beneath him. He had heard Jill directing his father to Fiona's door, and then Jill had come back into the room and John had quickly closed the door behind her.

"What's wrong with you?"

John had silenced her by raising his finger to his lips, then, crossing the room, picked up the phone and dialled Fiona's number. He could hear the phone ringing in her flat.

"Oh come on, Scott, what the hell's going on?"

"Long story. It's just that...uh...it could be embarrassing for Aunt Fiona if that guy finds me here." Which was no answer at all. Jill was still in the dark, but that couldn't be helped. Then, much to John's relief, Fiona had answered the phone.

A few moments after David had gone to fetch the beer, there was a knock on David's door. "It's okay," Fiona's voice called softly. "It's me."

Jill opened the door. Fiona, carrying an armload of John's clothing, slipped into the room. "Quick," she ordered Jill. "There are some of Scott's things inside the front door. Bring them in here."

Jill hesitated, but some of the fierce urgency in Fiona's voice had rubbed off onto her. She moved to the door. Fiona halted John when he made to follow her.

"Not you. It's not worth the risk."

"You haven't told him?" He didn't really believe she would, but he had to ask.

"Of course not," Fiona briskly assured him. "I just can't boot him out, either, or he'll get suspicious. I've asked him to stay the night."

Another jolt. She wasn't making it any easier. "You what?"

Fiona laid her hand on John's shoulder. Her fingers were strong. "Calm down," she said. "It'll be all right. You stay here with Jill."

Jill — there was another problem. "What'll I tell her? She's already wondering what the hell's going on."

Fiona bared her teeth in a determined smile. Her hand dropped from his shoulder. "Just tell her it's none of her business. She's good like that."

Maybe, but John still wasn't convinced. But before he had a chance to say anything Jill was back in the room with another bundle of his clothes.

"That's the lot?" she asked breathlessly.

Fiona nodded. "Good girl." She crossed to the door.

"Right, I'm off."

"Aunt Fiona," John called after her, but she waved him away impatiently.

"Oh, for heaven's sake!" she snapped, closing the door firmly behind her.

Still carrying his clothes, Jill looked at John. "Where do you want these?"

"I don't know."

So she dumped them unceremoniously on the floor.

John had no choice but to remain in Jill's room. His father was in there with Fiona, and John was undoubtedly the sole topic of conversation. He could hear their muted voices through the walls, the occasional muted chink of glass on glass. Jill's room still reeked strongly of fresh paint.

Jill was making a bed up for him on the floor. She looked up. "Hey, how about a bit of a hand? It *is* your bed."

"Huh?" John's thoughts had gradually been turning in another direction. His father had come here to look for him, had taken the trouble, would stand by him. "Ah . . . just leave it for a sec, will you? I might not need it."

He just couldn't keep on running and starting at every sound. It had to stop sometime, and there was always the chance that things mightn't turn out to be as bad as he expected. It was even possible that the police were already closing in on the real murderer. He walked across to the door, his mind in turmoil.

"You're not going in there, are you?" Jill said quietly behind him.

"I don't know. Maybe." He turned back to her and gave her a bleak smile. "I'm sorry for all the hassles. I mean it."

Jill shrugged it off. "No worries," she said with a smile. "One of these days just fill me in, huh?"

That much he owed her. "Sure," he said, and let himself out of the room.

Still undecided, apprehensive, he crept down the hall to Fiona's door. Reaching the door, he leaned closer to it. He could hear their voices more clearly now. Every nerve in his body was strained towards hearing what they were saying in there. He hardly dared breathe. He heard Fiona's voice.

"David, if you found out where John was, what would you do?"

"I'm not sure," he heard his father reply. "I think I know . . . but . . . I'm not sure."

"What do you think you'd do?"

"Hand him over to the police. I guess that's what I'd do. I'd dob him in."

Choking back a sob, John hurried back along the hall to Jill's room.

48

The party was going along marvellously, and Patricia Hamilton was pleased. She looked approvingly around at the guests, absorbed the chatter and returned the smiles. She moved graciously among the groups, stopping here, pausing there, making sure everyone had their glasses filled, passing the canapes. Through the doors that opened onto the terrace, the moonlight lightly gilded the branches of the trees and shimmered across the still expanse of the swimming pool. A warm, beautiful night. A beautiful party. Everybody looked so *well,* so lively and interesting. Simon looked particularly handsome. Patricia definitely approved. She felt happy, quite within her element, which was why she moved so easily among this very supple, upwardly mobile, most *acceptable* group of people.

Simon was talking to Angela, who — bother the girl; couldn't she even *try?* — was looking bored, glancing around the room abstractedly, her attention obviously wandering. It didn't matter that Simon might be talking about his car, his latest skiing holiday, or the bottle of Para 53 he had picked up at a wine auction the other day, which he wouldn't drink but put to one side as an investment. It didn't matter about any of these things, about tennis or golf, or sailing, or what was happening at the stock exchange. There were some things you had to accept even if they were sometimes a crashing bore. One had to compromise, make allowances, move upwards all the time.

Yes, that was how it had to be. Just as she'd had to compromise with regard to Gordon. But Gordon had been a godsend. He had come along just at the right time, had fallen hopelessly in love with her, had taken her away from Manly up to his country property, Woombai, and there she had made her plans for him to put in a manager so they could move to the city where she felt his background and social and financial contacts could be put to better use. It had all fitted in so nicely. He had come to see Fiona Thompson to discuss the property she had inherited, which adjoined Woombai, and which he had undertaken to manage on her behalf in return for the use of the water that originated on her property.

He had come to see Fiona, and had seen Patricia — and that had been it. He had been smitten straight away. To Patricia, he had been a lifeline, and she had grabbed it eagerly. Certainly there'd had to be compromises, but the stakes had been high, and she'd had to ride along with them. If only Angela could see things the same way, and realise that her future was something to which she needed to give the closest attention.

She saw young Scott Edwards standing across the room, staring at Angela and Simon, and once again experienced a small reservation over the wisdom of inviting him. It had seemed a good idea at the time. Wayne had thought so, and he had almost convinced his stepmother. Why not? he had suggested, and Patricia had asked him if he was joking.

"Not joking," he had said with a smirk. "Angela feels awkward with him around, so I just can't help feeling it might be useful, that's all."

Patricia had thought about it. Possibly it could work. Scott was so gauche, Simon so assured, and when she saw them together, surely Angela would see the futility of wasting her time and emotions on someone like Scott

Edwards — an employee at the stud after all, but nothing more than that. So she had sent him an invitation, and he had come.

"What if Angela sees the two of them together and decides she prefers Scott?" she had asked Wayne earlier in the evening, before the guests had started to arrive. The doubts had never been too far away.

Wayne had given her a philosophical smile. "Well, at least we won't have gone down without a fight," he had said, which wasn't all that helpful. Anyway, it was too late now for misgivings. The die was cast. She just hoped she had done the right thing.

She had opened the door to Scott. He had grinned at her. "Dressed and pressed," he had said, which she thought was just a little too familiar.

"So I see," she had said coolly, keeping him at a distance. She had directed him into the living room where Angela and Wayne were. Angela hadn't been at all pleased to see him, and had studiously avoided him. Then Simon had arrived with his mother, the formidable Mrs Armstrong, and Angela had made a show of staying with him. They had danced together, quite energetically.

She saw Angela move away from Simon's side, and say something to Scott. Scott was smiling. Angela looked angry. She swung away from him, and Patricia smiled happily to herself. Perhaps she had been worrying needlessly after all. She went to look for Mrs Armstrong. Now *there* was a woman who needed to be impressed. So much depended on it. If only Angela could appreciate the trouble she was taking on her behalf.

49

It had taken John less time than he'd expected to recover from the deep hurt he had felt on hearing his father's words through Fiona's closed door. He had spent a restless night in Jill's flat but the next day, after David had left, Fiona's warmth and support had helped ease the pain. Face it, John told himself, he'd really known all along that his father would "dob him in" at the first opportunity. The words he'd overheard had changed nothing — except to give him an increased awareness that he must cope with his predicament alone. Sure, there was always Fiona, but the ultimate responsibility was his. He knew that now, had learned the hard way, and the lesson had given him a new inner strength.

It was in this frame of mind that John had arrived at the Hamiltons' party. So far, John was not impressed by the way Angela was carrying on. He thought she was trying a little too hard. Her smile was too bright, she seemed totally distracted, constantly aware of him but pretending not to be. John wasn't feeling as uncomfortable as he might have done; he knew something Angela didn't, and that gave him a sensation, not of power exactly, but of containment, the possessor of a perspective that was available to no one else in this house. So he could study Angela and feel more or less detached. He was aware of Patricia Hamilton's distaste for him, but that didn't seem to matter so much now. If she only knew the truth about him, who he really was. She would choke on her home-made pate. He sipped his beer. He was almost enjoying himself.

Simon Armstrong was one of those guys it was easy to categorise. He was a creep. Arrogance born of money was stamped all over those smooth, tanned features. Spoilt and loud — he was one of a type John had no time for. Poor Angela. He smiled to himself. Angela moved away from the group of which she and Simon formed a part, and walked across the room to him. She was frowning, her lips were tight. She stopped in front of him.

"I suppose you think you're very funny," she challenged him.

"Funny?"

She gave him an annoyed look. "What are you smirking at?"

"Just pleased to see my first impression of Simon was spot on," John answered mildly.

Angela glared at him, opened her mouth to retort, closed it again, then abruptly flounced away, rattled.

People chattered and drifted. The music was loud and the air was heavy with smoke. Food was served. Simon escorted Angela into the dining room. John drifted in behind them. There was a crowd around the table. John waited until he could find a space. There were piles of food.

"Having a good time?"

John looked around. Wayne Hamilton was standing just behind him, his plate full.

"Not bad," John told him in a steady voice.

They smiled at each other, and their smiles contained a great deal of mistrust. Since John had started work out at the stud, they had reached a sort of uneasy accommodation, each of them recognising that they were stuck with each other for the time being, and there was nothing either of them could do about it. Wayne nodded towards Simon at the table.

"What do you think of lover-boy?"

John made a face. "I don't. Not if I can help it."

Wayne's smile widened. "I feel the same," he said lightly. "It's a real shame, though, that Angela's thinking of marrying him."

And that hurt. It really did. It was almost as if John had just been dealt a savage body blow. *Marriage?* Angela? That was something else again. It was bad enough the two of them going around together, but to get married . . . He felt suddenly deflated, lost, and the voices around him sounded more loudly in his ears. Married? Angela and the creep, who could never make her happy — surely not, bringing up his kids in a nice house in one of the better suburbs, tennis club, mothers' club, country club, while he would be out making money, pots of it. And that didn't count for anything, not the sort of life he was likely to give her. Not happy, not unhappy, but somewhere in a limbo, living together, but not really loving each other, and, hell, in the end she would turn out to be just like her mother — *their* mother, for God's sake! She didn't know what she was doing — John convinced himself of that. He had to talk to her, get things straight. He didn't feel hungry any more.

He followed Angela and Simon into the living room. They sat down together on a sofa and began to eat the food that was piled high on their plates. John moved across to them. Angela looked up at him.

"Can't you find anywhere to sit?" she asked coldly.

John was determined. He wasn't going to be brushed off. "Can I speak with you?"

"Sure," Angela said unenthusiastically. "Go ahead."

Simon was watching them with a puzzled expression, obviously picking up the tension in their voices. "Alone, if that's okay," John said.

She was going to be difficult. "I don't mind Simon listening."

"Well, I do."

Then Simon was on his feet, belligerent, his head thrust forward. "She doesn't want to speak to you," he growled.

John stood his ground. If it was going to come to a fight, he didn't mind. Just let the creep throw the first punch. Already there were people looking at them. Angela stood up and smiled at Simon. The last thing she would want was a brawl.

"It's all right, Simon," she said quietly.

Simon looked cheated. Big hero, John thought, ready to step in to protect the lady's honour. "You don't have to," Simon muttered.

"I know." Angela handed him her plate. "I won't be long. Promise."

Angela led the way out of the room to her father's study. She looked very cool in green. In the study she turned to face John. "Okay, I'm listening," she said expressionlessly.

It wasn't going to be easy. "I don't want you making a big mistake," he said.

There was no warmth in Angela's smile. "That's kind of you. What particular mistake did you have in mind?"

John gestured towards the door, but it was meant to go beyond that. "Marrying him."

Angela was taken by surprise. For a moment she let her guard slip. Then she recovered herself. "And why should that be a mistake?"

"You know why. You'd be doing it to get back at me."

"Talk about an ego," Angela scoffed.

"The only time you've turned on to him tonight has been when I've been looking." It was true. That smile of hers that was much too bright. Like her laugh now that was too brittle.

"You've got to be joking," she said in a tone of wonder that struck John as being patently false. "I couldn't care less about you." She moved across to the door. "If I want to get married, I'll do it — whether you like the idea or not."

She walked out of the room, leaving John with the feeling that he had made a right mess of things.

50

Patricia couldn't believe her luck. It was everything she had hoped for, had worked so hard to achieve. It was wonderful news. She was so happy. Angela had done it at last, just when Patricia thought she was showing a distressing lack of interest. She had come through — and with flying colours. Her first reaction when Angela had come to her with the exciting news had been astonishment tinged with disbelief. Then when she realised that the girl was being perfectly serious, a warmth flowed through her, and what a sweet sensation that was. Hopes, aspirations, dreams — all were bearing fruit at last. Patricia was absolutely delighted. She couldn't wait to tell everyone the news.

Angela was standing with Simon in the hallway. They were holding hands, and what a handsome couple they made. Simon was grinning from ear to ear. Patricia couldn't resist the urge to hug her daughter again.

"Oh, darling. I'm delighted, I really am."

Patricia was pleased, Simon was pleased, but Angela didn't look as pleased as she might have done. She gave her mother a quick, nervous smile.

"We thought you would be," she said a little flatly.

Patricia turned to Simon and embraced him as well. "If

I'd chosen you myself I couldn't have done any better." And how true that was! Simon Armstrong's credentials couldn't have been any better. She straightened. "I'd better get everyone into the living room."

"What for?" Angela wanted to know.

"To make the announcement, of course."

Carried away by the momentum of her happiness, Patricia almost danced into the living room. She felt quite weightless, as if she were floating on air. She held up her arms for attention. "Everyone!" she called. "I want you all in the living room. I've got an announcement to make."

She waited until they had all gathered in the living room, enjoying every moment of it, the suspense she was creating. She could see the interest she had aroused reflected in the faces of the guests as they filed into the room. She noticed Angela and Simon talking in urgent whispers in the hallway. Angela didn't look very pleased — but that couldn't be helped. Then an awful thought struck Patricia. What if Angela was already beginning to have second thoughts, was already regretting a decision made on the spur of the moment? No, no, abruptly, ruthlessly, she rejected such an unacceptable notion. No time to lose. She saw Gordon standing with John. Neither of them knew what was going on. The news would be just as much a surprise to them as to everyone else.

They were still straggling in from the other rooms, from the terrace. Patricia waited until they were all assembled in front of her.

"Everyone here?" She looked around her approvingly, and saw that everyone was. She nodded. "Good. Now the announcement I'm about to make is something that gives me a great deal of happiness, and I'd be less than honest if I didn't tell you it's something I've hoped for for a long time." How strong and vibrant her voice sounded, how true. She might have been standing on the stage of a great theatre, her voice carrying boldly to every part of it. How marvellously in control she was. She smiled at Angela and Simon who were hovering a little apprehensively in the background, and beckoned them to come forward. They shuffled and looked uncomfortable. Patricia's voice rose to a new pitch. This was it. "Angela and Simon have just told me they're going to be married."

And what a marvellous reaction that simple statement brought. The horrified look on Scott Edwards' face was enough to make it worthwhile. Simon and Angela were looking even more awkward, and there was a puzzled look on poor Gordon's face. But everyone else was showing their pleasure, smiling and clapping, murmuring their approval, and offering their congratulations to the young couple. Everyone that was, Patricia noticed suddenly, except Mrs Armstrong, Simon's mother, who was gazing stonily in front of her. Patricia realised she had made a blunder, had been guilty of a gross breach of protocol. She should have consulted with Mrs Armstrong first before precipitously launching into her announcement. She saw with a niggling sensation of dismay that didn't really threaten her euphoria that there was some patching up work to be done.

51

The implications of what she had done were beginning to sink in. Angela was appalled. She had rushed blindly into something from which it would be hard to extricate herself. She had been too quick, too impulsive, impelled by the overwhelming urge to get back at Scott Edwards. It wasn't even that she *liked* Simon very much. It was just that he had been there, at hand, and she had wilfully used him. She knew how unfair she had been, stringing Simon along like that, but she couldn't help herself — or so she told herself now. She looked at Simon sitting next to her on the stairs, quite drunk on champagne, and decided she had seen enough of him for one night.

"It's time you went home," she said. It was late. All the other guests had gone, and the house had a deserted, forlorn look about it in the aftermath of so much activity. Scott Edwards had stormed out just after her mother had made her announcement. Mrs Armstrong had left, grim-faced, shortly afterwards, ignoring Patricia's efforts to placate her.

Simon sipped his drink. "It's early yet." His words were slightly slurred.

"No it isn't. Everyone else has gone." Angela stood up, and taking his arm, pulled him to his feet. He swayed, and some champagne sloshed over the side of his glass.

"I haven't finished my drink," he complained.

Angela took the glass out of his hand. "You've had enough," she said sharply.

He lurched towards her, seeming to have some difficulty in focussing properly. "I'd rather stay here."

He tried to put his arms around her, but Angela deftly stepped out of the way. "I'm not in the mood." Simon pouted. "It's been a long night," Angela pointed out to him. "Go home and sort things out with your mother."

"I knew there was a reason I didn't want to go home," he said ruefully.

Angela moved across the hall and opened the front door. Simon stalled. "One more drink and then I'll go."

Angela shook her head. She had to be firm with him. She kissed him on the cheek. "I'll see you tomorrow," she said and practically shoved him out the door, which she closed quickly behind him before he could make any further protest. Angela was tired. It had been a long, eventful night.

On the way back to the staircase she looked into the living room. Her mother was emptying the ashtrays into a plastic bag. Gordon Hamilton was smoking a last pipe before turning in.

"I'm going to bed," Angela announced.

Patricia straightened and crossed the room to the door where Angela was standing. "Simon's gone?" she asked. She sounded surprised.

Angela nodded. "I would have brought him in," she said, "but he wasn't making much sense."

Smoke rose lazily from Gordon's pipe. He smiled. "You should never mix your drinks," he remarked.

"Sit with us for a while," Patricia suggested to her daughter.

What? To gloat, so she could tell her how proud she was? Angela shook her head.

"I'm too tired, Mother."

"Five minutes." Patricia's tone was eager. "We should

talk. It's not every night you get engaged."

Angela shook her head. "I'm sorry Mother — but I really am exhausted. But if you're worried about Mrs Armstrong, forget it," she said, unable to keep the bitterness out of her voice. "Simon will hang in there." Then she brightened. "See you in the morning."

All she wanted to do was go to bed and maybe cry a little.

52

Susan watched Bill tinkering with the engine of the utility with mounting irritability. Marvellous. Let's go bush for the weekend, a bit of shooting, bushwalking, swimming — and now look what had happened. Something had gone wrong with the engine, and now Bill was trying to fix it with no success at all, it seemed.

"I told you we should have used the company car." Bill shot her a savage look, but said nothing. "This one's on its last legs." It would have made much more sense to use the car Mrs Selmer had provided for him.

"I'll have it fixed in a minute."

"You said that ten minutes ago."

"Get off my back, will you."

They glowered at each other for a long moment, then Susan turned away and stalked to the side of the road, where she stood idly kicking stones. With a heavy sigh, Bill straightened and followed her.

"I'm only cranky because I know you're right."

That was better. Neither of them wanted a fight. Susan eagerly grasped at the chance. Up until now everything had been fantastic. The honeymoon had been everything she had expected it to be, and they had already moved into their new house.

"I guess I don't know when to shut up," she said with a smile, throwing herself against him, hugging and kissing him. Bill lightly returned her kiss, careful not to touch her with his greasy hands.

"I've got a job to do." He grinned. "Don't worry. We'll be back on the road soon."

Susan didn't exactly share his confidence, but she kept her silence. She looked around her, at the gently rolling countryside. There were trees and hills, a creek.

"Why don't we camp around here?" she suggested. "Looks a nice spot."

Bill shrugged. "I'm easy."

It was, after all, what they had intended to do — find a nice spot and camp there. "I'll pitch the tent," she said.

"You'd better leave it to me," Bill said.

She laughed. "I'm not helpless, you know," she lightly chided him.

Bill shrugged. "Go for your life."

She struggled with the tent, aware that he was watching her, but determined not to let it rattle her. She battled with ropes, the tent swayed. She swore under her breath. She struggled on. Bill finished what he needed to do with the ailing engine and wiped his hands on a rag. He lowered the hood and moved across to her side. She gave him a quick, exasperated look.

"One word out of you and I'll . . ."

"I was just going to say you're doing a great job," he broke in with a laugh.

Yeah, sure, very smart. Releasing the rope which she had been trying to secure, she held up her hand. "I've broken two fingernails trying to put the stupid thing up. Look."

The rope was slackening. The tent was beginning to fold in on itself. "Watch it!" Bill shouted, leaping forward and grabbing the rope.

Together they pulled on the rope, and Bill secured it in a practised way. Susan smiled at him fondly. Bill straightened, and brushed his hands together.

"I'll get the rifle," he said. "Soon as you've finished, give us a shout."

Susan groaned. "I don't know if I'll have any energy left."

"You'd better," Bill said, assuming a mock-serious expression. "I'm counting on you to pot a couple of rabbits for dinner."

Susan raised her eyes skyward, and thought of the house they had left behind in Melbourne. "And to think I gave up a weekend of painting for this," she groaned.

Susan had never fired a rifle in her life, so Bill decided a little time would be well spent giving her a few tips before they went after rabbits in earnest. He lined up a row of tin cans on a small rise, then told Susan to try and pick them off, after carefully instructing her what to do. She fired off several rounds but none of them found their mark. With each shot that went wide, she became increasingly more annoyed and frustrated.

"You'll never win a prize," Bill told her gently.

Susan had the rifle sighted again. "I can't understand it," she exclaimed, disappointed. "I did everything you told me to do."

"You're jerking the trigger," he told her. "You've got to squeeze it, gently . . ." he took the rifle from her, and raising it to his shoulder, took aim, ". . . like this." His finger squeezed back on the trigger, there was a sharp report then a resounding clang as the bullet hit one of the cans which went flying backwards. He held the rifle back out to Susan, who shook her head. She was feeling quite discouraged.

"You might as well use the last couple of shots," she suggested. "I'm just wasting ammunition."

Bill still held out the rifle. "Don't give up," he urged. "You can do it."

Susan hesitated, then still with the feeling that she would only be wasting more time and bullets, she took back the rifle and aimed again. The tin can was very clear in the sight. Gently, very gently, she squeezed back on the trigger, careful not to jerk it this time. There was a slight kick against her shoulder as the weapon recoiled, a sharp crack in her ears, then the moment of jubilation when she saw the can rock to the impact of the bullet. She hadn't hit it dead-centre, but at least she had hit it — and that was something.

"You see?" Bill said behind her.

She saw. Now it seemed easy. Squeeze the trigger gently — that was all she'd had to do. "I don't believe it," she laughed.

"I told you you'd get the hang of it. Have another go."

Susan raised the rifle again. "Hey," Bill said suddenly. "A bit to the left. Hang on . . . I think I saw something move in the bushes there."

Susan lowered the rifle. Bill was staring to one side into the bushes. Without taking his eyes from the spot, he reached out and took the rifle from Susan.

"Hey!" she protested.

Ignoring her, he quickly brought up the rifle, took aim and fired.

Hard on the echo of the shot there was flurry in the bushes, then a rabbit bounded free of them into the clearing. Bill squeezed the trigger again, but this time there was no shot, only a click. The chamber was empty. Bill swore savagely. The rabbit seemed to run out of momentum. Its movements became slower and slower as it swung back into the bushes out of sight.

"What happened?" Susan asked.

"A rabbit."

"Did you get it?"

"Not sure."

Bill was running forward. Susan followed him. They crashed through the bushes. Then Bill stopped. Susan came to a halt beside him. The wounded rabbit was lying in front of them, covered in blood, its body quivering as it gasped its final breaths.

"I got him," Bill cried excitedly.

Susan stared in horror at the stricken animal. "It's still

alive," she whispered.

"It won't last long."

"You. . . you're not going to leave him like that?" The sight of the blood, the fear in the creature's eyes, was upsetting her.

"What can I do?" There was an edge to Bill's voice.

"But it's in pain." She didn't want to look, she couldn't look.

There was no trace left of Bill's former excitement. He seemed to be very much on the defensive now. "You don't have to look."

It was dying — dying slowly and in great pain. Those fear-filled eyes, the entrails hanging out . . . "How can you be so cruel?"

"Give it a rest, will you?" He was becoming angry.

She knew the unsettling effect she was having on him, but that couldn't be helped. The animal was *suffering.*

Taking her roughly by the arm, Bill steered her away. "Come on."

She shook him away. "We've got to do something," she cried shrilly, moving closer to the dying rabbit. Bill grabbed her arm again, his fingers digging ruthlessly into her flesh so that she gave a small cry of pain.

"Don't be bloody stupid, Susan," he grated through clenched teeth as he swung her aside. "Get back to the camp."

Gripping the rifle, he stalked back towards the rabbit. Susan ran after him, stumbling on the uneven ground. "What are you going to do?" she gasped.

"Finish it off, of course," he shouted back at her. Bringing the rifle around in his hands, he wielded it by the barrel, raising it above his head, his feet apart, braced, and Susan knew precisely what he was about to do.

"*No!*"

He brought the butt of the rifle hard down on the squirming animal at his feet. There was a sodden thump. Susan looked at Bill's face, saw the naked fury there, and shuddered. She had never seen him look like that before, taken over completely by his rage as he brought the rifle butt down again then again on the lifeless, bloody, unrecognisable object at his feet.

Then, as quickly as it had come, Bill's rage subsided. He looked up and caught the expression in her eyes. He looked away. "It was the kindest thing to do," he said in a shaken voice.

All Susan could do was gape at him. She had just seen a side of him she never knew existed — and for the first time since he had made it and she had dismissed it as being rubbish, she remembered the accusation John had made about Bill. Sam Selmer's murder — John had claimed Bill had done it, and she hadn't believed him. Now, just having been witness to the rage that had carried him away, she wasn't so sure. When he was like that, he could be capable of anything — even murder. What if John was right? God, the thought was too awful to even contemplate.

53

John leaned on the fence and watched Angela and Simon Armstrong riding down the path between the paddocks towards the trees. They rode well, in a practised sort of way, relaxed on the saddle. The girl he had dreamt about — and now, of course, he knew why he had dreamt about her, had experienced her emotions as if from a distance. Something to do with the genes, one of those mysteries nobody had ever properly explained as far as he knew. A bond, a kinship that couldn't have been any closer, the result of a split cell, divided, separated and brought up many hundreds of miles apart. And yet, despite the distances, the difference in their upbringing in style and substance, the bond had remained, inextricable, indistinguishable — and still Angela didn't know it existed.

"Saddle Mercury for me."

"I've already saddled Gemma."

"Good. Then Simon can ride Gemma, and I'll ride Mercury."

"Your father said Stan's the only one allowed to exercise Mercury."

"I'm giving you an order."

"I take my orders from your father."

She had been imperious, and he had been immovable —

and in the end, saving face as best she could, she had told Simon, when he joined them, that she would take Gemma while he rode Bandit. "Bandit's a real man's horse," she had said, giving Simon a kiss and John a hard look.

She had already made it clear to him that, if she had her way, he wouldn't be working at the stud. He was just an employee, she had said, and he should remember that. Wayne Hamilton had been with them at the time, and John couldn't fail to notice the smug look on his face.

With one foot up on the fence railing, resting his chin on his folded arms, he stared after the two riders. Angela was looking her best, fresh, in tight-fitting jodhpurs and a checked shirt, a ribbon holding her hair in place. The sunlight had glinted from her brand-new engagement ring. Even so, John could sense she wasn't happy. He knew her too well.

"There they go, sweeping off into a beautiful day. The young lovers — what a perfect picture they make."

John pushed himself away from the fence, and turned to face Wayne who had come up behind him.

"So?"

Wayne shrugged. He was smiling in a nasty way. "So what? Can't a guy make an observation or two if he wants?"

John glared at him. There was still a deal of hostility between them. He didn't like the expression on Wayne's face. "Maybe there are times when nobody wants to know," he said coldly. "Smart-arse remarks like that . . ."

Wayne laughed. "Still got the hots for her, hey?"

John's facial muscles were set hard. He held himself back with difficulty. "Don't try me," he growled.

"Try you?" Wayne assumed an expression of mock innocence. "You're away beyond me, fella."

The figures on horseback were getting smaller. Soon they would be among the trees. "Go away, you're boring me."

"Yeah?" Wayne's eyes were wide. "What's the matter with you? You think you're someone special? You weren't the first, you know."

John lunged forward. It was his sister he was talking about. He could feel the warmth rushing up into his face. His fists clenched. "What's that supposed to mean?" he demanded.

Wayne stood his ground, his lips curved in a mocking smile. "Come on, don't tell me you're so naive," he sneered. "All the guys she's had, in the backs of cars, you name it, and if you . . ."

It was then that John threw the first punch, putting all his force behind it, and watching with grim satisfaction as Wayne, a ribbon of blood appearing at the corner of his mouth, staggered backwards, and losing his balance collapsed into the dust.

54

If only he had said something instead of remaining silent, quixotic, protecting Angela. If he had told the truth, and not just stood there, dusty and dishevelled after the fight with Wayne, Gordon Hamilton wouldn't have felt compelled to sack him outright. Now, as it was, he had to find Scott and offer him his job back. He had been too hasty, had accepted Wayne's side of the story — although he hadn't had much choice in the face of Scott's sullen silence. Wayne's side of the story? What was that after all? "He just walked up and laid into me," Wayne had said. Nothing, no reason — the fight had been about nothing. So Gordon had had no choice really. He'd had to give Scott his marching orders. Fighting was one thing he would never tolerate. He had been sorry to lose Scott, he was a good worker, but it couldn't have been helped.

Then, later, the truth had come out — and it was as he had really suspected all along. One of the other stable-hands had overheard the remark Wayne had made to Scott about Angela, and had broken up the ensuing brawl. So it had been Wayne's fault. Scott had simply reacted in the way he would be expected to react, as he himself would react. He had done Scott an injustice, and now it was up to him to put it right.

This on top of everything else, the grim financial position they were now in, partly the fault of the drought, partly the slump in the stock market, and partly because the stud wasn't producing the return it should. At least the transport division was thriving. That was the one bright spot, keeping them out of the hands of the receivers, at least for the moment. He hoped they could survive the crisis and get by without selling anything, but they still needed to cut back on their spending. He had made that perfectly clear to everyone.

Below him, at the foot of the hill, Manly nestled on its strip between harbour and ocean and washed up onto the hillside opposite. Gordon turned into the street where Scott lived, and with a start, realised just how well he knew it. He found the number, and that brought another shock of recognition. He had come here, often, to see Fiona, and it was there, on those same steps, that he first saw the woman he was later to marry. He experienced a strange sort of exhilaration. After all these years. Fiona Thompson! Scott had talked about his Aunt Fiona. The same woman. Small world. Same house. Patricia had been sitting on the steps in the sunshine, nursing her baby. She had been quite lost in those days, so uncertain of things. He took the steps two at a time, and knocked on the front door.

"I'm coming," a familiar voice called from inside, and Gordon smiled. Same old Fiona.

The door opened, and there was Fiona looking at him, curiously at first, and then with dawning recognition. "Well, well, well," she said at last, opening the door wider.

"Hello, Fiona."

"Surprise a girl next time." Fiona smiled and shook her head in wonder. "Gordon Hamilton!"

Gordon was feeling good. A place of pleasant memories. He followed Fiona inside. "I'm honoured," Fiona said. "But why the visit? Something to do with the property?"

Gordon shook his head. "I came to see Scott," he told her.

He saw the surprise that registered on Fiona's face as she turned in the living room doorway and looked at him. "I was surprised to find you were the Aunt Fiona he talked about," he went on.

Fiona smiled tightly. "Small world."

"You can say that again."

"Isn't Scott at the stud?" Fiona asked.

Awkward question. "No," Gordon replied. "I . . . ah . . . sacked him this morning."

The smile was abruptly wiped from Fiona's face. "What did he do?"

"It was a misunderstanding," Gordon told her. "There was a fight. I thought Scott started it. But he didn't. Wayne did. Wayne's my son."

Fiona looked thoughtful. "So you've come to apologise?"

Gordon nodded. "And offer him his job back."

"Well . . . he must be off somewhere licking his wounds," Fiona said. "Do you want to wait?"

Gordon glanced at his watch. It was getting on, and there were business matters he had to attend to. "Ah . . . I'd like to, but I don't really have the time."

"Not to worry," Fiona said cheerfully. "I'll tell him everything's okay. You can catch up with him at the stud tomorrow."

That was fine by Gordon. "You're sure you haven't got time for a cup of tea?" Fiona pressed him.

Gordon was tempted. He looked at his watch again. Things to do, but they could wait a few minutes longer. "Why not?"

"Or something stronger?"

"No, tea's fine."

Fiona moved out to the kitchen. Gordon looked around the room. It might have been only yesterday since he was last there, standing where he was standing now. "Does Scott know about our business connection?" he called to Fiona in the other room.

Water poured into the kettle. "No. Does he need to?"

"That's up to you." He sensed the reserve in Fiona's

voice, the suggestion that Scott really didn't need to know. He looked up as she appeared in the doorway.

"Scott's a great one for being independent," she said. "When he came home and started talking about the Hamiltons I didn't let on I knew you. If he found out he'd probably think I was behind him getting the job."

Reasonable, reasonable. Gordon nodded. "Okay. I won't say anything."

"If it ever comes up," Fiona went on, "I'll tell him." She changed the subject. "How's the property going?"

The property. Woombai. Cut down on the spending. "With the drought, the water from your place has been a godsend."

One didn't need to go into matters too deeply. Complications built upon complications. Now she was laughing. Easy-going Fiona.

"Don't tell me that," she said. "I'll be upping the percentage."

"You should come and visit the place," Gordon suggested. "You'd be surprised how much it's changed."

Fiona's smile just seemed to die and wither away. It was still there, but there was no longer any substance to it. "It would rake up too many unhappy memories," she said quietly. "It's good just to know it's there."

Areas not touched or probed. The sadness in Fiona's voice was unmistakeable. Gordon tried to laugh it away. "You're as bad as me," he said. "A sentimentalist."

Fiona rallied. Even so her smile was a little watery. "From way back," she said, moving back into the kitchen. "The water must be boiling."

55

"Guess who I saw yesterday?"

Patricia wasn't really interested. She had been to the opera the night before and had met a lot of people for supper afterwards. "I couldn't even begin to imagine."

Gordon was already dressed and having his breakfast. Patricia had only just got up. It had been very late when she got back.

"Fiona Thompson."

That did it. The day had started off promisingly enough, sunny and bright, and there were a number of things Patricia had planned to do. Now, suddenly, at the mention of that woman's name, she no longer had the zest.

"Really?" She tried to keep her voice disinterested. "Where did you bump into her?"

"I didn't. I went to see her."

He might as well have struck her. It didn't help that he should sound so offhand about it. "Why?" Her tone was sharp.

Gordon sipped his tea. "I needed to see Scott, and it turns out she's the Aunt Fiona he told us about."

Patricia took a deep breath. Scott, Fiona Thompson — why did she feel things were ranged so venomously against her, that her back was to the wall? Last night had been so pleasant. She had been with people she liked and admired. "Well, that explains a lot," she said icily.

Gordon put down his cup. "What do you mean?"

The answer was obvious. "The reason he's hanging around. Fiona knows Angela's illegitimate. It wouldn't surprise me if she and Scott were up to something."

Gordon laughed. He wasn't taking her seriously at all. "Like what?"

Patricia spoke slowly, distinctly. She fought back her rising sense of outrage. Betrayal lurked at every corner. "Imagine what would happen to the wedding plans if that snippet of information got out. There *is* such a thing as blackmail."

Gordon shook his head. There were times when he really did irritate her, when he was so cool and reasonable. "Don't be stupid," he said. "I'm sure the whole thing's a coincidence."

"Well, I'm not," Patricia retorted.

Gordon went on being reasonable and infuriating. "If Fiona wanted to pull something like that she would have done it before now."

Patricia was thinking hard. Her thoughts were running away with her. Something had to be done. She knew what she had to do. "I wouldn't have mentioned if I'd known how you'd react." Gordon was watching her with an expression of concern. "What about today?" he asked, switching to a new tack. "What are your plans?"

"Nothing much," she replied automatically. "One or two visits to make, that's all."

One visit in particular. Back to Manly, back to the past. Something that needed to be sorted out. The drab house, a feeling of impending doom, going back, reliving things, sights and sounds, a world from which she had escaped — or was that merely an illusion? Could she ever successfully and unequivocally put that part of her life behind her once and for all? She had thought so — until now. Fiona answered the door, wearing leotards. Patricia bore straight in, not giving her a chance even to register surprise.

"Are you alone?"

Fiona was obviously collecting herself. "Just me and the record player. I was doing my exercises."

"Can I come in?"

"Sure." Fiona stood back to let her visitor pass into the hallway. Music was playing in the other room.

"I had hoped I would never have to see you again," Patricia remarked.

"I'd always looked forward to it."

Patricia ignored the sarcasm. "Had you? I wonder."

"Now listen," Fiona retorted angrily, "I don't know why you're here, but don't come barging into my house playing Lady Muck."

So that was how it was going to be, was it? The battle lines were drawn. Patricia could give as good as she could take. "I know Gordon came to see you yesterday," she said tartly. "I don't know what you talked about."

The two women faced each other. "Not about you," Fiona snapped.

Patricia held the other woman's unflinching stare. "Gordon doesn't know *all* that happened here before he met me. I intend keeping it that way."

Fiona snorted. "Sounds like a healthy, open marriage."

Patricia ignored the remark. "He knows about Angela, of course, but nothing else," she said. "No one does. And I've got Angela all set to make a very good marriage."

"I've read about it," Fiona said sternly. "In the papers."

Patricia forged on. She was hard. There was so much at stake. All her plans . . . "Not you, not Scott, not anyone, is going to wreck that."

"Why do you think we'd want to?" Fiona demanded.

"It's too much of a coincidence," Patricia told her. "Out of the blue your nephew turns up and thinks he can start telling Angela who she can and can't marry."

Fiona bared her teeth in a mirthless smile. "Not that *you'd* try to tell her, of course."

Patricia airily brushed the suggestion away. "And I won't let you embarrass me either. Or blackmail me."

Fiona blinked at her. "I beg your pardon," she said in a quiet, dangerous voice.

"If that's what you're thinking of," Patricia went on, "I can tell you now, there's no money."

Anger flared in Fiona's eyes. "How dare you!"

Patricia was undaunted. "We're almost broke."

The atmosphere was building up thickly between them. "I don't give a damn about your money," Fiona said firmly.

Patricia wasn't to be swayed. "I put a lot of effort into my family and I'm not going to let someone like you ruin it."

Fiona's cool finally snapped. Her face was livid, her eyes blazed. "Don't give me *family!*" she cried furiously. "Don't you *dare* mention family to me when you *dumped* half of yours. Took off with Gordon without a second's thought about who would look after the little boy, who would nurse him, who would *mother* him." Her finger quivered in the air between them. "You couldn't give a tuppeny damn about him."

Patricia stood rigid, momentarily quelled by the force of the tirade. "Well, I can't imagine it was too much of a problem," she said in a subdued voice.

"It wasn't easy," Fiona snapped, and Patricia saw the tears that welled up in her eyes, felt the force of her emotion. Fiona turned away, and suddenly Patricia realised that Fiona *had* looked after the boy.

"*You* brought him up?" she asked quietly.

"Till he was five." Fiona's voice was muffled.

And now it was all coming to Patricia, teetering on the brink of awesome knowledge, and there was no turning back from it, or stopping it form in front of her with blinding clarity. She felt weak.

"My God!" she whispered. "Your nephew."

Fiona turned back to her. The two women stared at each other, Patricia dreading what was to come next, but there was no way of avoiding it.

"Scott's my son?"

Fiona said nothing, but Patricia knew it was true. "Is Scott my son?" she asked again.

Fiona hesitated. There seemed to be a fierce struggle raging inside her. Finally she said quietly, "Yes, he is."

It had been a shock. Patricia still felt weak. She sat down. She had to rally, pull herself together. There were more questions to be asked.

"Does he know?"

The room with its familiar objects seemed to be closing in around Patricia. Fiona was watching her solemnly. "I had to tell him," she said. "The way he felt about Angela . . ." she shrugged, ". . .it was dangerous not to."

The point was taken. Patricia nodded. "But why is his name Edwards?" she asked, still suspicious. "Didn't his father keep him?"

"No," Fiona said quickly, looking away. "He stayed with me, then went to a family in Brisbane."

Was she telling the truth? Patricia couldn't be sure. She did sense an evasion in the other woman, though. It was awkward — a complication she didn't relish. Gordon didn't know about the twins; he thought there was only the one child, Angela. He had taken them away to the country, Patricia and her daughter. Now the boy had come back, snooping around, and that could mean serious trouble."

"Why the hell is he hanging around us?" she exclaimed bitterly.

Fiona was staring at her coldly. Damn the woman. Okay, she could think what she liked about her. Patricia didn't really *mean* to be callous — but until now everything had been so . . .*ordered.*

"For some reason, he wanted to find out what his mother was like," Fiona said deliberately. "Hardly worth the bother, I'd say."

"I couldn't agree more," Patricia returned, just as icily.

"You always did have the maternal instinct," Fiona said.

This was getting too much. The woman had no right to

judge her. She didn't know a thing, didn't know how hard she had struggled to make things just right for everyone. She stood up. "I didn't care about him twenty years ago. I don't give a damn about him now."

"I'll pass on the message," Fiona said drily.

"You do that." Patricia headed for the door. "And don't try to make any trouble. It won't do either of you any good."

She walked quickly out of the house that carried so many bad memories.

56

John noted the shock on Patricia Hamilton's face when she opened the door and saw him standing there. The unwelcome visitor. She wasn't pleased to see him. His mother wasn't pleased to see him.

"I'd like to talk to you," he said quickly before she could slam the door in his face.

"There's nothing to talk about."

Fiona had told him about Patricia's visit. She had told him under no circumstances should he go out to the Hamilton house and confront his mother. But now, here he was.

"I think there is. You are my mother, after all."

Patricia's face was fixed in a grimace of distaste. John felt like something the cat had dragged in, a mess unceremoniously deposited on the carpet. There's no point talking about it. Wayne and Angela are my children — not you."

"Weren't you ever curious about what happened to me?" John persisted.

"No." Her eyes were like gimlets. It was early afternoon. It had taken John all morning to work up the nerve to come out here and face her. "I want you to leave us alone. And, to begin with, you can give up your job at the stud."

As hard as nails she was. "Why should I?"

"I don't want you hanging around."

No beating around the bush. Straight out with it. She couldn't have put it more bluntly, and John guessed he had to accept that. "Okay," he said with a shrug. "Soon as I get another job I'll resign." That was fair enough. Patricia's face muscles relaxed. She looked relieved. John paused and studied her curiously. "Why did you leave us?" Then, when there was no reply, "It's not going to kill you to tell me that."

Patricia reflected for a few moments while John waited. She gnawed at her lower lip, then nodded. "In nineteen-sixty-one nice girls didn't get pregnant. Your father couldn't keep a job, I couldn't take one. We were . . . saddled with two children, nowhere to live, not a cent in the world. What would you have done?"

"I wouldn't have walked out," John said with feeling.

Patricia sighed. "If I'd married your father it would have fallen apart in six months. By the time you were born I hated him. At least this way, Angela had a chance."

She spoke calmly, matter-of-factly, which made John's revulsion more complete. "Yeah, to grow up and be like you," he said contemptuously. "To marry some guy she doesn't give a damn about."

Patricia gave a languid gesture of dismissal. "I want you to leave. We don't like each other. We never will."

John looked at her in disgust, then turning, walked heavily away. She couldn't have made herself more clear. The swimming pool sparkled brilliantly in the sunlight, and the bougainvillea was in full bloom.

57

Fiona's anger with John for having disobeyed her and gone to see his mother had passed as quickly as it had come. Maybe she couldn't blame him so much. "I actually feel sorry for her," he had said with a wry smile.

"Don't waste your energy," she had told him, then had dropped her bombshell. "I think I'll go to Melbourne tomorrow."

"What for?" John was gaping at her.

"I don't trust Patricia," she said. "She's just as likely to start making enquiries."

"So?" John's eyebrows were raised.

Fiona was brisk. She had made her plans. "So we can't sit on our backsides and wait for the police to come knocking. Not any more. Patricia's visit has changed everything."

John wasn't convinced. "Don't see there's anything else we can do," he remarked.

Fiona was moving up and down the room. She stopped abruptly and swung to face him. "What's Bill Todd's big trump card?" she asked.

"What do you mean?"

"Why don't the police suspect him?"

"He's got an alibi." John was looking at her in a puzzled way.

"Exactly." Fiona was triumphant. "His mother knows the truth. *She's* the one we should be working on. What's she like?"

"Nice," John replied. "Very nice."

Fiona's eyes were bright. "Solid citizen type?" John nodded. "Good," Fiona said. "If she's lying for him, it must be worrying her."

John was sceptical. "You can't just walk in and say 'tell the police John Palmer's innocent.' Why should she?"

"Conscience, my darling," Fiona said with a sweet smile. "I might have to stay down there for a few days. Get to know her. So expect me when you see me. I'm off to collect my ticket now. No time to lose. Mind's made up." She gave John a peck on the cheek on her way past. "I think we're onto something."

58

Fiona was in Melbourne, and John had a visitor. It was Wayne Hamilton — and John was more than a little surprised to see him. Wayne said he had come to apologise, no hard feelings and all that. John wasn't too sure about him. He was a little suspicious. But he didn't want any more hassles. He offered his visitor a beer.

Wayne was looking keenly around the flat. "You think I'm up myself, don't you?" he said without any animosity.

John lifted his shoulders in an offhand shrug. "Maybe we got off on the wrong foot."

"Maybe we did." Wayne was being most agreeable. He was smiling a lot. "I just got carried away, I guess."

"Forget it?" Why not? No point in carrying on a grudge.

"Okay." Wayne held out his hand. John took it. There was nothing more to be said. John was still mistrustful, Wayne still looking around the room, inquisitive, absorbing things.

"Where's your aunt?" he asked suddenly, dropping into an armchair.

"She's gone away for a few days." John sat down opposite him. It was all very cosy.

"Brisbane?"

"No, Melbourne," John replied before he had time to

think. It was out before he could stop it. He groaned inwardly. Have to work around this one, he thought, repair the damage.

"Got family there, too?" Wayne was leaning forward in his chair.

"No. It's business."

"Business woman, is she?"

"Yeah," John muttered, hoping that would be the end of it, but knowing it wouldn't. Wayne had the look of an eager-beaver young Assistant D.A. just about to break his first case wide open.

"What does she do?"

Oh hell. John gave a feeble laugh. "Would you believe, I don't know?"

"Sure I would," Wayne said suavely. "You're the trustworthy type."

Just then there was a knock at the door. John almost leapt out of his chair. A relief, the chance for a breather, no more questions for the time being. He opened the door with a flourish. Jill was standing there, looking rather put out. In her hand was a sheet of paper which John recognised. It was a note he had written to her earlier in the morning. She held up the sheet and read it in a peevish voice. " 'Don't waste your time on breakfast while Fiona's away. Scott'." She looked up at John. "What's the idea?" she demanded angrily.

John was thrown. It was the last thing he had expected. He had thought he was doing her a favour. "I thought I'd make things easier for you."

Jill was not aware that there was anyone else in the room with John. "Since when have you written me notes?" She was highly offended. "What you mean is, you don't want to have me around."

"Don't be silly." John tried to sound light, easy. It was only a misunderstanding after all. "I was trying to be helpful."

Her face was a mask. The anger smouldered in her eyes. "Thanks for nothing. I know you've been trying to give me the brush-off for some time now. The other day . . ." Her gestures were quick and sharp, her voice rose in pitch. "Talk about a hypocrite. I was good enough to tell your lies for you. Play the pregnant girlfriend."

In the heat of the moment, John forgot they weren't alone, that in the room behind him Wayne Hamilton could hear every word. "It's your hang-up, Jill," he remarked, "not mine."

"Maybe you should team up with Angela Hamilton after all," Jill sneered. "You'd make a good pair."

She flounced away, back to her own flat, and slammed the door behind her. John was about to follow her, to try and sort this thing out, when he suddenly remembered Wayne. With a slumping feeling of dismay, he realised he must have heard everything that was said out in the hallway. Closing the door, he turned back into the room where Wayne looked up at him with just a tinge of a questioning smile.

John took a deep breath. "You heard then?"

"I guess I couldn't help it. You both had your voices raised."

John sank down into the chair out of which he had leapt so eagerly a few moments before. "I guess it sounds pretty stupid," he said in a forlorn voice, and when Wayne nodded that helped not at all. "Jill and I cooked up the story between us. I wanted to get Angela off my back."

"I thought you were keen on her." Wayne was acting as if they were already great mates. Man to man, masculine understanding.

John shrugged. "It wasn't going anywhere," he explained. "And I didn't want to blow my chance of a job at the stud."

Wayne sipped his beer and looked at John, who didn't know if he was being believed. Wayne would probably go straight home now and tell Angela what he had heard.

"It sounds weird now," John continued. "But at the time it sounded like a good idea."

"It worked," Wayne observed, and John was relieved.

He seemed to have believed him. Wayne finished his beer and stood up. "Time I was going." he winked at John. "I'll remember that one next time a chick won't take no for an answer."

59

Wayne was just coming in through the front door as Angela walked out into the hallway from the living room. When he saw her he smiled.

"Just the person I was looking for."

Angela waved him away. "Sorry I can't say the same." She didn't like the way he was smirking. She turned away. He had something to tell her. She saw with some dismay that he was bubbling over with news which would more than likely depress her.

"Scott's girlfriend, Jill." Angela stopped at the foot of the stairs. Her hand tightly gripped the railing. She had known it wouldn't be pleasant. "The one who's supposed to be pregnant. Well, she isn't."

Angela turned slowly and stared at him. This was something she definitely hadn't expected to hear. Wayne was still smiling in a self-satisfied way. "I'd say they've been having a good laugh behind your back," he said, heading into the living room.

Yes, possibly. It seemed that way. Angela was hurt and angry — and curious to know more. Why had he done it? Why had he deceived her in such a way? She hated the thought of talking to Wayne about it, but she had to know more. Reluctantly, she moved into the living room where

Wayne was fixing himself a large Scotch.

"Why should he lie?" she asked.

Wayne dropped some ice into his glass. "Search me," he said casually. "Why did he lie about coming from Brisbane?" Angela fought back her rising anger. "Okay," Wayne went on. "He wanted to get rid of you, but didn't have the guts to say so." Angela tensed. All this was quite a blow to her. Get rid of her? *Her?* "Stick with Simon," Wayne urged. "The other one's a lost cause."

It was too depressing, shattering, and the wedding plans still had to be gone through. The announcements had been made, all the other arrangements put into train — and now Angela had even less zest for it than ever. She was listless, moved around automatically. All she could think about was Scott Edwards and the story he had made up just to get rid of her.

The following morning she didn't feel much better, but she was ready to try a little harder. Simon and his mother were coming over to put the final touches to the plans. Simon was in a particularly happy mood.

"I've got a surprise for you," he blurted out at last, unable to keep it bottled up any longer. He glanced across the littered coffee table to Mrs Armstrong. "You know Shane Tuncks, mother." She nodded and put down her coffee cup next to the clutter of seating plans and invitation mock-ups. "He's got a villa on Sirna. It's a Greek island off Crete. Tiny and romantic. One taverna and no tourists. The locals don't even speak English." Angela listened. A Greek island and monolingual locals. Fantastic. Oh, she knew what was coming. Deep blue water, the sun glaring from whitewashed walls — and Simon. "He's offered it to us for our honeymoon. What do you reckon? The two of us alone — for a whole month."

"What did she think? She didn't want to think. She forced herself to smile. "Sounds wonderful."

Simon grinned, full of confidence, deeply suntanned. "Knew you'd go for it."

Mrs Armstrong glanced at her watch. "I'd better head

off," she said, beginning to gather things up from the coffee table. Simon and Angela also began to pick up things. Simon's hand touched Angela's, and she involuntarily drew it away. Realising it didn't look good — appearances, after all — she reached out and gave his hand a squeeze. She smiled, then looked up to see Mrs Armstrong studying her with a thoughtful frown. Angela handed her the material she had gathered.

"There you go."

Mrs Armstrong packed the material in her bag, and stood up. "See me out, dear," she said to Angela, then to Simon, "I'll see you this evening, Simon."

Angela and Mrs Armstrong walked out into the hallway, Angela knew the older woman wanted to say something to her. "You don't love him, do you?" Mrs Armstrong said abruptly.

Angela was startled. This wasn't exactly what she had expected to hear. "Simon's my son," Mrs Armstrong went on gently, "and God forgive me for saying it, but if I didn't love him the thought of spending a month alone with him would drive me crazy." She was warm, sympathetic, and Angela said nothing. "If he wasn't head over heels he would have realised himself how you feel. So why are you going ahead with it?"

Angela felt uncomfortable. Of course the woman was right. She didn't know what to say. All she could do was clutch at straws. "The arrangements . . . everythin's organised. And mother . . ." Oh God, she would hit the roof.

"You and Simon are both young," Mrs Armstrong said, still warm, still comforting. "Don't ruin your lives. Get out now." Angela stared at her. Simon's mother was giving her an out. She didn't have to go through with something she didn't really want. Mrs Armstrong took her hand. "I took you for a sensible girl.

Angela couldn't look at her. "I . . . I was mixed up," she said awkwardly. "Someone had just . . . well, thrown me over, and . . . the more I was with you and Simon the harder it was to make the break. I didn't want to hurt him, and. . . I was afraid I'd lose your respect." It was good to talk like this, to get it out of her system. She looked the other woman squarely in the face. "Last night I found out something. . . Maybe there's a chance with the other guy after all." Maybe. Who could tell? "I might be kidding myself. I don't know."

Mrs Armstrong nodded thoughtfully. "I see." Then she smiled and chucked Angela under the chin. "Buck up," she said cheerfully. "I'd rather have you as a friend than a miserable daughter-in-law."

Angela felt a rush of gratitude, of warmth for this woman who was being so understanding. "Don't worry about your mother," Mrs Armstrong went on. "I'll phone her and break the news. But Simon's your problem. Don't be too hard on him. He's a funny boy, but I love him."

Angela smiled and nodded. She glanced at the living room door, then as Mrs Armstrong gave her a light kiss on the cheek and walked out the front door, she took a deep breath and moved back into the living room. She would be easy on him. She felt so much better now — quite strong in fact.

60

Wayne had done some snooping. He had gone back to the house in Manly, at lunch time, when no one was there. He was not sure what he would find, with only a vague notion that he would turn up something that would tell him more about Scott Edwards, who really was bugging him. And he had come up trumps. He had found Fiona Thompson's folio of newspaper clippings.

He was carrying it under his arm when he walked into the living room of the Hamilton house and saw Angela sitting on the sofa, looking quite worn out. He smiled.

"If it isn't the blushing bride," he greeted her.

"The wedding's off," she said sharply.

The smile broadened. "Oh? Simon find out you didn't qualify to wear white, did he?"

Angela's lip quivered. Her hand moved as if she were brushing something away. "Please don't," she said with feeling. It hadn't been easy. At first Simon had been querulous and disbelieving. He had been badly hurt.

Wayne perched on the arm of the sofa. "The sudden change of heart wouldn't have anything to do with Scott, would it?" Without waiting for a reply he tossed the folder into her lap. "Take a look at that."

Hesitantly, with an enquiring look up at Wayne, Angela

picked up the folder and opened it. She saw the clippings, a blurred mass of newsprint from which individual words seemed to leap out at her. "Murder" was one of those words. She saw a name, "John Palmer". There was a photograph . . .

"Lover boy's real name is John Palmer," Wayne said, easing himself up from the arm of the sofa and crossing the room to the telephone. "He's wanted for murder in Melbourne." He picked up the receiver and began to dial. Angela flicked through the book of clippings. There were stories of a young man who climbed a television tower in Melbourne, the same young man who was wanted to help police with their inquiries in connection with a brutal murder . . . The picture was undeniably of Scott — or the young man she knew as Scott Edwards. *Her* Scott. What did it mean? Wayne had finished dialling, and now he was speaking rather breathlessly into the mouthpiece. "Ah . . . yes . . . I have some information you might fine useful . . ."

Angela was galvanised into action. Leaping to her feet, she ran across the room, and grabbing up the cord that connected the phone to the wall socket, gave it a hard yank. The cord came free. The call was disconnected. Wayne looked at her disdainfully and replaced the receiver.

"Telecom won't like you," he remarked coolly and walked out into the hallway. Angela followed him. "Wayne!" she cried desperately. "You can't!"

Wayne was heading along the hall towards his father's study. "Watch me."

Catching up with him, she grabbed him by the elbow. "Scott would never do anything like that," she pleaded.

Wayne pulled himself free. "Your so-called 'Scott' is a little thug," he remarked. "He would have cheerfully beaten me to a pulp that day at the stud." He grunted. "There's a guy down south who wasn't so lucky."

Angela followed him into the study. He reached for the phone, but Angela wrenched it out of his hand. "Don't kid yourself you're helping the police," she cried. "You're just trying to get back at him."

He gave her a supercilious look. "You know you can't smash all the phones in Sydney."

He pushed her hand away. Angela saw how determined he was. He was going through with it. So, if there was nothing she could do to stop him, there was action of another sort she could take. She didn't have to waste any more time arguing with him, becoming more and more infuriated with his smugness and barely suppressed glee. Scott was out at the stud. She had to get to him, quickly. Wayne was already beginning to dial. She hurried away, scooping up her bag from the hall table and rummaging inside it for her car keys.

61

John was spreading straw when he saw the cloud of dust rising on the unmade road that turned into the stud. Then he saw the car coming at breakneck speed. It was Angela's car. The top was down. Angela's hair was blowing free in the wind. The car screeched to a halt beside the fence. Stones were flung up from beneath its locked wheels as it skidded dangerously close to the fence. The engine still running, Angela raised herself in the driver's seat.

"Scott!" she called, waving to him in an agitated fashion. "*Scott!*"

John was puzzled. Angela was the last person, he had expected to see, and it was obviously something urgent that had brought her here. Leaning the rake against the fence, he climbed through the rails and walked towards her.

"Hurry!" She was clearly desperate. Something had gone wrong. He increased his pace until he was almost running. Angela was still waving her arms. "Jump in. The police will be here any second!"

The police? Suddenly there was a spreading area of ice at the pit of his stomach. The police? What the hell had happened? He stopped beside the car and blinked at Angela. "Looking for John Palmer," she told him. Anxiety was written all over her face.

John scrambled into the car. This was bad news. "How . . . ?"

Angela threw the car into gear, and there was another flurry of stones and dust as she swung it in a tight circle, and with her foot right down, headed back towards the road. They turned onto the road. Briefly she told him what had happened. Trees flashed by on either side.

"Mightn't be a bad idea to work out where we're heading," she said, attempting lightness.

The wind buffeted John's face. He narrowed his eyes against it. "Why run the risk? Helping me?"

She drove expertly. They were heading south. "You didn't kill the man?" she asked in a tone that suggested she wouldn't believe him even if he told her he had.

"No."

"That's good enough for me."

"I wish other people were that easy to get on side," John remarked wrily.

Angela pulled into the side of the road and switched off the engine. There was a lot of shade beneath the trees. They were off the main road. She reached across and took John's hand. "Maybe I'm biased," she said, and he was awkwardly aware of the tenderness in her voice, the gentle pressure of her hand. It was dangerous, too close. His heart was pounding. He slid his hand from hers.

"Everything's getting out of hand," he muttered thickly. She looked at him in silent query. he explained. "I dragged Aunt Fiona into it. Now you. I don't know what I'm running for."

"You can't give yourself up," Angela said.

Why not? What else was there to do? John shook his head. "The cops are getting closer all the time," he said in a voice not untinged with self-pity. "Might as well save them the trouble."

"Don't be stupid!" Angela exclaimed angrily, then in a more subdued and comforting tone, told him, "Things aren't hopeless yet. Wayne won't dob me in. Daddy'd kill him if he did. That gives us a start. The police won't be looking for *my* car."

John had to accept that. He didn't have much choice. "Okay. What'll we do?"

"We need time," she said decisively. She thought for a moment. "Let's find a motel near here." John frowned. That didn't sound to him like a good idea at all. Angela misinterpreted his hesitation. "Simon and I have broken up, if that's the big worry." She waited. John still said nothing. All sorts of thoughts were crowding in his mind. Angela prodded him some more. "You can't go back to your aunt's, can you?"

John looked at her steadily. That was something he couldn't argue with. She had him there. Angela started the car, and they pulled off the grass verge back onto the road.

About twenty minutes later they found a motel with a "Vacancy" sign up on the board outside it. Angela stopped the car outside the building. They both glanced at it critically. It was quite an unprepossessing type of building.

"It mightn't rate five stars," Angela remarked matter-of-factly, "but it'll do." She reached for her bag and took out her purse. "Wait here. I'll book a double room."

John experienced a sinking sensation. It was impossible. "No," he said gently.

Angela smiled and brushed aside his doubts. "Come on, don't be silly . . ." She leaned across and kissed him lightly on the cheek. Then with a smile, swung herself out of the car and walked across to the reception office.

John watched her go. So young, so pretty, so trusting and full of love. Geez, what a mess! What a thing to happen! She didn't know a thing. She believed. . . no, more than believed — was certain in her own mind — that she was in love with him. And to show him how far she was prepared to go was on her way, her step light and confident, to book them into a motel room. It couldn't happen — it just couldn't. And what it boiled down to was that he had only two choices. He could either stay here and tell her that she was his sister — and that would be really traumatic for her — or he could just walk away, which, under the circumstances, seemed to him to be the only decent choice. Angela had disappeared inside the office. John wasted no time. His mind was made up, only one way to go now. Quickly, he stepped out of the car and walked away in the opposite direction, fast putting distance between himself and the motel from where Angela would be emerging at any moment to find him gone. She would try to find him. He walked faster, turning corners, not knowing where he was going, just walking.

The streets were busier. He passed a shopping mall and turned yet another corner. Ahead of him he noticed a cruising patrol car. It was coming towards him. Only one way to go. Get this business over, no more running. The police car was just cruising, not looking for him, its occupants probably not even aware of his existence . . . Suddenly, John was filled with new resolve, of relief even, as he stepped from the footpath, his arms raised, and positioned himself in the patrol car's path. The car stopped just in front of him, and he could see the enquiring looks on the faces of the two policemen through the windscreen. He lowered his hands onto the bonnet of the car, and most of the tension seemed to seep away from his body as he waited. Over at last. No more running.

62

Fiona had brought out the tarot cards. She looked down at the last card she had put on the table in front of her, and said, "Very interesting."

"What is it?" Kevin asked eagerly.

She gave him a mock-severe look. "Hold your horses," she said reprovingly. "You can't rush genius."

Fiona was settling down very well in Melbourne. She was almost one of the family. She had been rather taken aback when coming out to the Palmer house and meeting Beryl for the first time, Beryl had suggested she stay with them instead of in a motel which had been her intention. She had made the necessary noises of protest, then had accepted the offer. She had met Susan and Bill, and by working on Beryl in such a way as to make Beryl think the thought had originated with her, had had her invite Nora, Bill's mother, out for dinner.

Seeing how preoccupied Nora was throughout the meal, Fiona was confident of being able to put sufficient pressure on her to wear her down. Hence the tarot cards after dinner — truly a stroke of genius, Fiona thought. She could see Nora, who was sitting between her and young Kevin, with whom she was getting along famously, was quite edgy about it. Seated opposite Nora, Beryl picked up the box the cards had come from and looked at it sceptically.

"You really believe this stuff?" she asked.

"Half a million gypsies can't be wrong," Fiona said lightly. She glanced at the woman next to her. "Nora's go next."

Nora looked almost frightened. "No, I don't think so," she said in a subdued voice.

Fiona gave her a playful nudge with her elbow. "Of course it is."

"You haven't finished mine yet," Kevin protested.

"We've almost lost the vibrations." Fiona was enjoying herself hugely. She was playing a part. She looked at Kevin's card. The Magician. "The tenth card sums up the whole reading," she explained. "The Magician. It means . . . originality, imagination. You'll make a living with your brains."

Beryl chuckled. "And I was counting on him to support me in my old age."

Fiona shook her head gravely. "The Tarot never lies." A point made. She gathered in the cards and made a deck of them, then cutting the deck into halves, riffled them with her thumbs so that the cards interleaved. She felt more like a cardsharp than a fortune-teller, and there was some justification in that. "Okay," she said to Nora. "Touch the pack and concentrate." Nora did so. "Good," Fiona said after a brief silence. "I'll make it quick. The first card is the present." In a quick, practised movement no one else noticed, she dealt a card from the bottom of the pack. She placed the card face-up in the middle of the table. She smiled sweetly. "Ah, what did I tell you? The Lovers."

"Me?" Embarrassed, Nora shifted on her chair.

"Bill and Susan, I'd say," Beryl said with a quick, cynical glance at Fiona.

Fiona grinned. "I think Beryl has hit the nail on the head," she said. "Bill and Susan. Perfect harmony." She paused, and allowed a small frown to appear. "Unless the card's upside down."

Kevin looked from her to the card. "Then what?"

"Then you get a reverse meaning," Fiona explained, feeling rather important. They were all listening to her; she knew about these things, they didn't. "In this case . . ." she gave Nora a significant look, ". . . falling into a trap." She injected a little levity here, soften Nora up a bit, ready for the king-hit. "Poor Susan. Lucky it came out the right way." Now was the time. Both barrels. Fiona felt marvellously in control. "Now let's ask the cards something specific. Nora?"

"Bill." Nora spoke very quietly. Fiona noticed the small but telling quiver of the woman's lip. She pretended not to hear. String out out a bit more, build it up.

"Pardon, dear?"

"Ask about Bill," Nora said a little more firmly.

Fiona picked up the cards. "We'll start with childhood," she said authoritatively, laying a card on the table. "The Chariot, trouble . . . a loss of some kind."

It was easy when you knew the facts. Beryl had told her quite a lot about Bill, and in her inimitable way, Fiona had made it seem that she was only mildly interested in the subject.

"His father." Nora Todd's eyes were downcast.

His father — yes. "I'm sorry." Fiona shook her head. "A long period of upset. Clearing?" She paused. "Maybe Bill's future hold something brighter." She busied herself with the cards again, then with a flourish, played one out onto the table. She looked at it wide-eyed, and then emitted a gasp. Oh, what a ham she was.

"Le Pendu," she said in an awed whisper, and what a lot of awed meaning she put into that French term. She quickly scooped up the card. They were all watching her. "Misdeal," she said in a voice that was meant to sound insincere and hollow.

"Show us," Kevin urged.

"No." Fiona's voice was sepulchral.

"What was it?" Nora asked in a quavering voice.

Completely grave and appearing to come to a major decision she knew wouldn't be a happy one, but had to be made neverthless, Fiona put the card back down on the table. "The Hanged Man," she announced sombrely, pausing to let it sink in, at the same time noting the chill that had crept into Nora's expression. "Of course it may have a reverse meaning," she added with a hopefulness that was meant to sound forlorn.

But it was a straw which was eagerly grabbed by Nora. "Yes?"

Fiona was drawing the net closer. "Let me think." She thought; she made quite a show of it. "Lack of sacrifice . . . Like there's something Bill knows deep down he should say or do. But he's too scared to make the decision. Ah . . ." Abruptly, she reached forward and scooped up all the cards. "I'd better put these away," she said in a more cheerful tone. "They're just not behaving themselves today."

She looked at Nora, who was looking decidedly uneasy. Bingo, Fiona thought. Gotcha.

63

John's arrest created its own ripples. Angela learnt about it from Jill when she went to Manly to see if she could find him. She had not really expected he would be so foolish as to go back there, but she had gone there just in case, with the thought that possibly she would pick up a clue from someone as to where he might have gone.

He had been picked up, Jill told her. The police had come to visit her, and in fact they were still there when the call had come through to say Scott (John Palmer, they had called him) had been picked up. Angela choked back bitter tears. To think Wayne could have done such a thing... She could quite easily have killed him, done anything to wipe that self-satisfied smirk off his face.

Patricia Hamilton heard the news from Angela that same evening. Gordon was out. In fact, he was over at the Armstrongs, trying to patch things up. There was still a good chance that the wedding would go through if only Angela would stop being wilful — and now that Scott Edwards was in gaol...

Then Angela cried out angrily that if no one was going to help Scott, then she would. She would talk to her father when he got back and ask him to use the money they had intended to spend on the wedding for Scott's defence.

Patricia was horrified by the suggestion. Gordon would never agree to that, she said, and Angela told her that she might well be in for a shock. Patricia knew only too well how Angela was able to twist her stepfather around her little finger, and this severely dampened the feeling of relief that Scott was now out of the way and no longer posed any serious threat to the wedding plans going through. When Angela had gone up to her room, she fixed herself a strong drink; she had some serious thinking to do.

Fiona Thompson also heard the news from Jill. When she called from Melbourne and asked to speak to Scott, Jill told her what had happened. Fiona decided that it was time she took some direct action. So it was that Bill Todd heard the news from Fiona, a woman he mistrusted greatly from the moment he had met her because she asked questions, seemed to be prying, getting close to the nerve. In a voice loaded with doom, his mother had told him about the Tarot cards.

He was still half-asleep as he padded barefooted across the living room, pulling on a pair of jeans, to answer the urgent knocking at the front door. He rubbed the sleep out of his eyes. His hair was a mess. He opened the door, and immediately tensed when he saw who was standing there.

"What do you want?" he demanded gruffly.

Fiona's expression brooked no nonsense. She really was hawk-like. "It's time for some straight talk," she said flatly. "They've picked up John."

Jesus! Now Bill was fully awake. She might as well have thrown a bucket of ice-cold water over him. Fiona pushed past him into the hallway. "We both know it's for something you did," she said, giving him no time to recover his thoughts, to defend himself. All he could do was gape at her. "I'm a reasonable woman," she went on with some irony. "I'm giving you the chance to own up — if you're man enough."

At last the words came to him, along with a sense of outrage. Who was this interfering woman? What right . . .?

"What *is* this?" he spluttered. "Sunday School?"

"Or I can call the police and make a formal accusation," Fiona persisted. Her gaze was unflinching. "I'm not bluffing."

Maybe, maybe not. Bill was on edge. What *did* she know? "They wouldn't listen to you."

Fiona moved down the hall and picked up the telephone. Bill watched her. The bloody woman was taking over. He was frightened. Something was fluttering wildly inside him. "I'll owe you the ten cents," she said over her shoulder as she began to dial 0-0-0.

The rage was building up inside Bill. He could hit her, he could strangle her. "You want to make a fool of yourself, you go right ahead." The grateful thought that Susan was on night shift flashed through his panicked mind.

Fiona spoke into the mouthpiece. "Homicide, please."

During the short pause that followed Bill and Fiona were locked into a mutual glare. Then Fiona was speaking into the phone again. "Good evening. My name is Fiona Thompson. I'm down from Sydney to give you some important information concerning the Selmer murder . . . yes . . . I'll be waiting at nineteen Harris Street, Doveton . . . yes . . . yes . . . thank you."

She hung up, and with an air of triumph, turned back to Bill. "They're not going to thank you for dragging them out on a wild goose chase," he told her.

She smiled grimly. "Not so wild."

"I've got an alibi — remember?"

"I wouldn't count on it," Fiona said in an icy tone. "From what I've seen of your mother, she'll last about ten minutes if they really get to work on her."

Another jolt. His mother. She hadn't yet had to face any serious police interrogation. This woman was probably right. His mother had been very upset after all that weird business with the Tarot cards. Bill had scoffed when she had told him about it, and maybe he was trying to convince himself as much as her.

"What a con."

"Then how did she know so much about you?"

"Use your brains, Mum. She must have pumped Mrs Palmer earlier."

"Why?"

"I talked to Kevin. He reckons Fiona's seen John. Something she let slip."

"Since he. . . ?"

". . . killed Sam? Yeah. She's cooking up a way to get him off the hook. So. . . if she thinks she can palm the blame off on me, she's wasting her time. But we'll show her. I bet she expects us to keep away, but we'll go on seeing her. And we're going to act completely natural. The minute she sees she's barking up the wrong tree she'll pack up and go back where she came from."

But she hadn't packed up and gone back to where she had come from. She had come right here, like an avenging fury. By the time the two detectives arrived, Bill was fully dressed, he had shaved and combed his hair — and the waiting was pure agony for him. With a sense of crushing doom, he had heard the heavy footsteps mounting the steps outside, the knock on the door. Fiona opened it.

"Come in," she told the two heavily built men who stood in the hallway. They came in, and the bulk of them seemed to crowd the room. They introduced themselves, and showed their identification. Bill stood up with an effort. One of the detectives spoke to Fiona.

"You're Fiona Thompson, aren't you?"

"That's right."

The detective produced a small spiral-bound notebook and opened it. There was an address scrawled across the top page. He showed it to Fiona.

"Your address? Twenty-two Manly. . ."

"Forget the red tape," Fiona sharply cut him off. She gestured impatiently. The detective ignored her. Stolidly, he went on.

"Twenty-two Manly Terrace, Manly, New South Wales?"

Fiona nodded curtly. "That's me."

The detective closed the notebook decisively. "We've been looking for you, ma'am. We've had a report from the New South Wales Police earlier this evening. It's quite a serious charge — obstructing the course of justice. For harbouring a fugitive — namely John Palmer."

Bill looked sharply at the two policemen. Now this was something else again. He could sense a change of direction, a breath of hope, a reprieve. Fiona was protesting.

"But he's innocent." She pointed to Bill. "*He's* the one. *There's* your murderer. Ask his mother. You'll have all the proof you need."

The detective in his gray suit was showing a great deal of patience. "You can make a full statement down at the station." He looked quite sorrowful. "I would like to advise you of your rights."

"Rights?" Fiona's mouth fell open. Serves you right, Bill thought.

"Yes. I'm afraid you're under arrest."

64

The police had just left, and Nora Todd was still shaken. She had done what Bill had told her to do.

"Just stick to your guns and tell them exactly what you told them last time," he had urged her. "No need to get worked up. It'll only be a formality."

Now they had been and gone. Bill came out of the room. Nora was making a cup of tea. "What did I tell you?" Bill said confidently.

"I was sure he would pick me up on something," Nora said in a small voice. The jug was boiling. She switched it off.

"You were great," Bill said encouragingly. "I could hear."

Nora turned to him. Her eyes were brimming. "You've made me lie to the police," she said tremulously. "Billy, I want a proper reason for it."

For Christ's sake, why did she have to go on? Bill was starting to get angry. "You're not *believing* those crackpot stories, are you?" he demanded.

Nora stood her ground. "Tell me the truth and I'll never ask you again." A tear rolled out of one eye and made its way slowly down her cheek. "Why have I got to lie?"

Bill's sense of well-being had evaporated. In its place was

exasperation. If she could only let things be. "You're tired," he told her. "I'm not going to argue with you when you're tired. Go to bed. We'll talk it over tomorrow."

Nora poured boiling water into the teapot. She shook her head. "Bill, it might be a good idea if I kept out of your way for a while. I mean, every time I see Susan . . . I don't think I could face her."

A vein was beginning to throb at Bill's temple. "Oh hell!" he groaned. "Now I've heard everything."

"I've been staying here with you and Susan," Nora went on, and it seemed to Bill that her voice was gaining a little in strength and determination. "But now I don't think I can any more." She moved across to the telephone. "I've already packed my bag. Now I'll call a cab."

"You're staying, Mum," Bill said menacingly, advancing on her.

She backed away from him, alarm passing across her face. "So you can keep an eye on me?"

"Mum!" The anger in Bill was building up. There was a roaring in his ears. "Don't!" She began to dial. "I said don't!" He grabbed her arm, but she shrugged him away — and that was when Bill momentarily lost control. "Don't be stupid!" he shouted, and it seemed to him that the echoes of his voice were reverberating from vast distances. Fiercely grasping the phone out of her hand he smashed it hard down on the rest, at the same time flinging her angrily away from him. Then, like a wave that had just washed over him, the rage passed and he realised just what he had done. He felt drained. He dropped his hands, and avoided looking into his mother's horror-filled eyes. Then she began to cry. She sank onto the sofa and buried her face in her hands. The tears seeped out between her fingers. Bill was shocked. He hadn't meant to lose his temper like that. It had just come, without any warning. He dropped onto the sofa next to her, and put an arm around her. There was a tightness in his throat, and his own tears weren't very far away.

"Mum . . . Mum . . . I didn't mean it," he moaned, needing all the comfort he could get now. "I didn't mean it, Mum."

She lowered her hands and looked straight at him through smudged eyes. She knew — he could tell she knew. "What's going to happen to us, Billy?" she asked in a weak voice.

It was no use. He had come to the end of the road. He couldn't pretend any more. Yes, what *was* going to happen to him? He was in a state of total exhaustion. It was all catching up on him at last.

"I didn't mean to kill Sam," he said in a flat, expressionless voice. His mother was staring at him. No more lies, just the truth now. Bill looked everywhere but at her. "I went to ask for my job back. He told me to get out... wouldn't even give me my back pay." He was getting it out at last, the words were pouring out of him, and in a strange way, it made him feel better. "I...don't remember doing it. He got on the phone to call the police — and all I could think was 'you ungrateful bastard.' Then I guess...I hit him?" Guess? He *knew* he had hit him, had hit hard, with a crowbar, and there could be no mitigating that fact. "It's funny. After you've done something like that, you'd think you'd freak." He looked up at his mother, but she wasn't in focus. He glanced away again. "You know what I thought about?" he went on with some incredulity; sometimes it was like a dream he only partially recalled. "All the cop shows I'd seen. How the guy got away with it. I wiped the fingerprints off the bar and went out the back ...over the fence. If I'd gone out the front way I probably would've bumped into John."

There was a short silence while Bill considered the enormity of this possibility. It had been incredible luck. Nora tentatively broke the silence.

"I'm as much to blame as you are." Bill looked up at her again in surprise. What the hell was she on about? "For what John's been through," she elaborated.

Now that was overdoing it a bit. Bill snapped his annoyance. "That was his own fault. He shouldn't have run."

"Bill . . ."

"He's innocent," Bill broke in before she could go any further. "If he'd stayed put none of it would have happened. Now they've got him it'll be okay." She was giving him a funny look. She didn't understand. "They're not going to send an innocent bloke to gaol."

"It's happened before," Nora offered dubiously.

"I'm telling you, Mum, they won't," Bill said peevishly. "The best thing to do is keep our mouths shut and it'll blow over."

Did she believe this? Did she want to believe this? Would it have made things any easier if she did? "Billy . . ."

"You want me to go to gaol," he challenged her aggressively.

"Of course not."

"Right. Just keep your mouth shut." He pulled himself up onto his feet. The anger was returning. He forced his voice to keep to a low and reasonable pitch. "It's going to work out," he said. "If we don't say anything it'll work out for everybody."

65

Fiona was out on bail. The first thing she did on her release was head straight back to Bill Todd's house. It was rash of her, she knew, but while the trap was closing in all the time, the mechanism seemed to be faltering. It needed a push along. Bill was stunned to see her.

"I'm out on bail. Can I come in?"

"No you can't. Get out of here."

"You can't stop what's going to happen, Bill." She kept her gaze steady. "John's told the police his story. I've told them mine. It's only a matter of time."

Then she caught sight of Nora Todd hovering tentatively in the background. Following her line of vision, Bill turned his head. "Get back inside!" he snapped at his mother.

Fiona took advantage of the momentary diversion to push past him into the hallway. "I know you love him, Nora," she said to the woman who was timidly backing away from her, "but it's too late."

Bill grabbed her arm and swung her around. "If you don't get out of here," he hissed fiercely, "I'll call the cops."

Fiona looked at both of them. No point going on with it right now. But she could get in one last telling shot. "He is a murderer," she told Nora, who seemed to be shrinking against the wall. "I hope you can live with that. I guess that's all I came to say."

She was on her way out through the door when she heard Susan's sleepy voice come from the bedroom. "Who was that, Bill?"

Bill closed the door firmly behind Fiona before making any reply.

But while Fiona knew Johnny was telling the truth, others were more sceptical. His father, in particular, put it down as just a crazy yarn. He shook his head in disbelief when Fiona told him.

"I've never been able to understand John," he said, puzzled, "but this takes the cake."

"It's the truth." Fiona had fixed them all a drink. She held out a glass to David, who took it, swigged, then gave a bitter laugh.

"You were there, were you?" Fiona didn't understand what he meant. "When Sam Selmer was killed," he said.

"There's no need to be smart," Fiona retorted, glancing at Beryl Palmer, who had believed her, had grasped eagerly at the straw she was holding out to her, and who was now frowning at her husband.

"He's conned you, Fiona," David went on relentlessly. "The police saw him there. Sam said his name, and he ran. What more proof do you need?"

Fiona was appalled. His own son. At least he could give him the benefit of the doubt. Beryl echoed Fiona's thoughts. "He's your son, David," she said quietly.

David glared at her and swigged some more of his drink. "And Bill's Susan's husband," he returned sharply. "I'm just using commonsense. You don't think I like it, do you?" he demanded. "Having to face the fact my son's a rotten little coward?"

Beryl's jaw was set in a firm line. There was a look of implacable toughness in her eyes. "Can we see Johnny today?"

David shrugged. "If we want to."

Beryl nodded. "Good. We'll go and talk to him. If he can look me straight in the eye and still say it, then I'll believe him."

Fiona smiled at her approvingly. Good on you, Beryl, she thought.

66

The time had come. There were things to be done. Matters to be arranged. His mother's words still rang in his ears. The tears had shone on her face.

"It's over, Billy. You know it as well as I do."

And, yes, he did know. He had seen as clearly as she did, unmistakeable, he had been living in a fool's paradise. Acknowledging his acceptance of the fact, she had stood up.

"I'll go home now. When Susan wakes up . . . you tell her. Then go to the police." There had been no form to her face; it seemed to have completely crumpled. She had hugged him tightly, briefly. "Don't make *me* do it, love."

She had gone, and Bill had been left alone. Arrangements to make. Things had to be left as tidy as possible for Susan, so she could cope — and God knew it was going to be hard enough on her as it was without having to worry about mortgages, the car payments and everyday household expenses. He sat quietly, under a tremendous strain, totting up figures, calculating this, calculating that, until it all began to swim in front of his eyes. He rubbed his eyes. He was bone weary — and frightened — but at least he was doing something, occupying himself with detail. He rose to his feet and stretched. His whole body was aching. He heard a sound from the other room.

"You awake, love?" he called.

Susan's voice came out to him. "I'll be out in a sec."

Oh hell, this was it. Bill went into the kitchen and filled the kettle. His hands were shaking. He came back out into the hallway just as Susan appeared, fresh from sleep, wearing a dressing gown and combing her hair. She looked just as fantastic at that moment, and this made what he was about to do even more intolerable to Bill. The end of the road, facing up to things at last, and Susan didn't suspect a thing.

"Had a beaut sleep," Susan said with a smile.

"Good." Bill tried to keep his voice and manner as natural as he could, not to let her even guess at the force of the tumult that was raging inside him. "I stuck the kettle on." Little things, little details — they all helped. A routine to follow.

"Thanks." Susan kissed him. "Any more news on John?" she asked.

A stab, a pang. How could he stop himself from shaking? The question caught him unawares. "No . . . ah . . . no, there isn't," he stammered, leading her into the sitting room. "Sit down for a minute, will you, love."

She sat down on the couch. The table in front of her was strewn with the papers Bill had been working on. He sat down next to her and nodded to the papers. "I've been fixing up all our papers," he told her. "Do you reckon you can take over these things? You know . . . house payments, furniture . . . that sort of stuff?"

Susan laughed. "Talk about lazy."

"No, no, look," Bill said seriously. It was not a time for joking. "It's just that . . . well, it seems crazy, me doing it all . . . and you've got time off during the day. It would be easier for you to do it."

"Of course I will." She looked at him curiously. "You okay?"

He was trying hard, but she could still see something was wrong. "Yeah, I'm fine." He picked up one of the sheets. "Right," he said, businesslike. "I've got it all down here. First of all the house payments . . ."

She laughed again, and clutched his arm. "Hold your horses. There's no rush, is there?"

Time was running out. "I want to explain it all now," he said gravely. "While I'm thinking about it."

For about an hour he went over the papers with her, detailing everything that needed to be done. They drank coffee and he constantly referred to the instructions he had written out for her.

"You sure you'll be able to handle it on your own?"

"Yeah, it's fine."

"Good."

Susan stood up and stretched, and Bill experienced a pang of desire for her. It wasn't fair. "I'd better get changed," she said.

Not now. He wasn't finished. The worst part was to come. Springing to his feet, he took her hand. "Don't go for a minute," he said urgently. "There are a couple of other things."

With a puzzled expression, Susan allowed herself to be eased back down onto the couch. She smiled fondly at him. "You're funny when you talk about money. You get so serious."

Bill managed a feeble smile. "You know I love you, don't you?"

Her dressing gown was partly open. Her breasts rose and fell. "Of course I do, stupid." Her tone suggested it was a pretty silly sort of question to ask. But that couldn't be helped. Bill had something important to say to her. He placed his hand on Susan's knee.

"You're the best thing that ever happened to me," he went on in a choked voice. "I was heading the right way to be a dero when I met you."

Susan made a show of impatience that didn't ring true. "You put yourself down too much," she reproached him. "You've got a hell of a lot going for you."

That was a laugh. What going for him? Absolute zero,

that was what. “I know we’ve had a few arguments since the wedding,” he said miserably after a short pause. “But that doesn’t mean I don’t love you or anything.”

Susan laughed uncertainly. “Stop it. You’ll have me thinking you’re going around with someone else.”

It was too much for him to handle. He had to tell her, now, no more putting it off. He was folding in on himself, nothing left, no substance. “I’m sorry, Susie,” he moaned.

There was fear now in her eyes, as if she knew something awful was coming. She couldn’t have mistaken the utter desolation in his voice. “I . . . His mouth hung open. He shook his head.

“What is it?” Susan prompted in a fearful voice.

He had to tell her. He had to force himself. The truth, no more running, no more hiding. “I . . . killed Sam Selmer.”

An hour later, fighting back the tears, Susan drove him to police headquarters.

“I want to go on my own,” Bill told her.

The tears were streaming down her face. “I love you,” she whispered.

Bill placed his hand on her arm, then he embraced her. It was to be their last embrace for a long, long time. It was quick and desperate. Bill pulled away.

“Don’t hang around,” he said quietly, trying to keep his voice steady, his own tears stinging his eyes. “Please.”

He opened the door and began to climb out. Susan grabbed for his hand. He held it briefly, squeezed it, then released it. He stepped out of the car.

He looked back once. He was about halfway up the steps to the main entrance to the building. He stood and watched Susan drive off, then, brokenly, his shoulders slumped, his feet dragging, began to climb the rest of the way to the top.

67

John was home again. There was champagne. It was a real celebration. Of course the news of Bill's arrest and Susan's sorrow had dampened their spirits a little, but Susan seemed to be rallying, accepting it, prepared to wait. David and Beryl had their arms around each other and David had even managed a gruff "Sorry, son . . ."

John raised his glass to Fiona. "I don't want to be boring," he began, "but I want you to know how much it . . . ah . . ." there was an irritation in his throat, and tears in his eyes, ". . . helped knowing you believed in me. And I . . ."

Fiona moved across to him and topped up his glass from the champagne bottle she was holding. She ruffled his hair. "If there's one thing I can't stand," she said gently, "it's a maudlin drunk."

It was all over now. No more fear, no more running. The cells had been cold and clammy, footsteps had echoed in the corridor outside. People had moaned and sobbed, orders were shouted.

"You told me the truth about Bill," Susan said to John, "and I didn't believe you. I let you down. I'm sorry."

"I understand," John said fervently. "Honest I do."

Later he thought about Angela Hamilton. She must

have heard, and he wondered what she would do. If she wrote to him or even came down to Melbourne . . . He shook his head, No, it was best she didn't, that they had no more contact with each other. It would be hard on her — on him, too, but it was for the best — and maybe she would come to accept the fact that he wanted to have nothing more to do with her. He could only hope . . . But not now. Susan had gone. Fiona was opening another bottle of champagne. He was tired. No more thinking today. There would be time for that tomorrow, and the day after that . . . plenty of time. Angela could live her life, he would live his. He was close to her, he would always be close to her . . .

That night he dreamt about a girl on a horse, galloping along the wet sand at the edge of the surf, her hair flying freely behind her.